American Beauty

A-List novels by Zoey Dean:

THE A-LIST

GIRLS ON FILM

BLONDE AMBITION

TALL COOL ONE

BACK IN BLACK

SOME LIKE IT HOT

AMERICAN BEAUTY

American Beauty

An A-List Novel

by
Zoey Dean

LITTLE, BROWN AND COMPANY
New York ⤳ Boston

Little, Brown and Company

Hachette Book Group USA
1271 Avenue of the Americas, New York, NY 10020
Visit our Web site at www.lb-teens.com

First Edition: September 2006

 Produced by Alloy Entertainment
151 West 26th Street, New York, NY 10001

ISBN-10: 0-316-01094-4
ISBN-13: 978-0-316-01094-8

10 9 8 7 6 5 4 3 2 1

CWO

Printed in the United States of America

To Lynn Weingarten and Cindy Eagan, without whom
I'd have much less time to shop.

Hope and curiosity about the future seemed better than guarantees. The unknown was always so attractive to me . . . and still is.

—Hedy Lamarr

Black Sweatshirt with a Bad Chanel Knock-off Scarf

"**A**nna Percy, you are a traitor to all that is good and holy. And to Manhattan"

Anna Percy smiled. Cynthia Baltres might be living in the intellectual mecca known as New York City, and Anna might now be living in the anti-intellectual sun-dappled overindulgent splendor of Beverly Hills. But whether there were three thousand miles or three blocks between them, it didn't matter. Cyn was still her best friend—one who could let fly with a friendly insult the way other uptown girls tossed off skimpy two-ply cashmere.

"Jealousy is oozing through my phone, Cyn," Anna teased, wriggling the discreet earpiece from her Motorola E815's headset to a more comfortable position. Her pearl-gray Lexus powered down Wilshire Boulevard; the Santa Monica mountains stood sentry to the north. Anna had just informed Cyn that she was driving to a pregraduation party aboard her friend Samantha Sharpe's yacht. Cyn had just informed Anna that she was stuck in the NYU library researching a final paper on pop culture references to the French Revolution and had also just admitted that a tiny part of her was actually enjoying working on it. "Anyway, what are you doing talking to me? You're in a *library*."

She turned left on Sawtelle, as Sam's directions had indicated. The neighborhood instantly got seedier—fancy buildings were replaced by low-priced Mexican restaurants, tire dealers, and the occasional strip club advertised by a dilapidated neon sign.

"What are they going to do, throw me out?" Cyn asked rhetorically. "The new research wing will be named for Uncle Georgie, who just left them a mint. The *Times* obit said he died from a heart attack, but the whole family knows it was actually . . . Well, let's just say he had a nasty habit of picking up boy-girls near the Holland Tunnel."

Diseased cross-dressing prostitutes seemed light years away from Anna's current life. Yes, she loved New York. It was officially her home, but a lot could be said for La La Land, despite the squalor of Sawtelle Boulevard. She smiled as she passed a red Prius with a surfboard sticking out the rear window whose twenty-something blond driver was talking on her cell, applying lip gloss, and allegedly keeping an eye on the road all at the same time. There were some things in life—commuter-friendly transvestite hookers—that could only be found in New York. There were others—triple-tasking Prius-driving surf bunnies—that existed only in L.A.

"When do you guys graduate?" Anna asked, making a conscious effort to pay more attention to the road.

"Two weeks."

"Mine is next Friday. It feels surreal, doesn't it? This huge rite of passage—"

"Oh please," Cyn scoffed. "This is not some ancient John Hughes flick; it's not such a big deal."

When they were in eighth grade, Cyn had rented all the John Hughes movies for Anna in an effort to broaden her friend's cultural horizons beyond the nineteenth-century British fiction with which she was already enamored. They'd watched *The Breakfast Club, Sixteen Candles,* and their all-time favorite, *Pretty in Pink.* For a few days after that one, they'd both dressed like Molly Ringwald as the lead character, Andie Walsh in quirky layers of lace, mismatched fabrics, and multiple shades of pink.

"I'll tell you what graduation really is," Cyn continued. "Intermission before we can get on with our real lives. Finally."

Anna smiled ruefully. In typical Cyn fashion, her friend had nailed the truth of the matter. Though loath to admit it, Anna had actually switched time zones and moved in with her father several months ago to be *more* like Cyn: wild, fearless, and sexy. Admittedly, the plan hadn't gone smoothly. Sometimes Anna wondered if the wild gene was simply missing from her DNA.

"Did you hear about the wait list at Middlebury?" Anna asked. Cyn's parents had both gone to the prestigious liberal arts college in Vermont, but Cyn hadn't gotten accepted there immediately. Instead, she'd been put on the dreaded wait list.

"Yes. And no."

"Meaning?"

"Meaning they didn't take me, the fuckers." Cyn went uncharacteristically silent; Anna could picture the sour look on her best friend's face. "So I'll be going to Colby, which is like Middlebury in Maine. It's okay. Some of my favorite writers went there."

"That's a good school," Anna assured her.

"And you're going to Yale. Only six hours away. Anyway, less about dumb-ass next year and more about the party," Cyn went on. "Please tell me you took my advice about the outfit."

Anna fingered the skinny strap of her eggshell-colored Egyptian cotton Anna Molinari dress edged in silver scalloped lace that fell below the knees of her long legs. She'd originally planned to wear a pale ice-blue vintage Chanel silk shift straight from her grandmother's armoire, but Cyn had nixed that idea, saying you couldn't wear Chanel silk on a boat. As it is utterly impossible to dry-clean away the smell of dead fish.

"Yes, I bought something," Anna replied, stopping for a red light at the corner of Venice Boulevard. "Cotton. Happy?"

"Deliriously. Do you look fantastic in it? No. Of course you do. Next question. Can Ben remove it with his teeth?"

Anna burst out laughing. "I haven't put that to the test. Anyway, he won't be there. He has to work. I'll see him tomorrow, though."

Ben Birnbaum was her very significant other. They'd randomly met on her flight to Los Angeles the day she was moving, the day before New Year's Eve. Since then, they'd been on again, off again, over and over. Ben was back in Los Angeles for summer break after his freshman year at Princeton, and now they were very much on again. And they had the whole summer ahead of them to prove it.

He had a summer job at Trieste, currently *the* hot club in L.A. Not that Anna was an expert on these things, but that is what Sam had told her. There was always a line down the block, and they were constantly flying in some cutting-edge DJ from Rome or London or Dubai.

Ben's job was both a good thing and a bad thing. Good because he was interested in learning the night-club business. Bad because the club was consistently overcrowded, full of incendiary girls who flirted outrageously with her boyfriend. Anna had witnessed that phenomenon firsthand.

"Wow, what a sucky charmed life you lead," Cyn joked warmly. "Want to hear about mine? Scott and I are totally over. I went to Bungalow 8 last night to drown my sorrows and got stuck in a banquette with some fat-ass loser masquerading as the son of the Japanese ambassador to the UN. Busted. The real son of the Japanese ambassador is in my history class. When I casually mentioned this, he mumbled something about needing to go talk to a friend and practically sprinted to the bathroom. I think he hid in there for the rest of the night."

Anna giggled as a skinny girl wearing all black, with a bull ring through her septum, and her buff, bald boyfriend stepped brazenly onto Sawtelle at the corner crosswalk of Washington Place. Cars whizzed by; Anna stopped completely as the couple crossed the street with their mouths in a lip-lock.

She was just about to share with Cyn the details of what she was witnessing when she felt the Lexus suddenly jerk forward—there was a sickening crunch of metal and a tinkling of shattered glass, and Anna's head smacked backward into the headrest.

Accident, she realized, even as her earpiece and phone were thrown to the floorboard. *Someone just hit me.* She reached down and grabbed the phone, instantly grateful that the air bags hadn't deployed.

"Oh my God, Cyn! I just had an accident!"

"Anna are you—?" Cyn started to say.

Anna quickly cut her off. "Don't worry, I'm totally fine but I have to go. I promise I'll call you later." And she clicked off her phone with unsteady hands.

Heart pounding, shaking with adrenaline, she turned around to see what had smacked her—a cherry-red Honda Civic dotted with rust spots was stopped on Sawtelle ten feet behind the crosswalk. Fortunately, her own engine was still running; she cut the steering wheel hard to the right and managed to ease the Lexus to the west side of the boulevard, directly in front of the red sign for Wild Women—yet another strip joint.

What am I supposed to do? Anna panicked to herself.

She'd been driving for two years, and this was her first accident. But she remembered what she'd learned in driver's
ed. In case of an accident, try and remain calm. Step one:
Turn off the engine. Step two: Make sure everyone in her
car was okay. Step three: Make sure the other driver wasn't
hurt. She stepped out of the Lexus to check. . . .

"What the fuck is the matter with you?"

Anna whirled. The driver of the Honda—a middle-
aged woman with a pale face that looked like it had been
smashed in a closing elevator door and never resumed its
normal shape—was striding over to her. Gray hair roots
led to a red ball of frizz tied back with a bad Chanel
knock-off scarf. She wore a black sweatsuit; pastel
puffed-paint pandas marched down the sleeves.

"Where the hell did you learn to drive?" the woman
barked throatily with the voice of a lifelong smoker.
"You stopped like a maniac! Don't deny it—you gave me
no chance to stop. You better get the fuck out of here
before the cops give you a moving violation."

Anna blinked in surprise. "B-b-b-but you hit *me*."

She quickly racked her brain. What now? Call the
cops? In New York, her mother's driver took Anna
wherever she wanted to go in their Mercedes town car.
On rare occasions Anna had hailed a taxicab, but that
was only when Reginald was sick or doing what he did
best—playing the ponies at Aqueduct racetrack.

"Are you even licensed to drive?"

"Of course I am," Anna fired back. "Let's just call the
police."

"Are you nuts?" The frizzy-haired woman's voice went up an octave and her face began twitching. Anna noticed the red lipstick that had crept past the lip line at the corners of her mouth melting down, like two mini scarlet fangs. "I bet you were on your cell phone. You want the cops? The cops will arrest you!"

Was that true? *Could* they arrest her? Dammit, if only Cyn were with her. Or Sam Sharpe, the self-assured friend whose party she was heading to. They'd know exactly what to do.

"Look. Just wait. Why don't you push your car off the road if you can't drive it?" Anna suggested, with more bravura than she actually felt. "You're holding up traffic."

The redhead got right in her face. "If I was you, I'd get my ass out of here."

Maybe she should. If her car was drivable, she could get it as far as a service station. *No*, she decided. You didn't leave the scene of an accident, no matter what. Then what? Wait, you were supposed to swap insurance information. Did you need to call the police here in California if there wasn't an injury involved?

Ben. Ben would definitely know what to do.

"I've got to make a phone call," Anna announced to the woman. "Go back to your car. I'll talk to you in a minute."

The other driver let out a scoff, rolled her eyes and stomped back over to her car. Anna took a deep breath and quickly assessed the damage to the Lexus. The oyster-gray rear bumper was severely dented; the right taillight had spider-glassed. A glance at the tailpipe revealed that the impact had bent it shut. So much for driving away from this mishap—she remembered enough from chemistry class to realize that she'd die from carbon monoxide poisoning before she even got to the service station.

Anna went back inside the car and dialed Ben. The phone rang, once, twice. Anna could feel the anxiety fluttering in her stomach. After three rings her heart was sinking; evidently, he couldn't come to the rescue this time. But just as she was about to hang up after the fourth ring . . .

"Yeah?"

Anna was taken aback by the brusqueness of his tone. "Hi, it's me."

"Hey, Anna." His voice immediately softened. "What's up?"

"Nothing. Well, I mean, I just got into a car accident."

"Jesus, what happened? Are you okay?" he asked quickly, his concern obvious in his voice. That made her feel better.

"I'm fine. It's nothing, just a fender bender, but—"

"Thank God you're okay. Whose fault was it?"

"Hers, I think. I'm going to trade license and insurance information. Do I need to call the police?"

"No police if there's no injury. Definitely get her license and insurance info and you'll be all set. Listen, I'm in the middle of a work thing. Glad to hear you're okay. I'll call you later to check in, I promise. 'Bye." He hung up.

Anna just sat there for a moment, trying not to get

upset. It wasn't fair to expect him to drop everything and come to her rescue, right? Actually, the whole damsel-in-distress thing wasn't very appealing. Well, it *was* appealing, actually, but she was definitely learning to take care of things herself these days.

Swap info. Then what? Call AAA. She remembered Django, her dad's driver and caretaker, had signed her up when she arrived in California. Wasn't there a card in the glove compartment? "Yes!" She found it and quickly dialed the road-service number. It only took her a minute or two to provide the monotone operator with all the pertinent information.

"Okay, just sit tight. There's been an oil tanker spill on the Ten at the Vermont Street interchange—we've got all our wreckers there; it's a total mess. We should have someone out to you in about two hours or so," said the operator. "Give or take an hour."

"B-But I'm on the street outside a strip club!" Anna sputtered. "Can't someone get here sooner than that?"

"Ma'am, I understand your frustration, but the California Highway Patrol told us to make clearing the freeway a priority, and that's what we've got to do. Is there anything else I can do for you? A tow truck will be with you as soon as one is available."

"No." Anna didn't know what else to say. "I don't think there—"

The operator hung up before Anna could finish the sentence. Damn. Now she was supposed to swap her license and insurance information with a shrieking harridan? As for Sam's party, the one that was supposed to kick off graduation week in less than an hour, her attendance was becoming more and more unlikely by the minute.

Anna decided it was a long shot, but she could at least try to contact her dad and see if he could help her. He was shuttling between Las Vegas, Los Angeles, and San Francisco these days, trying to negotiate the acquisition of an off-strip but still pricey hotel/casino for a group of men in Sausalito who wanted to turn it into a gay-and-lesbian-themed destination. But if luck was with her and Jonathan Percy was in Los Angeles, maybe he could get her out of this godforsaken neighborhood.

"Jonathan Percy." His brisk voice came through the phone.

"Dad, you're back!" Anna exclaimed. She quickly described the situation.

Her explanation was followed by dead silence. "I'd love to help you out myself, sweetheart," her dad said after the depressing delay, "but I'm swamped here. Look, it's just a fender bender. Swap the information, stay in your car and keep the doors locked at all times, and wait for Triple-A. Then take a cab right home."

Anna's fingers tightened on the phone. "Dad, that isn't reasonable."

"Well . . ." She could almost see her father tapping a Cross pen on his expansive granite desk. "How about if I send over my new intern? He's an ace; up all night wining and dining some real jerk-offs for me in Vegas—

helped make the deal happen. I gave him the day off. But if I ask, he'll come over."

Great. Her dad's intern hadn't slept all night, but her father thought nothing of waking the guy up to tend to his daughter? Maybe Jonathan Percy found it acceptable to impose like that, but Anna didn't. Besides, she remembered her last horrid encounter with one of her father's employees. Lloyd Millar. Anna had accompanied him on a drive to Las Casitas, a fabulous resort on the Pacific coast of Mexico that her father had also been helping a group acquire. Lloyd had been so obnoxious that the Mexican authorities nearly wouldn't let him cross the border.

"Dad, the last guy you sent my way was a Yeti in a bad Hawaiian shirt," she replied testily. "I'll wait for Triple-A. Sorry to have bothered you."

"Hold on, Anna. No need to cop an attitude."

Anna winced. Cop an attitude? Jonathan Percy tended to boomerang between businesslike precision and aging hipster slang, but she never got used to it.

"Really. Sit tight. I'm sending the new intern," he repeated patiently, as if she were a five-year-old begging for sweets at the Ralph's supermarket checkout counter. "His name is Caine Manning. He's twenty-two, Wharton grad. Helluva guy. He'll be there in thirty minutes. Tops. Okay. Ciao. Love you."

Anna sighed as her dad clicked off. Well, she wouldn't mind a little assistance sooner rather than later, but that didn't mean she couldn't take care of the situation herself in the meantime. She turned around to peer at the dreadful redhead, who had gotten back into her car. What was the next step? Exchange information. She took the registration and insurance card from the glove compartment, found her license in her bone leather Kate Spade hobo bag, and walked back to the Honda. The woman was trying—and failing—to get her car started.

"It won't run," the woman practically spat. "Thanks a fucking lot."

Anna believed in the virtue of *la politesse*, having been raised by a mother who considered good manners as important as personal hygiene. A lady did not curse out loud. A lady did not raise her voice. A lady remained gracious and in control at all times.

A lady didn't accept being cursed at.

"Now you listen to me, whatever your name is," she told the other driver, her voice shaky but her tone steely. "I have someone coming to help. He'll get here as soon as possible. In the meantime, unless you are ready to act like a human being, we are not speaking. I'll be in my car."

Take that, she thought, as she turned on her gold Sigerson Morrison leather-and-topaz sandals and headed back to the Lexus. *Anna Percy has* balls. *Well, figuratively speaking*. She glanced at her Jacob & Co. five-time-zone platinum-and-diamond watch, which featured a gemstone kite in each time zone—an early graduation gift from her mother, who was off in Italy seducing a very young muralist. Damn. Sam's yacht was supposed to leave soon. The unrealistic fantasy of making this party was growing fainter by the second. Not that it mattered; there was no point in holding everyone else up just because her car had been rear-ended by Cruella De Vil.

She got back in the pearl-gray Lexus and let her head fall onto the headrest. Then her cell rang. Ben. It had to be Ben.

"Hello?"

"Anna, Caine Manning." Not Ben. "Your dad's intern. He gave me your number. I just wanted to let you know that I'm on my way. I'm coming from Westwood; I'll be there in twenty minutes." His voice was assertive and deep. She instantly felt better.

"Thank you," she told him gratefully. "I really appreciate it."

"No problem. You can't miss me. Lots of tattoos. Okay, see you."

She clicked her phone shut. Huh? Tattoos? Her father had hired an intern with lots of tattoos? *No.* That had to be a joke.

Anna checked her watch again. She'd find out in nineteen minutes.

Four-Foot Eleven and as Bad-Ass as They Come

Anna was about to call Sam when an electric-blue Ford F-150 pickup truck pulled directly in front of her car. A brunette guy wearing distressed Levi's with holes in both knees hopped out of the cab of the pickup and strode back toward her. He wore an olive-green Brooks Brothers shirt with the sleeves rolled up; both forearms were indeed covered in tattoos. His deep chocolaty hair was slightly spiked in the front, his chin shadowed with light stubble. Silver hoop earrings hung from each earlobe.

Had to be him.

He tapped on her window. She pressed the down button and immediately noticed that one of his eyes was blue and the other was brown.

"Hey, Anna, I'm Caine Manning," he announced easily.

Anna got out, surprised to find herself looking up—way up—at him, since he was at least six-foot two, maybe six-foot three. She quickly filled him in and he soaked up all the details, nodding every once in a while.

"Okay, got it covered. Come with me, but let me do the talking—if that's okay with you?"

"Why not?"

Anna was proud of herself for having taken the initiative; if Caine could get the insurance and other information out of the driver of the Honda, so much the better. She saw him slap a smile on his face and head for the volatile redhead, who now appeared to be chomping on an entire pack of gum at once. Anna followed a few paces behind.

"Hi," Caine said amiably.

"Who the hell are you?" Before he could answer, the woman stabbed a stubby finger in Anna's direction. "This bitch is in so much trouble. I could get her arrested like that." She snapped her fingers in what would have been Caine's face, if he had been eight inches shorter.

His response was surprisingly muted, considering the traffic noise. "You and I both know that you'd be the one in trouble for following too close. Be grateful my client didn't call the police. She was simply obeying the law by stopping for a crossing pedestrian."

"Client?" She chomped furiously on her gum.

Caine nodded, then asked Frizzhead her name.

"Patrice McMasters," Frizzhead replied hesitantly, paling a couple of shades.

"Patrice, I take it you don't actually have insurance."

"Look . . ." She took a crumpled tissue from her

pants pocket and spat her enormous wad of gum into it, then threw it in the general direction of Wild Women. "I know that's against the law, too. But I can't lose my car. I need it to get to my job down at LAX."

Caine nodded. "Completely understandable."

"I'm just so damn stressed out, you know?" Patrice nodded too.

My God, Anna marveled. This was an entirely different woman from the one she'd dealt with previously. How had her dad's intern accomplished that?

Caine reached inside the back pocket of his jeans and pulled out a Tiffany money clip crammed with cash and ID cards. He flicked out a crisp manila business card.

"My friend is an Allstate agent in Redondo Beach," he explained with a calm grin. "Mention that you ran into me, Caine Manning—well, you might not want to use the words *ran into*, exactly."

This coaxed a weak smile from Patrice.

"Now, there's nothing that he can do about this accident, but my client is willing to walk away from this if you are, each responsible for her own repairs." He eyeballed Patrice's battered Honda. "I think you actually came out the worse for it, in fact. But there'll be no claims or lawsuits. Sound good?"

"Sounds good," Patrice agreed, perking up considerably. "But I've only got one problem. My car won't start."

"Let me take a look at that."

As Anna watched, Caine opened the hood of her cherry-red Civic and moved a few wires and cables around. Moments later, he was slamming the hood shut again. "I think your battery cable came loose when you hit my client. Try it now."

Patrice got back in and turned the key; the old Honda started right up.

"You're a lifesaver," she called through her open window.

"The license and insurance info," Anna told Caine softly. "Just to be sure."

"Smart." He nodded, then turned back to Patrice. "Ms. McMasters? I know we've got an agreement here. But let's exchange our information anyway, so in case there's a problem we can reach each other?" A pen and small pad of paper materialized from Caine's back pocket; he smoothly passed them through her cranked-down window. It was like watching a great hypnotist at work, Anna thought as Patrice copied down her information under Caine's watchful eye. He compared it to her driver's license and insurance card, then handed both back to her.

"Okay, 'bye now." Caine touched the hood of the Civic. "Drive safely. Check your radiator fluids when you get a chance."

Patrice raised a hand and started away as Anna and Caine headed back to her car and his truck. "I can't believe . . . I don't know how you . . ." She stopped, then started again. "*Thank you* doesn't even begin to cover it."

"Hey, no problem. She's broke and she was scared, that's all. No sense in suing her. Best thing to do is cut your losses and get on with it."

They reached the Lexus, where he leaned against Anna's front door. "Now, hop in my truck. Where ya headed?"

"Marina del Rey, for a party." She took her phone off the front seat. "If I'm going to leave my car, I need to call Triple-A and ask them to bring it to a Lexus dealership. Isn't there one in Beverly Hills?"

"There is," he confirmed.

"Great." Anna made the call, quickly explained the situation to the harried dispatcher, and then got into Caine's pickup. "I just want to thank you again—"

"No need." He smiled at her. Killer smile. He was so kind. Plus, he'd been able to read that shrew of a woman so well. He was right. She hadn't really been mean; she'd just been scared to death. Anna studied Caine's profile as he started the engine.

Well, well, well, wasn't he the intriguing one?

Five minutes later, they were tooling down Venice Boulevard toward Marina del Rey. Anna had called Sam to say she was indeed on her way after her first L.A. car accident, her first *ever* car accident. Sam said she was now an official Los Angelino and that they'd hold the boat.

Anna put her phone back in her hobo bag and turned to her father's associate.

"I'm curious," she began. "How'd you know that woman didn't have insurance?"

Caine shrugged. "I've always been good with people.

They give off all kinds of clues to what's really going on with them, especially things they're trying to hide."

"You should have been a detective."

"Not for me. Carmen and I don't want to work for The Man."

Anna stared at him quizzically. "Your girlfriend?"

"Carmen. My truck," he laughed, patting the dashboard.

She studied his large, callused hands on the wheel, and then the tattooed forearms. "An investment banking intern with tattoos and earrings. You can get away with that?"

"The earrings come out on workdays. I wear long sleeves at the office. Besides, your father has been known to loosen up now and then."

More than that, Anna thought, recalling how she'd come upon him stoned out of his mind a few weeks ago in the garden gazebo. Her tall and lanky father was a very handsome man who looked much younger than he was. He wore his hair spiked and had told his daughter that smoking a blunt now and then helped him unwind.

"What's the big tattoo on your right arm?"

Caine held it up; a stunningly beautiful woman was etched across his entire forearm, surrounded by lush seashells and swirling clouds. Her wavy hair was woven with vines; sunlight haloed her hair. The figure was vaguely familiar.

"Botticelli, right?" she asked, nudging her chin toward his arm.

He nodded with a half smile. "I guess you were paying attention in art history."

"My mother collects Italian painters."

"Don't you mean *paintings*?"

"Both, actually," Anna admitted. "What made you choose that one? Or is it too personal?"

They turned south on Ocean Avenue, picked up speed, and merged with the heavy late-afternoon traffic. "No big secret. My favorite grandmother was from Florence. Angelina Principesssa Filipepi," he explained.

"Oh my God. She was an actual descendant of Botticelli."

He gave her a curious glance, then changed lanes to maneuver past a slow-moving truck full of gardeners and lawn equipment. "How did you come up with that?"

"Botticelli's birth name was Alessandro Filipepi," Anna recalled. "Wasn't it?"

"Yeah. I just can't believe you knew that."

Anna waved a dismissive hand. "Oh, I'm a fount of useless information. I must have read it somewhere."

"Impressive. Well, my grandmother fancied herself a distant cousin of the artist—I have no idea whether or not that's true. She came to America when she was a girl, put herself through school, and taught art at Fremont High School in South Central for twenty-five years. She was like four-foot eleven and as bad-ass as they come."

Anna knew that South Central was probably the roughest section of Los Angeles.

"You got it to honor her. That's so sweet."

"Actually, we got drunk on Sambuca together one

night and we both got 'em," he admitted, laughing. "She raised me after my mom died. Hell of a lady."

Anna couldn't help but feel curious as to how and when his mother had died, but it was much too personal a question. She hated people who probed like that. What truly horrified her were the casual confidences she'd been privy to in ladies' rooms. Once, at the House of Blues, a girl with punked-out black hair and torn stockings—Anna had never met her before in her life, and had never seen her since—had given Anna a blow-by-blow description of her recent diagnosis and treatment for chlamydia.

"Hey, you want AC?" Caine offered. "I hate the stuff myself, but it's hard to hear you over the noise."

She nodded. He closed his windows and flipped on the air conditioning.

"So, you're on your way to a graduation party—your dad told me. I loved being that age; chilling with my friends, you know?"

The truth was, Anna wasn't yet terribly close with anyone at Beverly Hills High, with the exception of Samantha Sharpe.

"It's okay," she allowed. "But there are some girls who will be at this party who make cobras looks like cashmere kittens tucked in a wicker basket."

Caine's hearty laughter burst like fireworks. Anna grinned back, stealing a glimpse at his laughing profile. What a truly good guy he was, tattoos and all. Gratitude to him, and just general *liking*, bubbled up inside her. She could be friends with this guy. She really could.

"Are you busy tonight?" she blurted out impetuously, remembering why she'd come to Los Angeles in the first place. Nothing ventured, nothing gained. A person couldn't have too many friends; she guessed that Ben would really like Caine, too. "If you aren't, you ought to come with me. There'll be champagne at sea."

Caine raised an amused eyebrow. "Aren't I a little old for your crowd?"

"I know for a fact that you're only twenty-two." Anna could be spontaneous, but she was always prepared with the facts.

"There's light years between seventeen, eighteen, and twenty-one, twenty-two, trust me. Plus, I'm not really big on champagne."

"What, then?"

"Brew. Ice cold."

"How many kinds of beer are there in the world?"

Caine looked quizzical. "Can't say that I know."

"Well, however many kinds there are, my friend Sam will have them all on the yacht. Trust me."

He grinned. "Overkill. All a person needs is one great one." He reached over and slid a CD into Carmen's sound system and cranked it up.

"King Crimson. You know this? It's classic."

Anna shook her head, but listened for a minute. Heavy guitars and a strong drumbeat filled the air, and over them a man's intense but muffled voice. "I like it."

"And I like you," Caine said, flashing that killer grin again. "All righty, then. About this party . . . Count me in."

White Imitation of Christ Jeans Covered in Dog Shit

C ammie Sheppard was the daughter of a Hollywood *über*-agent; she had wined, dined, and reclined with a stellar variety of hot guys on hot yachts since her early teens. Yet even by her own grudging standards, the *Look Sharpe*—the new 120-foot yacht that Sam's father had acquired as the result of a three-picture, eighty-million-dollar deal with the most major of the major studios—was nothing short of spectacular. Now if only she could get this goddamn ocean wind to stop fucking up her hair. She was standing by the vessel's teak starboard railing, and every few seconds a gust of air would blow her vivid strawberry blond ringlets against her Bing My Cherry Plump Your Pucker lip-glossed mouth.

A perfected flick of one OPI ballet-slipper-pink-polished finger (French manicures were *so* last year) unstuck them, as two well-muscled arms snaked around Cammie's waist from behind, pressing her close. Adam Flood's left hand held the necks of two icy cold

Coronas. Cammie took one, lifted the glass bottle to her lips, and took a long swallow.

"Great view, huh?" Adam murmured softly into her ear. Cammie nodded in agreement, leaning further into her boyfriend's embrace. Adam wore khaki cargo shorts and a white linen button-up shirt from the Gap—unlike Cammie and so many of her friends, he had no compunctions about buying clothes without designer labels. And, also unlike Cammie, he'd just gotten a buzz cut that showed off the small blue star tattoo behind his left ear.

Cammie's clothes were a lot more upscale than Adam's, but, surprisingly, she didn't care. It hadn't taken long to pick her outfit from her cedar-lined walk-in closet: Seven For All Mankind jeans with a special-order Ferrari red leather low-slung belt encrusted with diamonds, and an Ella Moss kimono tee in hot pink held together by only a tiny clasp just below her cleavage so that it blew about her on the yacht, revealing miles of creamy alabaster skin. She didn't need to worry about a bra, since her large breasts were compliments of silicone and surgery, and remained unnaturally perky at all times. Her shoes were silvery white Jimmy Choo snakeskin pumps that hadn't even made it to market, courtesy of a 1970s movie star famous for a seminal film in the seventies in which she'd played a notorious female bank robber. This now-over-the-hill star had taken a liking to Cammie and had promised her early dibs on various fashion musts still offered to her by upscale designers who didn't seem to realize—as Cammie did—that the former star was Birds Eye. As in, frozen. As in, Q rating zero. As in, put her on *Hollywood Squares* if it was still on the air.

It was nearly sunset; the blazing sun low in a sky turned pink and purple, its reflection sparkling in the waters of the Pacific to the west. To either side of them were stretches of oak wood chaises covered in persimmon-toned linen, but most of the partygoers were gathered in the main salon. More accurately, gathered around the mahogany bar inlaid in gold with the titles of each of Jackson Sharpe's films, where three bartenders borrowed from the Elysian Fields private club for ladies-who-lunch poured Grey Goose vodka and Patrón tequila into waiting shot glasses.

Sam had redecorated the expansive room in keeping with the theme of her pregraduation party, the Seven Deadly Sins: Pride, Envy, Gluttony, Lust, Anger, Greed, and Sloth. The main salon had been transformed into the Sloth room; in addition to the central bar, an enormous statue of the Greek god Dionysus had been reconfigured into a Cristal-spouting fountain. The A-list graduating seniors from Beverly Hills High—and a few lucky A-minus-listers invited because they were hot enough, amusing enough, or weird enough to be entertaining—had draped themselves on lush ochre velvet chaises that had golden legs and were laden with gold goose-down throw pillows.

The crowded salon had been too much for Cammie,

so while Adam had stayed to get drinks, she'd ventured out onto the yacht's promenade deck.

Yet even the relative solitude and the beauty of the approaching evening couldn't quell the thoughts racing in her brain. Now that she was on the water, she found herself ruminating about her mother. More specifically, her dead mother, who ten years before had gone overboard off a boat off the coast of Santa Barbara and drowned.

It had been ruled an accident, possibly even suicide. Supposedly, Jeanne Reit Sheppard had been drinking, but Cammie couldn't recall ever once seeing her mother with a cocktail in her hand. Much of the official story didn't add up. Now Adam was helping her to unravel the mystery. They'd recently learned shocking information from a newly unsealed police document, that Sam's mom—who'd left Sam and her family to move to the east coast a year later—had been aboard the same boat that very same night, sleeping with Cammie's father.

At first, when Adam had brought her this report from the Santa Barbara police, Cammie had been pissed at him for getting it without her permission. She was still pissed. Or maybe she was just utterly stressed over the fact that after all this time she still didn't know the truth, or how knowing the real truth might affect her life, or—

"Thinking about your mom, right?" Adam guessed.

She leaned into him. "How did you know?"

"Considering where we are, it kind of makes sense."

"I am going to get some answers, you know. My dad gets back from Europe tonight and—"

"Nice tugboat," boomed an indiscreet voice from behind them.

Cammie turned. There was Jack Walker, his rust-colored hair spiked straight up, framing his Elvis Costello glasses.

Trust him to interrupt. Cammie thought that Jack invariably displayed the tact appropriate of his working-class roots—he was probably the only person on the *Look Sharpe* who'd ever set foot in Newark, New Jersey, much less been born there.

Jack was hand in hand with one of Cammie's lifelong friends, Dee Young. Cammie had seen them earlier at the bar: they'd had their arms around each other, and Dee had been laughing at something Jack had said. It made Cammie happy to see Dee that happy. In fact, she looked great too—her wispy blond bangs were swept over one pale blue eye. She'd gained a little weight on her petite five-foot frame; and while normally the words *gained weight* and *looked great* never occurred in the same paragraph in Cammieworld, this was an exception that proved the rule. Dee wore white twill Marc Jacobs cuffed trousers, two C&C California tanks—one turquoise, one robin's egg blue over it—and Indian flip-flops trimmed in blue satin and gilded sequins. Perfect for a party at sea.

Dee had always marched to her own metronome ever since Cammie had known her, but she'd had a serious psychological breakdown on a road trip to Las Vegas a few months before that had landed her in the Ojai Psychiatric Institute, where the high-priced staff—a day at Ojai cost more than the GDP of many island nations—had been able to diagnose a treatable chemical imbalance in her brain.

She'd come out of Ojai a different girl—happier, healthier, and much more self-confident. That was good. It was also boring as shit. Though Cammie was pleased that Dee had regained some sense of psychological equilibrium, she frankly missed the friend who flitted from kabbalah to Esalen and back again at the drop of a Ferragamo, and who'd insist on flying to Sonoma for a pinot noir spa soak because she'd just read about it in the *Los Angeles Times*. That Dee had been a lot more interesting.

"So guess who I saw at Ghost this afternoon?" Dee asked, wide-eyed, naming a boutique on Robertson Boulevard near West Hollywood that was famous for carrying designer sizes in negative numbers—in other words, smaller than size zero. "I was trying on this Dolce & Gabbana sequined slip dress, and I come out of the dressing room, and there was Pashima Nusbaum, about to buy these ugly Zippy Balenciaga by Nicolas Ghesquière shit-kicker boots."

"With *her* legs?" Cammie asked, since Pashima was built like an Oakland Raiders linebacker. "Were you able to keep down your lunch?"

"Care to fill me in?" Adam asked, cocking his head to

the side and raising his eyebrows, an amused expression on his face.

Jack groaned. "You don't really want to know, do you? It's gonna be a girl/shopping/bitch-slap fest."

"No, it won't," Dee insisted, kissing his cheek. "Pashima and her friend Stefanie Weinstock are the girls I told you about. You know, the ones giving the graduation party later in the week."

"Do they go to our school?" Adam looked perplexed.

"Nope. But it's not all that fascinating, Adam," Cammie opined, then put a hand on his arm. "Every year, Pacific Palisades High School and we have a joint pregraduation party. Last year it was thrown by our school, this year it's thrown by theirs. Pashima and Stefanie are the two most evil girls on the planet, but Pashima has the coolest house in Los Angeles. Well, besides Sam's. Her father, like, invented the *Internet*. It's Thursday night, and we're all going. It's tradition."

Adam didn't look impressed. "Why would you go to a party thrown by two girls you hate? You're not even going to remember their names next year."

"*You* may not remember—you're going to be at Pomona. But *I'm* going to be right here in Beverly Hills, running into them at the Ivy. I'll remember."

"Hey, that was your call," Adam reminded. "You're the one who didn't want to start college next year."

Cammie shrugged. "Next year? Any year. I deserve it. Anyway, why do you play basketball against kids that you hate?"

"To win," he admitted.

"Bingo. We outdo them. There's a contest as part of every party, but they don't announce it until, like, the day before."

"Am I going to be sorry if I ask why you hate them so much?" Jack queried.

"What they did . . ." Cammie frowned at the memory. "It's a long, ugly story, so I'll just describe one incident for you. After Stefanie moved to Pacific Palisades, like, a year and a half ago, Sam and I ran into her at and Pashima at Blue on Blue. Sam and I were sitting outside in the patio section, because the tourists sit inside and try to pretend they're somebody. So anyway, Stefanie and Pashima were with these two Abercrombie guys they were pathetically trying to impress."

"Just how long is this story?" Jack broke in.

"You asked, I'm answering," Cammie responded, in her most dignified tone. "Sam was having killer cramps, so I went with her to the bathroom. We get back and slide into our seats. Sam feels something squishy. She jumps up. The ass of her white Imitation of Christ jeans was covered in dog shit."

Jack recoiled. "This chick—"

"Yep. Put dog shit on her chair," Cammie filled in. "Like Sam wasn't self-conscious enough in fucking white jeans already. I told her not to buy them, but that's not the point."

"You're sure those girls did it?" Adam asked. Adam had been raised by two politically correct lawyer parents and was always trying to give people the benefit of the doubt.

"Fuck yes. They were falling all over each other laughing. Then Stefanie blew Sam a kiss and they ran out."

There was a long moment of dead silence.

Then Adam spoke. "Who gets off on that kind of cruelty?"

"Stefanie Weinstock," Cammie replied darkly. First her mother, then Stefanie and Pashima. Why was she spending all this time on such loathsome subjects? "Have you guys been through the boat? Let me take you on the tour." She was determined to get into a better mood.

"Sure," Adam agreed, "I've never been on an amusement park with gills before."

"Me neither, man," Jack agreed, putting his arm around Dee's tiny shoulders.

Cammie hid her inner yawn. Fine. She'd play tour guide for the *Look Sharpe*—Sam had invited her on the vessel's maiden voyage right after Jackson had acquired it, and she knew her way around.

Maybe it would take her mind off what promised to be a very ugly confrontation with her father. Damn. There she was, thinking about her dead mother again. This was the week before graduation; this was supposed to be a time to look to the future, but that obviously wouldn't be possible until she put the past to rest.

How she would accomplish that, she had no earthly idea.

Balancing Out the Baddies

"**O**kay. Who's in the mood for Greed?" Cammie stepped into a VIP guest bedroom suite that had been transformed into a gifting center; the girls' goody bags, by Bliss, were spread on a feather bed covered in a dark green crushed velvet quilted bedspread; the boys', by Fila, were on a matching fifteen-foot-long green sectional sofa.

Two party assistants dressed in black velvet cigarette pants and fitted women's tuxedo shirts knotted under the bust were in charge of handing out the bags. "What are your names, please?" the taller woman asked.

"Dee Young. Plus Adam Flood, Cammie Sheppard, and Jack Walker."

"Perfect," said the other assistant. "Cerise, you get the guys, I'll get the girls."

Adam was the first one to have a bag pressed into his hands. He opened it and peered inside.

"Jeez, there must be hundreds of dollars worth of stuff in here. How did they know this was . . . Okay, this is cool." He held up a small bottle that contained a miniature wooden version of the *Look Sharpe*.

"What a great Christmas present!" Dee exclaimed. God, she felt wonderful. Sure, there was a carefully prescribed cocktail of pills balancing out the baddies running in her brain, but she didn't think her good feelings were all due to pharmaceuticals. Nor were they due to that afternoon's oxygen facial and Escada shopping spree.

It was Jack. Smart, sexy, *deep* Jack. She had met him the night of the senior prom. Cammie had convinced Jack, whom Dee had never met before, to be Dee's date (well, technically her second date, since she was also escorted by an Ojai chaperone). The connection had been electric. They'd shared secrets.

He had told her all about his sister, Margie, back in New Jersey, the one who'd been brain damaged as an infant. What made Jack's sister happiest was watching reality television with her palms pressed against the TV screen. Together, they would watch *Survivor*, *Big Brother*, and *The Apprentice*. Dee could have sworn that she saw a glimmer of tears in his eyes when Jack talked about Margie.

And Dee had confessed how, some months ago, she'd told everyone she was pregnant with Ben Birnbaum's baby. Ben, who was Jack's best bud from college. Total lie. Dee had just wanted attention. And Jack had said he understood.

Cammie had fixed them up; Jack was in L.A. to work in Fox's reality programming division for the entire summer. Dee had gotten a lot of therapy at Ojai and had learned a lot about herself. She'd learned that she couldn't handle too much pressure in her life, which made her decide to go to Santa Monica Community College for at least a year, instead of one of the other schools she'd applied to, like UC Santa Cruz and Evergreen State College up in Washington. Thanks to Cammie, though, she had the best medicine of all: love. That thought was corny as shit, but Dee didn't care.

The tall assistant gave her an enormous Bliss bag, and Dee checked out the contents, squealing with delight as she tore open her treasure trove: Kiehl's pineapple facial scrub and seaweed clay mask; a real oceanic bath sponge; a Nars eye shadow palette in Sea, Sex & Sun; Lulu Frost drop earrings in gold and red coral; and a Rosa Chá beach tunic in shimmering turquoise chiffon swirling with sequined flowers in pink and orange, in size extra small. Last but not least, a red leather Gucci motorcycle jacket with her name set on the back in tiny rubies. Cammie's gift bag was the same, except instead of a long tunic, she got a London by London strapless tangerine one-piece bathing suit with strategic cutouts on the stomach and lower back.

The boys fared just as well, with baby-blue Lacoste polo shirts, Kiehl's Ultimate Man exfoliating scrub, and the male version of the Gucci motorcycle jacket in jet black.

They decided to leave their loot and pick it up later, which allowed Cammie to continue the tour. The *Look*

Sharpe was immense, with two upper decks for Jackson and his guests, and a lower deck for the crew. At two hundred and sixty-five feet, it was aquatic luxury at its best . . . not to mention at its most expensive.

Their next stop on the tour was the vaulted shipboard movie theater, crowded with partyers, which currently was screening a reel of guest spots that Jackson had done for his favorite shows—*Will & Grace* and *The West Wing*—in a futile effort to keep them on the air. Dee noted that quite a few couples in the theater were busy making out. It was then that Jack cupped his hand around her butt. She *loved* that about him; how he wanted her all the time.

After that, Cammie led the way to the main salon on the uppermost deck. "Oh look," she pronounced coolly as they stepped into a high-ceilinged atrium. "It's a double. Lust *and* Envy,"

In stark contrast to the rest of the ship, which was mainly muted reds and browns, this room was completely white, save for a dozen tall windows facing the stern. A throng of at least sixty kids was jammed around a white marble platform suspended from the ceiling. Adam and Jack led the way through the crowd to get a better look at whatever was fixating everyone so thoroughly. Then Jack lifted Dee up on his shoulders so she could see: Six girls, wearing nothing but pale lime-green bras, lacy panties, garter belts, and white patent leather Electra-2020 go-go boots, were dancing wildly on the platform, even helping up willing guys to gyrate with them.

"Looks like Sam snagged the Pussycat Dolls," Cammie noted. "Great idea, but she should have warned me."

Dee knew the Pussycat Dolls—a cabaret group fixture at the Roxy for many years; they were now chart-topping pop stars—and giggled. "You hate it if anyone thinks of anything fabulous before you do."

"Because I am usually the prime mover of that which is truly fabulous, Dee," Cammie responded.

"Yeah, that's right," Dee recalled.

"I don't get it," Adam mused loudly to be heard over the pulsing music. "Why name this room both Lust and Envy?"

"Isn't it obvious, man?" Jack replied, as he put Dee back on the hardwood floor. "The guys are drooling all over themselves, but the girls are analyzing whether or not they look as good as the Dolls." He leaned over to his new girlfriend and whispered, "You're way hotter than any of those girls."

"So is Cammie," Dee whispered back.

"You're hotter."

This thrilled her. He thought she was hotter than Cammie Sheppard? No one was hotter than Cammie Sheppard.

"Shall we press on?" Cammie suggested. "Pride is the full-service salon at the end of the deck. Anger is the piñatas at the stern."

"How about food?" Adam queried. "There's only so much I can take on an empty stomach."

"Downstairs is Gluttony."

Dee wasn't hungry. Not for food. What she was ravenous for was to tear each and every article of clothing off Jack's wiry body. "Why don't you guys nosh, and I'll . . . take Jack . . . to look at . . . the helipad," she invented.

"You do that," Cammie agreed; Dee was sure she knew full well what Dee's actual intentions were.

"Helipad?" Jack asked her, as soon as they were out of earshot. Dee winked. "You read my mind, babe," Jack said with a grin.

Dee led them back to one of the smaller rooms, stepped inside and flipped on a gold-plated light switch, which revealed a massive plasma screen on the wall, plus a small stage. Several chintz-covered maroon sofas and armchairs surrounded a marble table. A small square machine was hooked up to the plasma screen, as well as two microphones.

"It's a karaoke lounge," Jack laughed. "You ought to hear my version of Third Eye Blind's 'Forget Myself.'"

Then he was kissing her, easing her down to a vermillion loveseat piled with downy cushions. When he nuzzled the curve between her neck and her shoulder, goosebumps exploded on Dee's arms.

"Don't sing," she instructed. "I've got something else in mind. Please?"

Bitch in a BMW

The gorgeous bartender with the waist-length red ringlets handed Caine a Heineken and Anna a small green bottle of Kona Nigari water with a lime slice pressed around the rim, then inserted a straw through the bottle's small opening with a special hook. Kona Nigari was desalinated and heavily mineralized water that came from a pipe two thousand feet below the surface of the ocean off the coast of Hawaii. It retailed for nearly fifty dollars for two ounces, and had become quite the rage among Beverly Hills' cognoscenti.

Anna sipped it. It tasted like . . . water.

"Quite a boat," Caine remarked, as they strolled the upper deck. A DJ was spinning Coldplay; a few couples danced while dozens of others dotted the area—drinking, talking, laughing, and doing various versions of an upscale mating dance.

"Isn't it?" Anna agreed. She wanted to introduce Caine to Sam. "As soon as I see the hostess, I'll introduce you."

Anna turned around to see if she could spot Sam, but

no luck. She did, however, see Cammie and Adam. The
sight of Cammie made her smile mirthlessly. It had almost
become a point of twisted pride that Cammie Sheppard
didn't like her. Cammie was one of Sam's best friends, and
for a while Anna had tried to be open-minded, because
maybe there was some good lurking beneath Cammie's
outrageously sexy good looks. But she was Ben's former
girlfriend, which only exacerbated things, and before
Cammie had gotten together with Adam, she'd made it
clear on many occasions that she'd be happy to get Ben
back, if only to prove that she could. When it came to
Anna, Cammie Sheppard was 100 percent viper.

"Hello, Cammie." She quickly introduced Caine to
her and Adam. They both looked at him strangely.

"I didn't realize Ben had already dumped you,"
Cammie said, gathering her strawberry blond ringlets
into a bun on top of her head and then letting them fall
around her slim shoulders.

"He didn't," Anna replied, keeping her voice even.
"Ben had to work. Caine—"

"Let me guess. He's just a friend?" The way she said
it made it clear that she didn't believe it for an instant.

"Chill, Cam," Adam suggested easily, wrapping an arm
around Cammie's shoulders. Anna smiled. He was a great
guy. In fact, she and Adam had dated for a short while, and
she'd basically dropped him to get together with Ben again.
She wasn't proud of that, because Adam deserved the best,
and Anna knew this much: the best was *definitely* not
Cammie Sheppard. So what was he doing with her? Was it

that the sex was great? What was it that Cammie *did* that made her so intoxicating anyway?

"Really. Caine is my father's intern." Anna briefly explained about her car accident and how he had come to her rescue.

"Another Sir Galahad. Seems to be your type." Cammie's eyes flicked over Caine's tattoo-laden forearms. "Nice ink. See you."

"Nice to meet you, man," Adam said, before he and Cammie strolled away.

"So, no love lost between you two, huh?" Caine commented when Cammie and Adam were gone. They drifted along the starboard side of the *Look Sharpe*—three miles out to sea, they could see the marina and the Manhattan Beach shoreline bathed in the magnificent fire-red light of a perfect Pacific sunset.

"Exactly. For one thing, she's a witch. For another, she used to be with my boyfriend."

"Who broke it up?"

Anna was surprised that he cared. "Ben. Not to be with me, though. I met him long after that. She still acts as if we're romantic rivals."

"Hey, a woman scorned and all that." Caine stopped, leaned an elbow against the railing, and contemplated Anna. "So tell me about this boyfriend. Ben, did you say?"

Anna nodded. "He had to work. That's why he's not here."

Caine nodded. "I figured."

Anna flushed. "I thought you and I could be friends."

Caine threw his head back and let out an easy laugh. "I figured that, too."

Anna laughed with him. She liked Caine. A lot. "Ben is great!" she said, sounding ridiculously perky.

"I told you, I read people really well. You're a true-to-your-guy type. Correct?" He upended his beer and finished it.

"Honestly? Yes."

He hoisted the beer bottle as if in a toast. "Good for you. Not enough of your kind left in this world."

"Are you a true-to-your-girl type?"

"Most definitely."

Anna wondered who his last girlfriend was and why they'd ended, but she didn't ask.

They continued to walk until they reached the stern. There was a helipad back there, for when the yacht was already at sea and Jackson wanted to join the voyage. Just past the small two-seater chopper, Anna saw a massive, school-shaped piñata suspended from a weighted-and-jointed metal rod.

Gathered around it was a cheering crowd; in the center of the crowd, whacking at the piñata, were Parker Pinelli and Candace Lepore. Candace's mother was an extremely successful designer of hand-embroidered one-of-a-kind coats and jackets. Candace was apparently Parker's latest conquest. She fit all of his criteria: gorgeous, not all that bright, and filthy rich.

"Anna!" Sam scurried over on white Chloé kitten-heeled sandals, topped by a pair of dark denim Diesel jeans, which in turn were topped by a red-and-white polka-dot Anna Sui peasant top, dotted with seed pearls and crystals. The blouse fell past her hips, hiding the body part that Anna knew her friend liked the least. She hugged Anna warmly, gesturing at the piñata. "We're beating the shit out of Pacific Palisades High."

Then she took in Caine. "Hey, Anna," she said with a grin. "Who's your date?"

Caine extended his hand to Sam. "Caine Manning."

"Sam Sharpe. Nice to meet you. Thanks for getting Anna here in one piece. Excuse me!" Sam called to a stringy-haired, but still hot, waiter who was working the crowd with seafood hors d'oeuvres—fenneled jumbo prawns, raw oysters, and Beluga caviar on toast points. "Could you tell the captain to turn north? Ask him to anchor off of Barbra's place in Malibu."

"Thanks for waiting for me," Anna told her. "For a while there I didn't think I'd make it. I was stuck there in—"

"Take that, Stefanie Weinstock! You ridiculous BB!" Candace shrieked, battering away at the piñata. The crowd cheered so loudly that Anna couldn't finish her sentence.

Sam spread her hands wide. "Do I have the greatest friends in the world or what?"

"Who is Stefanie Weinstock?" Anna wondered aloud.

"Surely you jest," Sam chided. "You know. Bee-in-Bee."

"Bring Indian Beer?" Caine guessed.

Sam shook her head. "Admirable effort, but it stands for Bitch in BMW. She's legendary. She's—"

"And here's to you, Pashima Nusbaum, you ass-clown!" Candace took another swat at the piñata.

"Who are these girls?" Anna was baffled.

"Anna, Anna, Anna," Sam sighed. "You've lived among us for five months. Surely you've heard of Stefanie and Pashima."

"No, Sam, I haven't."

"Whatever." Sam waved a dismissive hand. "Can I help it if you transferred here the middle of senior year?" Then she grabbed Anna's wrist. "Caine, excuse us. We're about to do one of those things where two girls pretend they have to go pee so that they can talk. *In private.*"

The Girl's Back Is Like, Cro-Magnon

"Their names are Stefanie Weinstock and Pashima Nusbaum." Sam leaned out over the white-metal railing of the bow of the *Look Sharpe*. Anna stood next to her, brightly lit in the bow floodlights. "They deserve to be ruined. Especially Stefanie. Graduation week is the time to do it. Actually, their graduation party is the time to do it."

"I don't even know this girl," Anna protested. "Why would I want to dedicate my last week of high school to destroying her?"

Sam's face grew dark. "Just listen. Stefanie used to live in Beverly Hills. Her father is an orthodontist on Wilshire who was one of the first people who started using those clear braces, you know, like Tom Cruise had a few years back. Remember? It seemed like he actually thought no one could see them and from the mouth down he suddenly looked like he was about twelve except the rest of his face still looked forty so it was really weird?"

Anna shrugged as Sam plunged on. "We used to let

Stefanie hang out with us. She had zero style and even less class. She was a project, like in *Emma* or *Clueless*. Like that formerly fat girl, Maddy, who was living at Ben's house."

"Thank God that's over. She went back to Michigan early. But anyway, go on."

"Okay, so we taught Stefanie everything. How to flat-iron her hair. The right skin stuff. We got her to stop wearing purple nail polish. We took her for her first body wax, for God's sake! Talk about hairy—the girl's back is like, Cro-Magnon."

"She's hirsute. Got it."

Sam nodded. "She even came to sleepovers, where we told each other our deepest, darkest secrets. Then her parents got divorced and she moved to Burbank with her mother."

"So far I'm not hating the girl."

"Oh, you will. So, the mom married this asshole with a bad comb-over, who invented the dead-fish tie. I think she likes inventors."

Anna was totally lost now. "I have zero idea what you're—"

"The dead-fish tie," Sam repeated impatiently. "Shaped like a dead bass. No one we know would wear one, of course, but they became huge in places you'd only go on a forced march. You know, states with lots of strip malls, whatever."

"And . . . ?"

"And every discount mart in the country bought this

shit. The guy made a gazillion dollars. They bought an old mansion in Pacific Palisades, right on the ocean."

There was a table of cold hors d'oeuvres behind her; she plucked an iced shrimp from a silver tray and popped it into her mouth. "The point here is that Dee, Cammie, and I *made* this girl."

"Um, this actually doesn't make any sense. You were nice to her. And—"

"She turned against us!" Sam felt bile rise in her stomach. "Why? Who knows? I ask you, does Pinocchio hate Geppetto? Stefanie then used everything she knew about us to hurt us. How bad? She started a Web site called "OinkthePig; every line of it referred to me as Pig Sharpe."

Anna inhaled quickly. "Oh my God. That's unbelievably mean."

"She used to call Dee, have an entire conversation with her, and then claim she never called and that Dee was hearing voices."

"That's sick."

"Tell me about it."

"So, Stefanie and her best friend Pashima are giving the two-school pregraduation party at Pashima's house next Thursday," Sam concluded. She threw the tail of the shrimp overboard. "I want to teach them a lesson they'll never forget."

"Sam, this girl sounds awful. But to sink to her level . . ."

"That's the beauty of it." She opened her Kate Spade bag and took out a Stila lip gloss in Strawberry Tarte.

"And if you do, so what?"

Sam slicked her lips with gloss, then linked an arm through Anna's. "Revenge is best served cold, Anna dearest. Let's get back to your new boyfriend before he jumps ship."

"He's not my boyfriend!" She smiled and shook her head quickly.

"Yes, Anna," Sam said with a grin. "I know that you and Ben are joined at the hip. But Tattoo Boy is hot. Of course, at the moment I'm a rejected woman, so my cute radar is a little off."

Anna's hand fell on her arm. "This is about Eduardo."

"No, it isn't."

"Yes, it is. You're trying to take your mind off what happened with him."

"I *am* going to get Eduardo back. I am devising a game plan even as we speak. " As if to prove the point, she dug her ruby-and-diamond-encrusted Samsung phone out of her bag and pressed one of the speed-dial buttons.

"You're calling him?"

Sam shushed her friend—Eduardo's voice-mail message played.

"Hi, it's me again. Just give me a chance to explain, Eduardo. It's nothing like you think. Next time I call, answer. Please."

With a sigh, she dropped her phone into the back pocket of her pants.

"Still won't return your calls?" Anna asked hesitantly.

Sam shook her head, so frustrated. Eduardo Muñoz was the dashingly handsome son of a wealthy Peruvian government official. He and Sam had met when Anna and Sam had been on vacation in Mexico. Eduardo was a student at the Sorbonne in Paris and hadn't been able to take her to prom due to a family reunion in Mexico. By the end of the night, she'd had way too much to drink, and ended up kissing Parker Pinelli on the beach at the after party. It had been a horror-show moment: unbeknownst to Sam, Eduardo had jetted back to L.A. and showed up to surprise her . . . just in time to see the lip-lock in progress. After which Eduardo had walked away. He hadn't called Sam since, nor had he responded to any of the dozen phone messages she'd left for him in the couple weeks since.

"Try an e-mail," Anna suggested gently. "At least you'd get to explain yourself."

"He'll delete it."

"He might not. It's worth trying. I know he loves you."

"Let's go back to the piñatas," Sam declared, looking toward the crowd. "I want to sublimate my anger."

Two minutes later, Sam was wading into the midst of the piñata bashers—they still hadn't brought down the Pacific Palisades High School piñata—put two fingers in her mouth, and whistled.

"Everybody! Chill out for a second! I have an announcement to make."

Parker lowered the club. The crowd noise died down. Everyone waited.

"As we all know," Sam began, "this year Stefanie and Pashima are giving the big graduation party."

"Fuck Stefanie!" someone yelled, and the crowd booed in support.

Sam waved a hand to silence the noise. "Indeed. Parker, give me that club!"

Everyone cheered; Sam took the thick wooden stick from Parker and whacked the piñata with all her might. She wasn't one of those girls who lived at L.A. Fitness, but there was more than muscle mass fueling her. There was fury. After three smashing blows, the papier-mâché schoolhouse shattered. Instead of candy flying out, tiny plastic dolls scattered over the deck. They were all, oddly, headless.

Sam scooped one up. Written on its little T-shirt was the name "Stefanie," just as she had ordered. On the back were three letters: R.I.P. She chucked the headless doll over the side of the yacht. Dead in the water. Just like Stefanie would be at her party. Well, at least socially, which was sometimes worse than the real thing.

Sexy Blue Star

The yacht had docked at midnight; it was now nearly one in the morning. It occurred to Cammie that she must really, really love Adam. The proof was that they were zipping along the 10 freeway in Adam's mother's green Saturn. A *Saturn*.

Adam's right hand caressed her thigh. "You still want to do this tonight?"

This being "confront her father." Cammie knew he'd still be awake. He could never sleep when he returned from a business trip.

Did she still want to do it? Maybe she should just drag Adam up to her bedroom to make wild monkey love instead of dredging up the past. Sex was easier than dealing with emotions. Plus, she was so much better at it.

They'd talked about her mom on the boat. A little. Then she'd downed three cosmopolitans and spent the balance of the night dancing and partying.

"Cam?" Adam prompted again.

For a while, Cammie had wondered if her mother had ended her own life because she would rather be dead than be Cammie's mother. It was a heartbreaking notion; confirmation that on some level, Cammie wasn't sufficiently lovable. Now, with the information that Adam had brought to her, Cammie felt closer than ever to proving that her mother's death hadn't been a suicide or the result of some drunken accident.

"Adam?" She shifted in her seat.

"Yeah?"

"Is it nuts to think that Sam's mom and my dad murdered my mom?"

Saying it aloud certainly made it sound nuts.

Adam's knuckles tightened on the steering wheel. "You don't really think—"

"I think it's possible." She rushed on, afraid that if she stopped talking, the words would never come out. "You read the same police report. Sam's mom was on the yacht that night. My dad never told me about that. Then she moved away right after. Why? Why would Sam's mother do that to her own daughter?"

"Well, a whole lot of reasons that aren't *murder*." Adam shifted to the center lane and accelerated—there was no traffic on the 10; it was a rare, satisfying feeling to be cruising along at the actual speed limit.

"Just think about it," Cammie urged. "She never calls, never writes; she just pretends Sam doesn't exist."

"Still, Cammie. Jeez. That's quite an accusation."

"It's possible."

"Yeah, I know, but still . . . this isn't one of your dad's

TV shows. It's not going to tie up in a little bundle in sixty commercial-free minutes."

Cammie sat up and tossed her curls angrily. "Don't fucking patronize me. I mean it. My father is ruthless. Everyone knows it. He'll do anything to get what he wants. He'll do anything."

"You're talking about murder."

"*Anything*," she repeated. Tears sprang to her eyes and she dug her nails into her hands so keep herself from crying. "My mom loved me. I know she did. She would never, ever have left me unless . . ."

Adam draped his right arm around her. "I know how much it hurt you. I really do."

She didn't trust herself to say anything. Adam wanted to protect her from her fears, guard her from harm. It was so sweet. But every now and then, Cammie struggled with an ugly truth: Sometimes she didn't want sweet. She wanted tough, or dangerous, or just plain bad. She knew this was fucked up. She was *trying* not to want that anymore. Because Cammie almost always got what she wanted. Except when it came to love.

"When we get back to my house, my dad should be there." Cammie went on. "He's not going to avoid me," she reached up and grabbed Adam's hand, which was resting over her shoulder. "Will you please, please help me?"

Adam pulled the Saturn up to Clark Sheppard's immense spread high in the hills of Bel-Air. It was so quiet—you couldn't see or hear noise from another

mansion from the parking area. His quick hug gave
Cammie the strength to unlock the front door and tap
the code into the security system.

Moments later, they were inside—she went straight
to the front living room, with Adam close behind. It was
crammed with Louis XIV Bergere chairs and Finnish
traveling trunks–turned–coffee tables, all atop a soft
plush beige Berber carpet. Cammie didn't expect to find
her dad there, but his private home office was attached
to the living room. That was her real destination, and the
light was on under the door. A good sign.

He hated to be disturbed when he was working,
which was why Cammie didn't bother to knock—just
pushed open the big brass double doors.

To her surprise, his brushed-stainless-steel desk chair
was empty; the brass Levenger lamp turned to dim.
Could her father actually have gone to bed? If so, he was
losing his edge—what happened to the Clark Sheppard
who read every draft of every script and watched more
dailies than his directors?

She gazed around. Nothing. No sign of life. Just a
single page of paper sitting in the output tray of her
father's Xerox WorkCentre Pro 785 plain-paper fax
machine.

She went to it and read.

The fax was on Apex Agency stationery. In fact, it
had been addressed to her. After all the identifying crap
at the top—the To/From/Re/Number of Pages—the
message was a crystal-clear blow-off:

Cammie Sheppard,

Mr. Clark Sheppard arrived from Europe this evening as scheduled. However, due to his considerable workload, Mr. Sheppard asked us to inform you that he has checked into a bungalow at the Beverly Hills Hotel, and under no circumstances is he to be disturbed.

Many thanks,

Alleister Blaise

Personal assistant to Mr. Sheppard

"Bullshit," she declared.

Adam asked what was going on; Cammie gave him the fax, with plenty of editorializing to boot. Her father had arranged a disappearing act so as not to have to deal with her; she was certain of it.

"I'll be right back," she told Adam, distractedly. "Wait in the living room."

She sprinted upstairs to her closet, practically ripping off the clothes that she'd worn on the yacht. What does one wear when one goes to give one's father hell? She opted for a pair of Imitation of Christ jeans, a tiny lemon-yellow vintage T-shirt she'd picked up with Adam at the Coachella festival in Palm Springs, and Swarovski-studded flip-flops.

She was about to start back downstairs, but stopped to take a deliberate look at the half-finished wall mural of *Charlotte's Web*, her favorite childhood book. Her mother had died before she could complete it. Cammie had insisted that the mural move from the bedroom of her old house into the mansion. Sometimes she would stare at it, trying to remember the soft sounds of her mother's intonation of Wilbur, Templeton, and Charlotte.

Now, hard as she tried, Cammie couldn't remember that voice anymore.

Her hands flew to where her heart would be if she had one—who could afford a heart when going toe-to-toe with Clark Sheppard, the meanest man in Hollywood? If she went with her heart instead of her head, she would lose and her father would win. Hearts were soft sometimes; they made mistakes. Cammie couldn't afford to take that chance.

One sign of a great hotel is that it's just as busy at two o'clock in the morning as it is at two o'clock in the afternoon. The Beverly Hills Hotel was even busier—an endless line of cars and SUVs were waiting to pull into the valet roundabout. The three pink sandstone hotel towers were floodlit; tonight, the flagpoles displayed the flags of Ireland, Italy, and Israel, as well as the United States.

Finally, Adam was able to edge the Saturn forward under the roundabout's pink-and-white-striped canopy. A young uniformed valet with a white-blond buzz cut and startling blue eyes took the keys with the most supercilious of nods, somehow miffed that he'd even have to put a low-end vehicle like a Saturn in the parking area with all the Jaguars, Beemers, and Range Rovers.

Adam took the claim ticket, then held Cammie's elbow as they as they headed between the famous four columns and up the long red carpet that led to the double glass doors. "You're sure . . . ?"

"Stop asking me that."

Cammie slapped a cool smile on her face and went through the pink-and-white lobby, with its elegant seating areas, massive art deco chandelier, and huge potted plants, to the understated front desk, Adam just a step behind her. A uniformed young woman greeted her with a warm "Welcome to the Beverly Hills Hotel. May I help you?"

"Hello, Jara," Cammie replied sweetly, reading the young woman's name tag. Jara was very tall and slender, with a glossy chestnut brown bob. Obviously a wannabe model.

Cammie tapped a quizzical finger against her lower lip, deciding how to play the scene. "Wait. Didn't I see you in *Vogue* last month? Modeling that purple silk-charmeuse Proenza Schouler miniskirt?"

The young woman's face stretched into a glossy grin, showing off twin dimples. "I wish. I'm still shopping for an agent. How may I help you?"

"Well, Jara, I'm Cammie Sheppard; my *father*, Clark Sheppard, is staying in one of the bungalows, and it's *urgent* that I see him."

"One moment, please." Jara crossed to her manager, a tan guy who bore a startling resemblance to a Ken doll. After a brief conference, she returned. "I'm sorry, but Mr. Sheppard has specified that no one is to disturb him."

Cammie grabbed the edge of the burnished walnut counter. "Maybe you didn't hear me." Her voice remained as calm as before. "I said I'm his *daughter*."

"I know. But he left very strict instructions."

"Oh, I see." Cammie's voice dripped gentle disdain. "So if I was being *assaulted*, or our *house was burning down*, or his wife was *having a heart attack*, you'd have to call his bungalow and leave a message on his voice mail?"

"Cammie." She felt Adam's hand on her arm but shook him off.

"Excuse me, but I'm having a little chat with Jara the wanna-be model. Now, where were we, Jara? Oh yes, you were about to tell me what bungalow my father is in."

Jara handed Cammie a heavy sheet of embossed hotel stationery. "May I suggest that you leave a note for him? I'll have one of the house staff deliver it."

With a cold smile, Cammie methodically tore the paper into little pieces and let them rain down on Jara's side of the desk. "Apex Agency gives this establishment hundreds of thousands of dollars a year in business. If you don't give me that bungalow number, I assure you, not only can you forget about a modeling agent *ever*, but you'll also end up working the night shift at the Holiday Inn."

Cammie saw Adam wince. Well, sometimes power was best applied discreetly, and then sometimes stronger measures were called for. Her father had taught her that lesson too.

Jara nodded coolly. "We all admire your father. We respect him. Which is exactly why we are following *his* orders, not yours. Have a lovely evening." With that, she politely smiled at the next customer, a Sikh gentleman in a turban. "Welcome to the Beverly Hills Hotel. How may I help you?"

Cammie was floored—she *always* struck fear into the hearts of bartenders, bellhops, waiters—pretty much anyone low on the food chain. This bony-ass bitch was not going to thwart her plans. She tried to take Adam's arm and start back into the lobby, but he didn't move.

"Well?" she challenged.

"First of all, stop ordering me around. It's ugly, nasty, bitchy, and pretty much all-around uncalled for. Are we clear?"

Oops. Gone too far.

"Sorry." She put her hand on his. "I'm just upset. And . . . and I know what we have to do. There's a path out back that leads to the bungalows."

"So?"

"So we knock on doors until we find my dad."

Adam was incredulous. "Not happening, Cammie. Not at two in the morning because you've got an issue with your father."

Is that all he thought this was? An *issue?*

"Fine. I can do this on my own."

"We don't think so."

Suddenly, two house detectives in impeccable Ted Lapidus suits were on either side of them. One was tall and thin with a short silver brush cut; the other was not much taller than Cammie but half again as wide as Adam . . . and none of it was fat.

"Miss, we think this would be a good time for you and your companion to go home," the tall one suggested.

"Do you know who I am?"

"Yes, Miss Sheppard. Which is why we're going to walk you to the door."

There was another lesson that Clark had taught her: Know when to retreat. It's better than being bloodied on the battlefield.

"Fine. We'll take care it of this morning."

Five minutes later, they were on their way back to Bel-Air. As Adam drove, Cammie felt a wave of pure exhaustion and was just the tiniest bit ashamed for the way she had acted. Not toward Jara, that stupid bitch, but toward Adam. Why did she always turn on the one person who she was certain actually loved her?

"Adam. I'm sorry." Her voice was low, sincere. "I hate myself when I treat you like that."

"I'm not particularly fond of you at those moments, either." After a silent beat that seemed to go on for an eternity, he relented. "You just had all this adrenaline built up to get into it with your father, and he thwarted you again. I got it."

"Tomorrow," she vowed. "Well, later today. He can't duck me forever." She reached over and caressed the sexy blue star behind his right ear. "Right now I just want to get naked and get in bed. I need to take advantage of you before you go away to college."

"Hey, that isn't for three more months. And it's only fifty miles from here."

"Smart decision."

His lip tugged upward. "Is that about my choice of school, or about what I'm about to say?"

"Both," she responded.

"In that case, yes."

Bohemian, Of-the-People Thing

"This is it?" Jack stared dumbfounded at a nondescript gray low-level building on a nondescript side street off Sunset Boulevard near Vermont Street—a scruffy neighborhood of auto body repair shops, adult bookstores, Mexican bodegas, and medical-supply distributors just across from Los Angeles Children's Hospital. "*This* is supposed to impress people?"

Dee opened up a small, discreet console on an exterior wall and punched in a numerical code. "The music industry is different than Hollywood," she replied in her breathy voice. "It's cooler to have that funky, bohemian, of-the-people thing. Wait till we're inside."

It was the next afternoon, Sunday—a warm and beautiful June day. Jack and Dee were standing in front of a single locked door paneled in deeply tinted glass. The only identification on the door was four numbers and four peeling white letters: RON'S. Jack was having a hard time believing this was a famous recording studio.

Last night, Dee had stayed with him in his tiny Santa Monica guesthouse. It had been blissful, as it had been every single time they were together. He still couldn't fathom how fast and how deeply he'd fallen for her. Back at Princeton, he and Ben had been pretty much hound dogs, at least before Ben had met Anna.

The last thing Jack had expected to happen to him on coming to Los Angeles was to meet a girl he cared about. But there was just something about Dee. She was so genuinely sweet, her innocence brought out the same protective instincts he had for his brain-damaged younger sister. Not that Dee was brain damaged—far from it—but she had the same lack of guile as Margie.

This lack of guile was in stark contrast to her skills in bed, where she was anything but innocent. She'd confessed to him that many of her previous boyfriends had turned out to be gay, which had kind of led to her trying extra hard. He wasn't complaining.

"Funky, bohemian kinda thing," Jack repeated. "Yeah, I'm down with that."

He chuckled, because what rich Los Angelinos knew about real working-class life was exactly nothing. Not like him. Take his own parents, for example: his pop worked the freight yards and barely made enough scratch to supply the family with Kraft mac and cheese. Jack wasn't bitter about his background. In fact, he wore it as a kind of badge of honor, especially in this town. Oh sure, he had serious plans to create his own reality show and become very rich, very young. He knew he had the brains, and with his internship at Fox in the reality TV department, he'd soon have the connections to go with it. But he would never turn into one of them. He called them the richies. Pretentious pricks.

A loud buzzer sounded, and Dee pulled the door open. "We're in," she announced happily, leading him down a stark gray corridor. "Are you sure you're ready to meet my parents?"

"As long as your dad won't put me in a band. I already warned you about my singing."

"He won't," Dee grinned.

"Then we're cool."

It was a unique way to spend a Sunday afternoon. Dee's father—a major record producer—had invited Dee, who had invited Jack, to a showcase for a new band called Evolution. Jack was a bit uncertain about the outing. Meeting the Girlfriend's Parents seemed like a big-ass step. On the other hand, so far, so good. He hadn't yet found himself with that nauseous fight-or-flight feeling he usually got when a relationship got too serious.

The corridor was long; the walls were bright red and covered in signed album covers that had obviously been recorded at the studio. Dee explained that her father, Graham Young, had produced several of the old albums, but was now also moving into music management. He would be managing Evolution, as well as producing their first CD.

They came to the end of the hallway; harsh fluorescent lighting showed that they had three choices: the left fork went to the recording studios and sound booths, the right to a kitchen, conference room, and administrative office. Straight ahead, beyond a sliding glass door, was an outdoor lounge with two long maroon picnic tables.

Dee tugged him toward the conference room and kitchen. "Come on. I'll give you a quick tour before we hear the band. And meet my parents!" She stopped a moment and nibbled at her lower lip. "Maybe I should have had Beloved do your chart before you met them. In case this is an inauspicious moment."

"Come again?"

"Beloved. My mom's assistant. Amazing astrologer. She knew Angelina Jolie was pregnant before Angelina did."

Huh? Every so often, Jack wondered if Dee was still just the teeniest bit . . . off.

The conference room was no great shakes—boxes of files covered the entire surface of the portable folding table, two drum kits were disassembled in the corner, and a couple of electric guitars sat on swiveling chairs. "Not much," Dee acknowledged. "You hungry? There'll be a buffet where the band plays. Organic. Mom's caterer is Mother Earth on Melrose—mung beans, tofu . . ."

Jack shuddered. "I'll take a big, fat pass on that one. I told you, back in New Jersey, as organic as my family got was Chef Boyardee."

"I know. I hope I did okay."

She walked him into a crowded kitchenette and pointed at a line of boxes and cans on the mosaic-tiled counter: SpaghettiOs with meatballs, Hostess Sno-Balls, and Little Debbie Zebra Cakes. This blew Jack away. They were the foods—the *exact* foods—he'd told her he'd loved as a kid.

"I wanted you to feel at home here." She smiled her giant smile and her cornflower-blue eyes lit up.

"You are too much, girl."

She opened a can of SpaghettiOs and poured the contents into a plastic bowl, then popped the bowl in the microwave. Meanwhile, he studied the signed photos of famous musicians that lined the kitchen walls. It was fascinating. Bebe Winans with a burrito, Bette Midler eating a Hawaiian pizza, Jello Biafra with a bowl of Jell-O, Rollins with a slice of pizza, the guys in Green Day holding up a large suckling pig. He had zero idea what that was about, but it was damn funny.

Just as the chrome microwave chimed, a voice from behind them chirped, "Hello, you crazy kids!"

The voice was soft, babylike—a dead ringer for Dee's. Jack turned to see a tiny woman whose sleek blond hair hung perfectly down her back like Donatella Versace's, only this woman had eye-skimming bangs. She had big, round, blue eyes that were just a tad googly, and a nose that was so small it was hard to imagine that it hadn't, at some point, seen the pointy end of a scalpel. She was wearing bubble-gum-pink Cargo gloss, gobs of Lancôme bronzer, and a fuchsia Tory B tunic spangled with crystals, white Juicy Couture linen pants, and bare feet with French-manicured toes. She was about Dee's height and had the same build plus twenty-five years and twenty pounds.

Instantly, Jack knew who it was.

"Hi, Cici!" Dee cried. It surprised Jack that Dee called her mother by her first name. "Wow, you look so cute!"

"Thanks, honey; I hope you don't mind. I nicked the threads from your closet. The tunic hides everything in the middle, thank God. I can hardly breathe in your pants. But after a couple more days on the fat flush diet, I'll be skinnier than you. People will think I'm your older sister, not your mother." She stepped toward Jack. "Well, you must be the guy I've been hearing so much about."

"Cici, this is my friend Jack Walker." Jack relaxed visibly at the word *friend*. Dee hadn't used the *b*-word. Boyfriend. "He just finished his first year at Princeton. He's friends with Ben Birnbaum."

"Oh my God, Ben's father is just the best plastic surgeon in the world," Cici gushed. "I know women whose lives the man has saved. *Saved*."

"Burn victims?" Jack asked half-facetiously. He scratched his chin, trying to keep a straight face.

"Hardly." She made a gesture at her chin to indicate hanging jowls, then a similar motion at her breasts. "One day you wake up and your whole body is just falling to the floor. It's terrifying," She grabbed Jack's arm. "I think we need to all be very, very upfront about our feelings, our lives, our *essence*, don't you?"

Fuck no. It's no one's damn business.

"Like, take the word *crazy*," Cici went on, not letting go of his arm. "What does it mean, really?"

"It's just a label," Dee agreed. "A *mean* label."

"Wait until you hear Evolution." Her mother beamed, her googly eyes bulging a little. "They're so in tune with their essence. I named the band, you know. Evolution. As in, evolved to a higher plane."

"Gotta love it," Jack commented. He now had a sneaking suspicion as to why Dee had gone off the deep end. It was genetic.

The microwave beeped and Dee handed him the steaming bowl. As he speared a few SpaghettiOs, a short, red-faced white guy stepped into the kitchen. He had the build of a snowman; a small round head atop a larger round stomach, which led to two sticklike legs in baggy gangsta-style jeans. There was serious bling around his neck. This look would have been acceptable, even expected, in the music industry, had the man not been forty-five years old.

"Hi, Daddy," Dee called out.

Graham Young was too livid to return her greeting. "Have you seen Armando?" He was carrying a glass bowl of creamy Alfredo sauce, which he flung into a garbage can. "What the fuck is that cook trying to do? He knows my lead guitar player is lactose intolerant!"

"Honey," Cici pointed out. "It's tofu. Not to worry."

He ran and literally fished the bowl out of the trash. "Oh. Why didn't anyone tell me?"

Okay, Jack decided. The whole family was insane. Suddenly, Graham Young noticed his daughter.

"Babykins! Kitten!" He scooped Dee up in his arms,

then stopped suddenly and turned to Jack. "So, you must be the guy I keep hearing about."

The guy he kept hearing about?

Jack set his SpaghettiOs on a counter and offered him his hand. "Jack Walker. Nice to meet you, sir."

"Sir. He calls me sir!" Dee's father chortled. "Funny guy. Cici, do you know where the new guitar strings are? Cody needs them."

"Beloved put them in his dressing room," Cici explained, as her Sidekick began to sing inside her purple Balenciaga bag.

"Dad, can you put me down now?"

"Sure, sweetheart."

"Beloved's of the Baha'i faith," Dee went on. "Very spiritual. Her name used to be Ethel."

Jack nodded. "I can see why she changed it."

"Listen, it was great to meet you." Graham nodded vigorously to Jack. "Now I gotta go." He zoomed out of the kitchen.

Cici smiled, as if her husband was the most normal person on earth. "So, kids. How about if we go hear the band?"

Evolution was comprised of four American guys in their early twenties who had met at an English boarding school outside the town of York, where they'd practiced in front of the roaring fireplace in their dormitory's common room. Even though they were privileged kids from rich families, Graham Young had retooled them into the Beatles circa *Yellow Submarine*. He'd even had the lead singer—formerly Sam Gebhardt—legally change his name to Darwin.

The studio performance space was crowded—A and R reps from top record labels, music editors from *Rolling Stone* and *L.A. Weekly*, plus programming execs from MTV, VH1, and the other cable music channels all huddled around the good tables. The guys were all dressed in some variation on white T-shirts and jeans; the women seemed to have agreed that since it was a Sunday, sundresses were in order. Jack was glad that he fit in, with jeans and a navy blue New York Yankees T-shirt.

Cici and Graham had redecorated the room for the showcase, opting for an Indian subcontinent motif; tapestry rugs from Bombay were layered artfully on the hardwood floor. On top of the rugs were twenty or so squashy velvet pillows edged in delicate fringe. Sweet-smelling incense burned slowly in various metal holders studded with golden stars and moons. Cici was busy adding to the olfactory assault, scurrying around the room and fanning a huge feather over a large abalone shell that spilled sage smoke into every nook and cranny.

"My mom is spiritually cleansing the room," Dee explained, as they stood in the back of the space, taking in the scene.

"Good to know. Let's sit down."

They found some unused pillows toward the back, since the industry guests were supposed to be closest to the band. Once everyone was settled, the Ravi Shankhar music that had been playing faded out, the lights dimmed, and Evolution took their place on the stage. Before they began, though, a shaman shuffled in, wearing a long red ceremonial gown of indiscriminate origin. He carried a long wooden branchlike item that tinkled with every step, and took a place behind the band.

"It's a rain stick," Dee whispered excitedly.

Jack had studied rain sticks in a Latin American lit course—they were hollowed, dried cactuses filled with pebbles. Both ends were capped and sealed, with the pebbles trapped inside. When the stick was moved, the pebbles ran over the interior thorns, making the sound of rain. They were traditionally used to serenade the gods in hopes of bringing moisture to the land.

What this had to do with Evolution was lost on him.

Then the shaman left the stage and the floppy-haired brunette lead singer mumbled into the microphone, "This first one is called 'Monsoon.'" Then they started to play. To Jack's surprise—no, shock—the band sounded pretty talented. He looked over at Dee, who was swaying happily to the melody.

Then he felt her small hand journey northward from his knee to his thigh to—

Damn. It was a good thing it was dark in there.

"Cici?" He heard her lean over to her mother. "I'm going to show Jack where the bathroom is."

Dee led Jack out of the showcase room; they made a hard right down a narrow corridor, Dee trying door handles all the way. Finally, one opened: behind it was a tiny closet packed with brooms, an ancient vacuum cleaner, and a crusty mop.

She pulled him inside and shut the door.

Damn, this girl was smoking. Jack pressed her against the wall as darkness enveloped them. He moved his mouth to the spot where the top of her dress melded into her petal-soft skin. Her hands were totally tangled in his hair, and he couldn't control how much he wanted her. . . .

Neither of them knew how much time had passed when they realized that the music had ended.

"Jack, what happened?" Dee whispered urgently.

He stopped and listened—people were shuffling past them in their hallway, chattering excitedly about what they'd just heard.

"I think it's over."

"We have to get out—my dad will flip!"

Fuck. She wasn't really going to leave him like this, was she? How the hell was he supposed to go out there with a tent in his jeans?

"Um, Dee, there's a problem." He touched her hand on the difficulty.

"Just tell Captain Winky to come out and play later."

Before he could explain that Captain Winky was not under his conscious control, he saw her push the closet door open, her baby-blue eyes squinting with the sudden appearance of light.

Then, out of nowhere, Graham wheeled around the corner and watched them slip out. But if he was unhappy at the sight of Jack, his daughter, and an open broom closet, his words belied it. "DreamWorks wants to make a deal," he reported efficiently. "What did you think?"

"I think they're great, Daddy," Dee gushed. "Really. Jack did too."

Thanks, kids. I have to go kibbitz with the Columbia guy. Again, nice to have met you, Jack."

"You too, sir."

Graham fixed his gaze on him, then on the closet door, and then on him again. "Excellent. I'm glad you were here. And Jack? One more thing. Hurt my little girl, I'll eat you for lunch."

Crimson Crime

I f you wanted the perfect Los Angeles double hamburger, you went to In-N-Out Burger. If you needed a vintage terry-cloth jumpsuit, you haunted the thrift shops on Melrose. If you craved utter and total indulgence, you hauled your Dior-clad ass to Le Petite Retreat day spa.

Le Petite Retreat was *the* spa of the moment. Its clientele included Heidi, Kate (after her latest rehab), Nicky (but definitely not Paris, who rendered everything she touched post-hip), and Gwyneth, when she was in town. Sam knew for a fact that there would be a five-page-with-glossy-photos spread on Le Petite in the next issue of *Vogue*. Hence, this Sunday afternoon outing with her friends would be their last and best chance to go before the tourists and wanna-bes swarmed the place.

It was always so much work to find the spa of tomorrow.

A-list models and movie stars, as opposed to A-list television stars, were the only ones who could get into

Le Petite without a month's advance notice. Sam Sharpe had A-list-movie-star clout because of "Action Jackson," as he was called, which was why she was treating Anna, Cammie, and Dee to a Sunday afternoon at Le Petite as a graduation present. Of course, she was treating herself, too.

Naturally, this spa afternoon was part of a still-forming larger plan—a strategic plan, in fact—to win Eduardo back. Every woman looked more beautiful after a spa day. It was absolutely crucial that Sam look her best to carry out her mission, no matter what shape it ultimately took, which was why it was absolutely crucial that she spend an afternoon at Le Petite. Eduardo was a wonderful guy who, through some magical alchemy of the stars, really loved her. She was not going to let one stupid night make the whole thing disappear.

She'd decided to begin with the outside. Yes, she was ridiculously rich and semifamous, due to her very famous father and her own occasional mentions and photos in *CosmoGirl!* and *Teen People*. She had the best of everything and had taken advantage of every beautifying service known to womankind short of actually going under the knife. Yet she was still not really beautiful.

Maybe if she'd lived in Duluth or Salt Lake City or one of those places where women thought wearing a size twelve was just fine, she could have dealt with her own physical shortcomings. But Beverly Hills? Sam's deadly sin was worse than the seven she'd used as a theme for her pre-graduation party on the boat: hers was lack of perfection.

The great thing about Eduardo had been—and would be again, she vowed—that he really and truly loved her exactly as she was. They'd even made love with the lights on. That had been tough on her; she'd studied him like he was a canary in a coal mine for signs of disgust while viewing her dimpled thighs. But all she saw was lust. And love. On the worldwide guy scale of one to ten, Eduardo was an eleven. He had fallen really, deeply, and truly for Sam. Then she had gone and fucked it all up.

Well, how the hell was she supposed to know he was going to surprise her and show up at the prom after-party? In real life, guys as fine as Eduardo didn't do things like that for girls who looked like her. Talk about your suspension of disbelief. She'd tried to reconnect with him since then: phone calls, e-mails, all the usual ways. Nothing worked. It was time to get more creative. Whatever her plan would be, step one involved being buffed, scrubbed, rubbed, painted, and primped into a state of Le Petite polish. If, God forbid, her efforts bore no fruit, she'd at least look as good as she ever did.

Roger, one of her father's many drivers, dropped her at Le Petite, and she stepped through the glass door into the circular lobby. It was all white, with a soaring twenty-foot ceiling that featured a massive skylight. A waterfall trickled musically into an indoor koi pond—lights on the waterfall morphed through the spectrum of colors, all pulsing in time to the New Age music that emanated from inside the pebbled white walls. Large, slender aquamarine vases had been placed here and there on small black pedestals; each held a single purple orchid. The spa staff—invariably slender, mostly platinum blond—wafted through in white saris and loose-fitting pants, specially designed for the spa by Vera Wang. Each staff member had a "third eye" jewel glued to the middle of his or her forehead.

Her friends were already there, on different white couches, as if they'd never met. Anna looked up from her *New Yorker* magazine; Cammie continued a cell phone conversation.

"Hi, Sam." Anna stood and kissed Sam on the cheek. "This place is beautiful. Thanks for inviting me."

"That was Dee," Cammie reported, dropping her Razr cell phone into her mint-green-and-baby-pink Kate Spade hobo bag. "She can't come—I didn't catch exactly why—probably boning Jack. She said she tried to call but, Sam, your phone is off."

Sam pulled her Samsung out of her chocolate-brown fringed Kenneth Cole purse. Dee was right; the battery pack had come loose. *Shit.* What if Eduardo had tried to call, hit her voice mail, and decided not to leave a message? She couldn't have it on during the spa session; cell phones in Le Petite were strictly forbidden. Even for her.

"Ah, Miss Sharpe, welcome. I am Batsheva, at your service." The girl greeting her had beautiful almond-shaped eyes and a lush raven braid down her back. She wore the regulation white outfit and had a ruby in the center of her forehead. She gestured toward Anna and

Cammie with one graceful arm. "Please call me Sheva. And these are your guests?"

"Yes; meet Anna and Cammie."

Sheva nodded. "I will be your personal valet for the afternoon. If you need anything at all, I am but a chime away." She handed Sam a small white disc on a wristband. "You press the disc like so—" Sheva pressed the disc; an identical bracelet on her own wrist chimed loudly. "When you chime, I chime, you see, and then I will come see to your every need. I hope that is satisfactory."

"Sure," Sam agreed, donning her bracelet. "Thanks."

Sheva gave a small bow. "Most excellent. Now if all three of you would be so good as to follow me?"

She led the way through a pristine hallway, then down some steps and into the ladies' changing room. There was a row of doors with brass handles. Each girl's name had been precalligraphied on a faux-brass nameplate. Nice touch.

Sam entered the SAM door to get undressed. Her cubicle—at least as large as her oversized bathroom and dressing area at her dad's estate—contained a graceful white velvet divan, a private sunken whirlpool, and a white leather massage table. Hanging on the back of the door she found an Italian Frette spa robe monogrammed with the Le Petite logo and silk thong slippers. There was even a white velvet head wrap to protect her hair during her facial.

The treatments had all been prearranged. They'd each begin with an aquasonic lymphatic microdermabrasion facial on the massage tables in their chambers to firm, oxygenate, and rejuvenate the skin by detoxing the lymph system.

A moment later, Sheva knocked discreetly and asked if she might come in. She handed Sam a bone china cup of herbal tea, and then asked if Sam would prefer jasmine, eucalyptus, or primrose scent in her room. Sam picked jasmine. Sheva pressed a button on a panel. Moments later the aroma of fresh flowers subtly filled the air.

Then another female entered and Sheva departed. This young woman, who called herself Natasha, wore the same outfit as Sheva, save for the third eye glued to her forehead. Hers was a blue sapphire. She had a blond crew cut and the perfectly chiseled bone structure to pull it off. "Lie back and clear your mind," Natasha instructed, in a voice that had the faintest of Russian accents. "Enjoy your facial."

Sam closed her eyes, and as Natasha's hands pressed firmly on the lymph nodes around her eyes, over and over, she drifted away on a magic carpet of bliss. If she were a guy, she could imagine marrying Natasha for her hands alone. In fact, Sam didn't realize that Natasha had finished and exited until she heard the chime go off on her wrist.

A moment later, Sheva reentered her chamber. "So, you are ready to meet Cammie and Anna at the copper tubs?"

The attendant led Sam out of her chamber and down

an entirely different white hallway that finally opened into a large bath area with a dozen massive copper tubs. Given the choice of hydrotherapy bath options, Sam had opted for the Peppermint Ginger Plunge, wherein she would soak in aromatherapy oils of eucalyptus, ginger, and peppermint that were said to energize and invigorate the body and the spirit. For Anna, she'd selected the Aqua Latte & Floral Medley—essential oils of lavender, rose, and sage. Finally, Cammie would experience the Green Tea Escape, soaking in rose petal oil and essence of green tea.

"How's life?" Sam giggled to her friends, who were already in their respective baths.

"Amazing," Anna rhapsodized as she lowered herself deeper into the scented water. "It put me to sleep."

"Me too, and that never happens." Sam noticed less of an edge than usual to Cammie's voice, as Sheva helped her into her steaming copper tub, bowed, and exited.

She sank into the bubbling water, her eyes closing of their own volition. "Oh my God. This might be the best thing I ever felt in my life."

"In that case, you better tell Eduardo to step up his game," Cammie commented, from Sam's other side. "That is, if he ever speaks to you again."

Sam reopened her eyes. Trust Cammie to say just the thing guaranteed to bring the tension roaring back. "That was bitchy."

"You're right." Cammie nodded quickly. "Sorry. I'm dealing with all this shit about my father."

Had Cammie Sheppard apologized? Cammie *never* apologized. Sam knew Cammie was referring to what had happened on that yacht. She turned her head and dropped her voice so Anna wouldn't overhear.

"So how's that going?"

"It isn't. My father keeps ducking me. I *am* going to confront him tonight. If I have to have him kidnapped and tied to his Eames management chair, I will."

"I know you will."

Forty-five minutes later, when all three girls were bubbled into pink submission, their attendants came back to wrap them in fluffy white seven-hundred-thread-count Egyptian cotton towels. Then they were given aromatherapy pulse-point massages by various attendants while three other minions tended to their manis and pedis. Sam opted for the spa's Crimson Crime polish, mixed with flecks of real twenty-four-karat gold.

"I have one more treat for you guys," Sam announced as their fingernails and toenails dried. Three professional makeup artists appeared, along with Sheva.

"Ladies, your new 3D-Lashes are semipermanent eyelash extensions," their spa envoy explained. "They will be applied one at a time to your existing eyelashes with a special waterproof bond that will not be disturbed by makeup remover. They will stay on for two months. If you wish to remove them, simply return to us and we will use our special polypeptide bond remover to gently take them off. But they are so weightless, so utterly and totally natural, that we have not yet had a client choose to remove them. More likely you will decide to return in six or seven weeks to have new ones applied."

Anna hesitated. "They don't look fake?"

"I assure you that they are absolutely undetectable," Sheva promised. "We offer them in Jet Black, Espresso Brown, Burgundy Red, Velvet Purple, Midnight Blue, and Mountain Green. Please inform your trained technician the color of 3D-Lashes you wish to have." She gave her little half-bow again and left.

Anna leaned close to Sam. "How can they look completely natural if they're 'Velvet Purple'?"

Sam grinned and shook her head. "Go for brown, Anna. You aren't the Velvet Purple type."

Ninety minutes later, all three girls were batting their new eyelashes into magnifying mirrors handed to them by their lash technicians.

"This rocks," Sam marveled. "I really can't see where they're attached at all."

"Oh, I am so adding this to my regular beauty routine," Cammie said, admiring her Jet Black lashes. "This is great."

"Thanks, Sam," Anna added gratefully. "This has been a really fantastic graduation present. I won't be able to figure out how to outdo you."

"Knowing you? A check to Make-A-Wish in Sam's name," Cammie suggested sarcastically.

"I'll take that as a compliment," Anna replied serenely.

Sam blinked her eyes at the mirror one more time. The lashes looked long and thick and made her brown eyes appear—well, if not enormous, at least a little bit bigger. Huh. *Très* hot. They would look great for Stefanie's party, for graduation and, most importantly, for Operation Eduardo. She was going to bat these eyelashes back into his life if it was the last thing she did.

Body-art Babe

Anna had been lost in thought during most of the afternoon of pampering at Le Petite Retreat. Just when she'd thought everything was perfect with Ben, things were making her wonder about that assessment.

She understood why he hadn't been able to go with her to Sam's pregraduation party. He had work at Trieste, and he couldn't very well make his own hours there, but when she'd called him about her car accident, he'd been so . . . short. True, she'd assured him that it was only a fender bender. Yet he hadn't seemed very concerned.

Then there was the phone call this morning. They'd had plans for a couple of days for Sunday night; he'd talked about dinner someplace special. But this morning he'd sounded vague and removed. Yes, they'd definitely go out, maybe pick up a burger. How had "someplace special" morphed into a burger? Anna had no idea.

While she and Cammie were waiting for Sam to settle their bill at Le Petite—Sam insisted again that it was her treat—Anna took her Motorola out of her battered Louis Vuitton Speedy 15 purse. She considered calling Ben. Just as she was about to punch in his speed-dial number, it rang.

Fabulous. Great minds were thinking alike. But she didn't recognize the number on the caller ID.

"Hello?"

"Anna, hey," said a sexy male voice that unfortunately did not belong to Ben. "It's Caine Manning."

"Caine?" She was surprised he was calling. Then she winced, wishing she hadn't said his name aloud, since Sam and Cammie were now both staring at her with great interest. She drifted to the other side of the white lobby and faced the blank wall to continue the conversation. "How are you?"

"Great. Just wanted to thank you for the party last night. And to tell you I called the body shop that has your car. They're moving it to the top of the list."

Anna was bemused. Caine was so utterly different from Ben in his level of efficiency. "That's great. Really. Did they say when it would be ready?"

"A week . . . I've arranged for a loaner."

"You may be the most practical guy I've ever met," she teased.

"Oh yeah, that's me. The tattoos are just to throw the world off. So listen, I was supposed to do this Excel project for your dad tonight, but I finished early. I know you like classic art; I was wondering if you liked classical music?"

"Love it."

"I've got a line on two ducats to the philharmonic at Descanso Gardens tonight. They're doing the Tchaikovsky violin concerto. Would you like to go?"

Anna paused, but before she could mention anything about her plans with Ben, Caine spoke up again. "I know you might be busy with your boyfriend. That's cool. If not, I was thinking we could make a night of it. Modest Mouse is jamming at my bud's loft in Pasadena around midnight."

God, that sounded like it would be fun, if she hadn't already had plans with Ben—plans she would have been excited about if not for that very weird phone call with him.

"It's a wonderful invitation. But I indeed already made plans with my boyfriend."

"Okay, well, that's cool. How serious is it between you two anyway?" he asked smoothly, as casually as if he were inquiring about the weather.

It was a good question. Certainly their relationship was intense. Ben had been her very first—and to date, only—lover. But she still couldn't shake a niggling disquiet about that afternoon's phone call.

"I don't know how to quantify something like that. We aren't seeing other people."

"Well, I'd be lying if I didn't say that I'm disappointed, but that's fine. Have fun. So, would you mind if I called you anyway? As *friends*," he added with gravitas.

Anna laughed. Wow, she was flattered.

"As friends," she agreed.

"So I'm thinking you have, what, a week more of high school?"

Out of the corner of her eye Anna saw Sheva return with Sam's bill and Sam sign the paper without even glancing at it. "Correct assumption," she confirmed.

"Excellent. Boyfriends have been known to come and go. Keep that in mind."

"I hope you can find someone else to use that ticket tonight—"

"Oh, I don't think that'll be too much of a problem," Caine chided easily. "Hey, have a good time. What's his name again?"

"Ben."

"Ben. Right. Have fun with *Ben*. I'll talk to you soon."

Anna hung up. She couldn't keep a smile from tugging at her lips.

"That's quite a smirk you're wearing," Cammie observed, as Anna crossed the lobby back to the main desk. "Is Caine getting 'Anna' tattooed on his ass? Or is his ass already fully inked?"

Anna didn't bother to respond. Why stoop to her subzero level?

"Okay, we're out of here," Sam announced, carelessly throwing the receipt into her purse. "What did Body-art Babe want?"

"He has tickets for the philharmonic. But I've got plans with Ben."

"You don't seem like his type," Cammie mused.

"He'd do Rose McGowan over Keira any day. Or maybe both at the same time. Which is *so* not your lack-of-style."

That stung; Anna knew she was hardly the exotic sex goddess type. Was that what was bothering Ben? Was she not sexy enough? No, that was silly.

"He was just being friendly," she insisted, as they pushed out the spa's massive oak front door into the late afternoon Beverly Hills sunshine. The valet arrived in Cammie's BMW immediately. When she was gone, Anna impetuously turned to Sam. "Do you think you can tell if something is wrong in your relationship, even if the other person doesn't say anything?"

Sam slipped on her oversized white Chanel sunglasses. "You and Ben?"

"Nothing happened," she hastily added. "It's more like . . . a feeling."

"Come right out and ask him," Sam decreed. "It's the only way."

Anna gave Sam a big hug and thanked her for the great gift, then waited for the valet to bring over her dad's gray 1995 Porsche 911, which she'd been driving with the Lexus in the shop. A puff of wind blew Anna's hair across her face. When she flicked it back, the back of her hand brushed against her newly lengthened eyelashes.

She wondered if Ben would notice. She'd never been big on the idea of "feminine intuition." Yet she couldn't get over the feeling that something was going on with him, and whatever it was, it was bad.

Her Guy Looked Luscious

"So, have you been to Chinatown?" Ben asked, as if they were two strangers chatting each other up in the checkout line at Gelson's supermarket.

"Only in New York," Anna replied. "I didn't even know there was one here."

He nodded—that was the end of the exchange—and motored his father's new jet-black CL65 AMG Mercedes with the twin turbo-charged V-12 engine through the streets downtown Los Angeles. Anna had been pleased when he'd called to suggest they eat in Chinatown. It sounded like fun—a step up from In-N-Out Burger for sure. She'd dressed down for the occasion: her oldest and most faded jeans, a blue no-name long-sleeved thermal undershirt with tiny yellow daisies on it that she'd purchased with Cyn at Cheap Threads on the Lower East Side, and a pair of gold Chanel ballet flats she'd owned for so long that she actually couldn't even remember when or where she'd acquired them.

They rolled past the Staples Center on their way to whatever Chinese restaurant they were headed to; Anna studied Ben's profile as he drove. She loved every line of his face, the way his large, capable hands looked on the steering wheel, the pull of his muscular thighs against the legs of his Levis. The faded blue of his much-washed Fila tennis shirt contrasted nicely with his summer tan. All in all, she would have to say that her guy looked luscious.

Her guy. He *was* her guy, wasn't he? So why had he been acting so peculiar? It wasn't her imagination, she was sure of it. Even when he'd picked her up a half-hour before, he hadn't managed more than a perfunctory kiss on her cheek. What was *that* about?

Five silent minutes later, Ben had pulled in front of Ocean Seafood on Lower North Broadway.

"Good thing there's valet parking," he remarked, as he came around the car and took the claim ticket from the short, stocky valet. "This car would get ripped off within like five minutes on the street." He put his hand on the small of her back to guide her toward the front door of the restaurant. "You're in for a treat. This is my favorite Chinese in the city."

"Do you think Chinese people in China go out for American food?" Anna mused. She was certain Ben would laugh at that, goofy as it was. But he didn't. In fact, he barely seemed to have heard her. Still, he held the massive red wooden front door open for her like a proper gentleman. As she passed him, she tried to catch his eye, to find that special spark they always had together. Nothing.

Anna shuddered. *What* was going on?

"Smells great in here, huh?" Ben remarked once they were inside. It was the kind of thing that a person might say to a business acquaintance.

Ocean Seafood was crowded—at least twenty people were milling around the entrance with glasses of wine in one hand, waiting for tables to open up—but Ben led Anna through the crowd and motioned to a diminutive middle-aged woman in a floorlength black silk floral Chinese dress.

"Ben!" she said, then flashed a smile that had to have been aided by either massive whitening agents, porcelain veneers, or both. "Welcome back. And welcome to your friend. Table for two?"

He nodded.

Welcome back? Anna was perplexed. Okay, he'd been here before, he'd already told her that. The hostess knew him by name, which meant he had been here quite a bit. Yet he'd never taken her to this place, never even mentioned it before.

"Follow me, please."

They walked through the large restaurant, past rows of hanging orange and white Chinese lanterns, until the hostess seated them at an orange banquette.

"You order for us, okay Jade?" Ben suggested.

He even knew her first name.

"Happy to do so, " Jade replied with another super-white grin. "Very good. I'll send beer."

There was ice water in tall tumblers already on the table. Anna took a sip as they sat in silence. Where was their easy banter?

"You're pretty confident I'm going to like what she brings," she finally teased him.

He grinned and reached across the table for her hand. "I'd bet on it."

Whew. That was better.

Anna looked around. There was a row of huge salt-water aquariums by the far wall, each of them easily two hundred gallons or more. She could make out crabs, multicolored rockfish, and sea bass. One entire tank had been reserved for dark, spiny lobsters.

She turned back to Ben. Played with her fork. Tried to figure out what to say. Nothing came to her brilliant mind, nothing at all.

"Ben . . . is something wrong?" she blurted.

His eyebrows rose. "No, nothing. Why?"

"Well, you're so quiet."

"Thinking about work."

"How did it go last night?"

"Okay. They stuck me on the door again. At least I didn't have to make a thousand smoothies. Why don't you tell me more about Sam's party?"

"Well like I said before, the theme was Seven Deadly Sins and . . ." She rambled on, giving every detail she could think of. But for some reason that she couldn't quite fathom, she didn't mention that she'd been there with Caine. Maybe she was just feeling perverse, but she felt as if Ben was keeping something from her. Why should this dinner be a one-way confessional?

A young Chinese waiter dressed in white hustled over to their table with three huge platefuls of food: a platter of steamed shrimp, roasted sea bass, and a tray of sizzling Pacific oysters.

They dug in. The food was as good as it looked, and eating gave them both something to do. Jade stopped by their table every two minutes to make sure that Ben was satisfied, to make sure that Ben gave her regards to his parents, to make sure Ben introduced her properly to the lovely lady, and to make sure that the lovely lady was comfortable and happy.

They ate. They ate some more. They even held hands again. About the only thing they didn't do, really, was the one thing Anna really wanted to do: talk.

An hour and a half later they were on the ticket buyer's line at the Grove, the magnificent multiplex movie theater in the farmer's market complex in Hancock Park, within striking distance of the CBS television studios. The theater was stunning, with a semicircular art deco high-gloss facade separating it from the market proper, plus a vertical sign reading THE GROVE that soared thirty feet into the air.

They'd decided to go see the new David Lynch film, though Anna had agreed with some trepidation. She wasn't a big moviegoer by nature, and had been completely nauseated by *Blue Velvet*. Yet she'd loved *The Straight Story*, which was why she thought she'd give

Rocket to Russia a try. Evidently about five hundred other Los Angelinos had made the same decision. The line to buy tickets snaked back nearly to the glass doors.

"What time does it start?" she asked Ben.

"Eight. And it's a two-and-a-half-hour film, which means—"

"Anna?"

Anna turned around. The line was one of those parallel velvet rope queues, with four or five different routes to get to the ticket seller. Standing in the next queue was Caine Manning. He was alone, in gray Calvin Klein khakis and a black T-shirt, short-sleeved, so that his tattoos showed. There was a copy of *Spin* under his arm. She felt herself flush, as if she'd been caught doing something. She still hadn't told Ben that she'd been with Caine at Sam's party. Yet Anna had been raised well. Her mother had always emphasized the importance of appearing unfazed. So she smiled at Caine as if running into him at the Grove was the loveliest surprise in the world.

"Hey! I thought you were going to the symphony."

He ducked under the rope. "I ended up giving the tickets to a friend." His eyes moved to Ben. "So. This is the guy, huh?"

"Umm, you just gave up your place in line," Anna pointed out.

Caine gestured into the expansive theater. "I'm not worried. I'm going to *Best of the Best, Part Seven,* the karate movie. Somehow I don't think this is a big chop-socky crowd." He held out a hand toward Ben. "Hi, I'm Caine Manning."

"Ben. Birnbaum." Ben slipped a proprietary arm around Anna's shoulders. "You two know each other, I take it?"

"Yeah, I'm her ex-husband," Caine deadpanned. "What, she didn't tell you about that? Or Caine Junior, either? The custody battle was a bitch."

Anna laughed.

"Caine is my father's intern," she explained, hoping that would erase the scowl from Ben's face, and praying that Caine wouldn't mention Sam's party.

No such luck.

"And occasional daughter-rescuer," Caine put in. "Hey, I had a great time on the boat by the way. . . ."

Caine went on—it had been nice of Anna to invite him after Ben couldn't help her out after her accident. "She told me all about you. You've got a great lady, there."

Ben nodded and fixed his eyes on Caine's heavily tattooed right forearm. "I didn't know that Jonathan Percy was into hiring rockers."

"Hey, we've all got our own thing. I like tattoos, rock 'n' roll, late nights, smart ladies, and wise old men. Don't hold it against me." He leaned backwards on the heels of his black Converse All Stars. "So, I'll get back in my line. Nice to meet you, Ben." He ducked back under the velvet rope. "Gotta love Jackie Chan when he beats the crap out of the bad guys. Sublimates aggression better than *Grand Theft Auto: San Andreas.* You into Jackie Chan, Ben?"

"No," Ben replied bluntly.

Their line edged forward. Caine pulled a twenty-dollar bill out of his wallet. "Man, they charge a mint for a flick these days, huh? It would be cheaper in Minnesota. But then I'd have to actually *be in Minnesota.*"

"Does he ever shut up?" Ben muttered under his breath, putting his arm around Anna as their line moved forward. "I have to say, there's something about that guy that I don't like."

Well, I do like him, Anna thought. Besides, running into him is what got you to put your arm around me. Maybe a little competition isn't such a bad thing after all.

The movie was good, really good, about an autistic boy who builds a toy rocket ship that he plans to ride all the way to Russia, and his peculiar friendship with an elderly Russian lady who was a neighbor's housekeeper. Anna had found it touching. She'd found it even more touching when she'd glanced at Ben in the stadium-style seat next to hers and seen an actual tear roll down his cheek when the boy allowed the Russian lady to hug him for the first time.

That tear . . . It was just so . . . Ben. The Ben she knew. The Ben she was pretty sure she loved.

After the movie, they'd gone straight back to Anna's house. The exterior was dark as they pulled into the circular driveway, since Jonathan Percy had left late that afternoon on an overnight to San Francisco—he had a dinner planned with his casino clients. Ben stopped the Mercedes by the front door. "So," he began.

"So."

It had definitely been a tense evening. Until the last couple of days, she and Ben had had an infinite number of things to talk about. Everything from family to literature, from their hopes for the future to their regrets about the past. True, when they'd first met on Anna's flight to California, their attraction had been entirely physical. She'd found him incredibly hot, remembering the moment when he'd stood in the first-class aisle and pulled a Princeton sweatshirt over his head, revealing a V-cut body and rippling abs. There'd been plenty of opportunities since to indulge her admiration of that godlike form, but their connection had always been more than that.

"You liked the movie?"

She nodded. "A lot more than I thought I would."

Uh-oh. Here they were again. two strangers talking. The French had a word for how it made her feel: *dépaysée*. Like being a stranger in her own country. She hated it.

One more try. She mustered what she hoped was a sexy smile.

"I've got a great idea. My dad's out of town. Which means . . . the place is empty. So my question is . . ." She leaned over and kissed him seductively right next to his lips. "Are you coming in?"

Ben was out of the car and around to the right side of the Mercedes before she could get the door open herself. To her surprise, he picked her up and carried her to the front door. It was such an unexpected, romantic gesture. One part of her was thrilled. Another part of her was watching the part of her that was thrilled and decided it was almost excruciatingly corny. The thrilled part won out and kissed him. Then they both realized that he'd have to put her down to allow her to unlock the door, which made them both burst into laughter.

Once they were inside the mirrored foyer, Anna's back was to the priceless Ming vase that was a replacement for the one she had carelessly broken her first night in Los Angeles. There was no danger of that happening now. They were kissing intensely, holding each other close. She was whispering how much she cared for him, how much she wanted him to carry her up the stairs to her bedroom. She had this dramatic vision from *Gone with the Wind*—a guilty pleasure she'd read between *Vanity Fair* and *The Portrait of a Lady*—of Rhett Butler doing just that to Scarlett.

Ben reached down and picked her up, just as easily as when he'd brought her inside the house. Then they were in the hallway, then in her room. She managed to reach the dimmer switch as they entered—soft yellow light bathed the cream-colored walls.

"You know," he remarked, "I don't know that I've ever been in this room before."

He put her down gently and Anna watched him take it all in: the antique French bed covered with needle-point pillows, the matching nineteenth-century French teak furniture she'd ordered when she realized that this room in her father's house would be her home for a while. The bookshelves were filled with all the classic literature she'd had shipped from Manhattan; her over-sized oak rolltop desk was one that she'd purchased from an antique dealer in Los Feliz who didn't want to part with it because he swore that F. Scott Fitzgerald had once been the owner. It held a Fujitsu LifeBook laptop with the monitor currently twisted to forty-five degrees, some notebooks, and a champagne flute filled with calligraphy pens.

"Whoa. That's strange"

"What?"

"No media. Except for that laptop." He smiled and pointed at her desk. "No TV, no MP3 player, no iPod, not even a clock radio. You keep it simple."

Anna edged over to the dimmer switch and dialed it down a notch. "Yes. I do like to keep it simple. Sometimes."

They kissed again. And again. A moment later, they were on her bed, which is where the weird night that Anna thought she was in the process of salvaging . . .

Ben rolled away from her.

"Umm," he mumbled.

What the hell did *umm* mean?

"Is something wrong?" She sat up leaning on her elbows.

"No."

Why was she certain his "no" meant "yes"?

"You don't want to . . ."

She couldn't bring herself to finish the sentence. It was too humiliating.

"We don't have to have sex every time we're alone."

"You don't want to make love to me?" Anna thought her voice sounded like a child's.

"I love to make love to you. I really do."

"Then why not . . . ?"

Her voice trailed off again, and she lay back down beside him, wondering whether she was being unreasonable. There was some truth to what he was saying—there was no law that said they had to have sex whenever they could. The night had been off-kilter from the start. On the other hand, there was also a chance that this was yet another sign that something had recently gone terribly wrong in their relationship.

She gazed at him—fingers interlocked behind his head, eyes closed—and then nestled into the warm place between his left tricep and chest. "Ben?"

"Yeah?" He didn't open his eyes.

"Are we okay?"

He finally looked down at her. "We're great. I mean it. I don't want to be anywhere tonight but right here."

Her eyes met his. "Okay, then."

Yet Anna was anything but okay; his words had sent her brain into Anna Percy overdrive. Part of her believed him. If he was lying, it would have been just as easy for him to have made an excuse outside and left. Instead, he'd done his best imitation of Rhett Butler and carried her over the threshold. You couldn't fake that.

Could you?

Dinner for One from L.A. Farm

The rail-thin doorman in the cobalt blue uniform peered dubiously at Sam through a pair of old-fashioned horn-rimmed spectacles.

"You say you're Samantha Sharpe? *Jackson* Sharpe's daughter?"

"No, I'm Ozzy Osbourne's daughter," she replied, voice dripping sarcasm.

The doorman nodded. "Knew it! You took off a few pounds—looking good."

Sam gritted her teeth. Every time someone mistook her for a thinner Kelly Osbourne it made her insane. "Let's try this again, shall we? I *am* Jackson Sharpe's daughter. As in: let my people in the building, or you'll be misidentifying celebrities in a really long unemployment line."

He looked intimidated but still didn't budge. "This is the most exclusive residence on Wilshire Boulevard. We have some famous people living here. Celebrities and such. I can't let you in because you say you're somebody, Miss."

Oh for God's sake. Yet Sam came prepared for occasions such as this. She dug into her pocketbook—Adobe Designs with Indian feathers and dragonflies hand-tooled into the mahogany leather, a recent gift from her dangerously young stepmother, Poppy, in the name of "family solidarity"—and found the clipping from the *Variety* story about the opening of principal photography on *Ben-Hur*. There was a photo of her and her father on the set, standing beside one of the old Roman chariots. The caption identified her as Jackson Sharpe's daughter, Sam Sharpe.

"Consider this my photo ID," she snapped, thrusting the clipping at the doorman.

He peered at the photo, asked if he could get her father's autograph—like she somehow carried that around too—and hastily let her in.

It was after eleven o'clock on Sunday night, and part of Sam really couldn't blame the doorman for giving her the third degree. He was, after all, the keeper of the gate of the Pinnacle West condominium building at the corner of Wilshire Boulevard and Comstock, one of the most exclusive buildings on the Wilshire corridor of high-rises that ran from where the 405 freeway crossed Wilshire practically to the ocean. Sam had always found this little stretch of condos in sprawling Los Angeles reminiscent of Miami Beach. If you wanted to live in an apartment, Manhattan or Paris were acceptable options. Who would do it in Los Angeles? Still, the condos in these buildings changed hands for low to mid-seven-figure sums, and there was no dearth of clients at Sotheby's or even Coldwell-Banker to purchase them.

Eduardo lived in a condo, evidently owned by the Peruvian government, in this very building. Sam had never been to his place, but she'd managed to track down the information from a crisscross telephone directory on the Internet. Which condo unit was his, she wasn't sure, because he still wasn't returning her calls. She'd left plaintive messages, sweet messages, funny messages, and finally frustrated messages, none of which he'd chosen to answer.

Now, she'd had enough. It was okay for him to be mad at her—hell, *she* would have been mad at her, if she'd seen him do what she'd done on prom night—but it was time to get over it and, as they said in Hollywood, move on to another level.

She'd dressed carefully for a mission of persuasion: her most flattering Escada black velvet jeans with the silver rivets, a red cashmere Gucci V-necked sweater she'd bought at a trunk sale at the Shed restaurant in Santa Fe, and her favorite white-leather-and-crystal sandals from Jimmy Choo. Then she'd climbed into the black Hummer and buzzed over to his building.

"So, how's the shooting going on *Ben-Hur?*" the doorman asked, hovering over her. "Word is your dad's starting to go over budget."

Christ, was *everyone* in this town in showbusiness?

Sam put her hand out without answering. "May I have the article back, please? And can you tell me if Eduardo Munoz is here?"

He nodded. "Now, what did you have in mind?"

"Some people need to get to Eduardo—it's a little surprise I'm planning."

Then he frowned. "I don't know. . . ."

Sam pulled a few twenty-dollar bills from the back pocket of her jeans, having stashed them there just in case. She slapped them into his palm and curled his fist around the money. "Better?"

The doorman smiled and pocketed the money. "Much."

"Good. Stand aside. You're about to see genius in action."

Eduardo was relaxing on his hand-tooled-in-Lima living room sofa, reading a book on the conflict in the Middle East, when someone knocked on the front door of his suite. Strange. The doorman always buzzed him if there were visitors. Maybe it was one of his neighbors stopping by.

He marked his spot with a red felt bookmark and went to the front foyer. Security in the building was so good that he had no worries about simply opening the door for whoever was knocking.

Three middle-aged men in tuxedos, with white towels over their right arms, stood before him. Between them was a silver room-service warming box on wheels.

"Eduardo Munoz?" the oldest looking of the three asked.

"Yes? May I help you?"

"Dinner for one from L.A. Farm," the man continued. He consulted a small card. "Ceviche of arugula with beets, goat cheese, and pine nuts. Crispy Thai shrimp. *Loup de mer* in a white saffron sauce with snow peas. A cornucopia of berries and sorbet. And two different wines: a Chassagne-Montrachet '87 for dinner, followed by a private-label Gewürztraminer with dessert. I trust this will be satisfactory."

Eduardo was confused; not only because he hadn't placed the order, but because whoever had placed it knew him well: they'd ordered his favorite foods and his two favorite wines.

His stomach rumbled. Only now did he remember that he'd neglected to eat dinner. Funny how little he'd been interested in food since he'd seen Samantha kissing another guy on the beach. He felt just slightly sick most of the time. Lovesick, maybe. But he was determined to get over it. Certainly he'd get over her. Eventually. Even if his body kept telling a different story.

"Who ordered this for me?"

"A friend," the lead waiter replied. "May we come in and set up for you, sir?"

"Please." Eduardo opened the door wider and ushered them in. L.A. Farm was a terrific restaurant. "Set up in my dining room. You're sure you can't tell me who is responsible for this?"

"The gift-giver prefers that we not say," the older gentleman explained, as, with a flourish, he set down a snowy white tablecloth. Then the three men arranged the food on the table, leaving the sorbet in the freezer section until he wanted it. Finally, the youngest, roundest gentleman held out Eduardo's chair.

"Thanks." He took a seat.

"If there is nothing else," the lead waiter told him, "simply call the number on the silver cart when you wish for us to return and gather our things."

"Thank you very much," Eduardo said.

The wine was opened; then the waitstaff departed. Eduardo poured himself a crystal goblet of the French white wine and took a small sip. Heavenly. A smile tugged at the edges of his mouth. Who would do something like this?

That was when he heard another knock on the door.

"Come in, it's open!" he called.

The door opened. It was the lead waiter again. "I'm sorry, Mr. Munoz. We neglected to bring in one thing. Patrick?" He turned to the front door, where a second waiter carried in something long and cardboard under his arm. He set it on the chair opposite Eduardo—the cutout had been manufactured to bend at the knees.

"Your dining companion, Mr. Munoz," Patrick told him.

Eduardo found himself sitting across from a life-size full-color cardboard replica of Sam. She was wearing tennis clothes, exactly the ones she'd had on in Mexico the first time Eduardo had spent any time with her.

Words were scrawled in giant black letters across the front of the cutout's tennis shirt:

BON APPETIT. CALL ME.

Sam stepped outside and coolly handed the valet her parking stub. As desperately as she wanted to run upstairs to Eduardo's condo, pound on the door, and throw herself at his feet, she wasn't going to do it. In fact, she wasn't even going to stand around and wait to see if he came downstairs. Better to do what needed to be done, then depart.

More than anything she wanted this to work, but if it didn't, she would think of something else. Giving up was simply not an option.

While she waited for the Hummer, she checked her makeup in the small mirror that flipped up from her Bobbi Brown lip gloss trio, dug into her purse for her Touche Éclat, and touched up the area around her eyes. Then she checked her BlackBerry messages—she'd turned her cell off just before she went into the building. There was a message from Cammie, who reported that she hadn't been able to connect with her father tonight after all. She was feeling antsy; did Sam want to meet her for a drink?

Sam was game, even as she mentally counted the calories of a Mudslide. Cammie was at the Whiskey Blue bar at the W hotel in Westwood. The Whiskey Blue had recently turned into a favored industry hangout, both because of its potent cocktails and its central location.

Though it was a Sunday night, the bar was jammed when she arrived. As she threaded her way through the dense, upscale-chic crowd toward the bar, she marveled again at the fantastic décor that had been the talk of the town when the place had first opened. Huge square red and black panels formed ninety-degree angles along one wall; nestled against their base were low-slung flat wooden tables with even more low-slung cushioned high-tech couches that formed cozy conversation nooks. The floor was jet-black slate, with a row of wooden rectangular on-edge abstract sculptures that ended in square tabletops ready for plates and drinks.

The bar itself was a marvel, with a long blond-wood countertop, square brown-and-yellow wooden chairs instead of bar stools, and square red lights at intervals across the top. The effect was anything other than square. Sam spotted Cammie on one of the bar chairs between Thailand's Princess Duangthipchot—whose hair reached her ass and who'd turned into a total party animal of late—and a DreamWorks exec whose last initial was not *S* or *K*.

"Hey." Cammie kissed her cheek. She was wearing a miniscule hand-crocheted Missoni dress shot through with orange, tan, and avocado-green threads. It was cut almost to her navel, showing off tons of immaculate skin. She looked stunning as usual. Cammie peered at her. "Where've you been?"

"Operation Eduardo."

"Go for it. How'd it go?" She smiled, then motioned to the bartender—Sam ordered a Mudslide.

"I'll tell you tomorrow. Or the next day. If he calls me, I'm a genius. If he doesn't, I'm pathetic." The DreamWorks exec got up; Sam slid into his seat.

"I hope it works out." Cammie took a long suck on her Tequila Santa Ana Sunrise, which had half the usual orange juice. "My father's holed up at the Beverly Hills Hotel and still won't see me."

A young Asian bartender with a pierced lip and black-on-black clothes pushed Sam her drink. She thought of all the reasons that Clark might be at the Beverly Hills Hotel, 99 percent of which had to do with him cheating on his aging actress wife, but kept silent. Cammie needed support now, not a reality check. She tasted her Mudslide. Outstanding. Maybe the rum was what gave her the inspiration, if not the courage, for what she said next.

"I'm going to help you."

"Right." Cammie cleared her throat dubiously. "You're going to airdrop down the chimney into his bungalow?"

"No. There was another person on the boat the night your mom died. Remember?"

"Your mother. Who told the police she had sex with my dad on the boat. I know the whole story—I told *you*, for God's sake." Cammie drained her glass. The bartender motioned like he was ready to make her another, but she shook her head.

"Maybe we don't know the whole story," Sam reasoned. "Maybe my mom didn't tell the cops everything."

"Sam. Think. You haven't spoken to your mother since the twenty-first century. She lives who-the-fuck-knows-where. What makes you think she's ready to spill her guts to Dominick Dunne? Or to you?"

Good point.

"I wonder if she realizes I'm about to graduate from high school?" Sam pondered. "Or going to film school at USC?"

Cammie offered a shrug. "How could she possibly know? You didn't tell her. Your father didn't tell her. She doesn't get the school newspaper, and somehow I doubt that she's a regular reader of your father's Web page of family news. Do you even know where she is?"

"No. But I'm going to find out. I'll hire someone to find her. And then, I'm—we're—going to talk to her."

"We are?"

"Yes. Okay, so the bitch doesn't give a shit about me," Sam went on. "Fine. Got the memo. But she was with your mom the night she died. I say she owes you an explanation."

"You'd do that for me?"

Sam couldn't believe it—Cammie's tone was reasonable. No, not reasonable. Grateful and appreciative. It reminded her of when they were little girls, and Cammie had been afraid to swim underwater despite months of lessons at the Riviera Country Club. Sam recalled how Cammie had been playing with one of her mother's necklaces in the Sharpes' enormous backyard pool. Suddenly, the necklace had slipped from her grasp and

settled like the Heart of the Ocean diamond on the bottom of the pool. Sam had offered then to do a surface
dive and retrieve it. It seemed like Cammie had said the
exact same words in response. "You'd do that for me?"

"Yeah, of course," Sam replied now, as she had then.

"I don't deserve that kind of loyalty."

"Cam, come on. We've been best friends forever."

Cammie played with the stem of her glass. "I don't
exactly excel at it. Friendship, I mean."

Sam waved a dismissive hand. "Whatever. Neither
do I."

"Can you handle two favors in one night?" Cammie
bit her lower lip.

"Just call me Sam of Arc. What do you need?"

"Are you busy in the morning?"

She shook her head.

"Well." Cammie motioned to the bartender for two
more drinks. "Now you are."

Sun Rising in the West

"Stay with him," Cammie instructed. They were roaring down the 405 freeway south, tailing Clark Sheppard, who was on his way to work at the set of *Hermosa Beach*. "Gray 2003 BMW Z8 convertible, two red roll bars in the back, California vanity plates that say CS APEX. Got it?"

Sam took a sip of the double espresso double latte with Splenda from the Beverly Hills Coffee Bean that Cammie had handed her when she'd picked her up at 7 a.m.

"Got it."

When Cammie had asked her the night before to drive to the Beverly Hills Hotel that morning so that she could follow her father—the goal being a confrontation—Sam had readily agreed. Cammie had found herself feeling grateful to her friend for the second time that evening. This was unusual; perhaps even unprecedented—it helped make up for the many months during which Cammie had thought she was losing her best friend to that snotty East Coast bag of bones known as Anna Percy.

Sam, indeed, had it covered. She stayed right behind Clark's car in her Hummer from the freeway to Manhattan Beach, and then from Manhattan Beach onto the Strand of Hermosa Beach, with its peculiar mix of surf shops, restaurants, and boutiques. Hermosa Beach was beautiful; the blue waters of the Pacific beckoned invitingly. Cammie, though, was a woman on a mission.

"The set for his show is ahead on the right."

"Cammie, I *know*."

They reached the small white hotel that was the main location as well as the production office for *Hermosa Beach*, the hour-long drama that had premiered this season to excellent ratings. Clark's agency had packaged it—they were responsible for the whole show, from show runners to writers to talent. As a result, they collected an even heftier agency fee than the normal 10 percent. Clark treated *Hermosa Beach* like it was his own. He loved to hang out in the writers' room, helping to fashion future episodes.

"Let him pull in alone," Cammie decided quickly.

"And?"

"I want him in a room. Cornered. No way out."

A few minutes later, after her father had parked his car, Cammie told Sam to pull into one of the parking spaces at the far end of the *Hermosa Beach* lot. The main entrance to the hotel was used only for filming; everyone else entered and exited via a side door protected by a flimsy green awning. They made their way to this side door. Just inside was a security desk, where a single balding guard with a pencil stuck behind his ear drummed his fingers on a Lucite clipboard.

"Cammie Sheppard," she announced with a dimpled smile. "My father forgot some papers."

She tapped her oversized cream Balenciaga bag, which contained nothing but a Too Faced face palette in Beach Bunny, a bubble-gum-pink Fendi wallet, and a ribbed Trojan condom. But the guard didn't know that.

"Go on back," he told Cammie. "Your dad's in the writers' room."

"Thank you." Cammie could feel her heart race, but she knew she could pull off nonchalance. "Hey, why don't you wait for me by the beach? This'll only take a minute."

"Sure thing," Sam replied, then mouthed a silent *good luck*.

Cammie knew the set well—she left the guard's desk behind and strode down a hallway that opened into the hotel lobby. Dressed to film, the lobby was decked out in beachy, white-blond wood furniture and cheerful puffy yellow cushions. A white baby grand piano stood in a corner near a Moroccan fireplace that looked real but was the handiwork of the production designer. Cammie had been here when huge lights blasted the room, and actors, makeup magicians, and techies with boom mikes scuttled around between takes.

Today, though, there was no filming. She felt like a ghost haunting the scene of its own demise.

The writers' room was on the other side of the

building, in the wing that had been converted into production offices. Just as she was leaving the lobby, she tripped over a thick bundle of cables snaking across the hardwood floor. Her coral Dolce & Gabbana stiletto flew off her foot; she angrily scooped it up and slammed it back on before she strode into another corridor.

"Cammie, is that you?" An over-chipper British voice rang out from one of the offices that lined both sides of the hall. It was her father's new assistant, Alleister, he of the good diction and pretentious spelling. "Come in for some coffee—I've got your favorite vanilla mocha beans. They're simply divine. I can brew a fresh pot—"

"By all means do that, Alleister," Cammie cooed, but shot by without stopping, her strawberry blond curls springing with each furious step. Two more doors and she'd be at her destination. The one she wanted was unmarked, with a chipped doorknob.

She squared her shoulders, then burst inside.

A small guy with a big nose, an oversized gray sweatshirt, and a dirty L.A. Lakers baseball cap was addressing the room—Danny Bluestone, young wunderkind co-exec producer of *HB*. Single-minded as she was, Cammie still remembered Anna having had a brief flirtation with Danny during one of her off periods with Ben. No shocker there. Anna seemed to have had brief flirtations with everyone.

All eyes in the room—the seven-person show writing staff, plus Clark—turned toward Cammie, although

Danny didn't stop talking. Writers' rooms had a reputation for being the most profane locations in America, and Danny was underscoring that rep as he waved a green dry-erase marker for emphasis.

"All right. Let's look at the story outline. Fucking Alexandra is trying to ruin Chyme for revenge. I ask: Who the fuck cares? Where's the fucking romance? This is a nighttime soap, so I'll repeat: *Where's the fucking romance?* Want to know what our watchers are asking? 'What's on the fucking *OC?*'"

Danny stopped talking; the room fell silent. Cammie took everything in: the writers, in their late twenties and thirties, sleep-deprived and rumpled; a token female writer (they were always either drop-dead gorgeous or lesbians who had Hollywood Gay Mafia clout, or both). Whiteboards covered in episode beats lined the walls. The center table was a mess—littered with old takeout containers, candy wrappers, and half-consumed bottles of Dasani. Anna saw Danny give Clark a curious look.

"Cammie?" her father inquired calmly, raising his dark eyebrows slightly in annoyance. He leaned back in a Herman Miller Aeron metal-and-mesh chair, with his black A. Testonis by Norvegese shoes up on the table. He was dressed more casually than usual, in gray slacks and a pink Budd's sport shirt with French cuffs. "This must be important, since you're interrupting a staff that makes roughly ten million dollars a season."

"Father." She was deliberately formal. "I need to talk to you."

"After this meeting."

"Now." *You've taught me well, Dad. I've learned from the best.* "Dad, you've given me no choice." Cammie felt the venom pump through her. "You've ignored me, avoided me, and hidden from me. Not today. I want some answers."

She took a step toward him, and saw that all the writers were now staring at her. No one challenged Clark Sheppard like this. They were watching the equivalent of the sun rising in the west and setting in the east.

Good. Maybe you guys can learn something from me.

"You. My mother. Sam's mother."

"Cammie, I told you. Later. Go shopping on the Strand. I'll take you to lunch, and we can talk as long as you'd like." He grinned hard and looked at his writers for affirmation, but everyone just stared at him, dumbstruck. "All these people are witnesses."

Cammie folded her arms. "We can definitely do lunch. But we're also going to do this. I know you were screwing Sam's mother. The police report says you were all on the boat the night that mom died. So it's time you told the truth. A simple yes or no will suffice. Did you kill Mom?"

Vermicelli Silk Sheets

Anna opened her eyes the next morning to find Ben staring into hers. He blinked quickly and then pulled away, as if he'd been caught doing something.

"Well," she mustered. "Good morning."

Did that sound faintly British? She winced at her own words.

"Morning," he mumbled, stretching out one long arm. His bare, tan, muscular chest beckoned. He'd slept last night just in his green Everglade-colored Patagonia Capilene boxers. The ones that had never come off.

She moved closer—wary, tense. "What time is it?" The sunlight was streaming through the window.

"Ten. You're late for school." He kissed the top of her head.

"No class for seniors this week. We just had a final paper for humanities and—"

"Let me guess. You turned it in last week."

"Last month, actually."

Because I wasn't sure when you'd be home, she mentally added, not daring to say it aloud in light of their

119

present state. *I didn't want to have to do it if you were home.*

He stroked her head. "I could definitely get used to waking up next to you."

As what, cuddly roommates?

Anna wondered if she was overreacting. It was maddening not to know—surely every couple had a glitch now and then. But to sleep in the same bed and not have sex . . . it wasn't like they'd been married for twenty years. She felt certain that if this was their first time, or if he was with a new girl to whom he was wildly attracted, he would not have been able to restrain himself the night before.

And yet he had. Apparently, easily.

"Got plans for today?" He ran his knuckles softly along the side of her neck, then shifted his weight so that his lips could brush hers.

Now? Now suddenly he wanted to make love? Hadn't she read somewhere that men preferred sex in the morning, while women preferred—

That line of thought was interrupted by a sizzling kiss. She couldn't help but respond. So . . . this meant everything was okay, didn't it? They were good.

She pulled him close and was gratified to hear him sigh in her ear. "Anna."

"Anna!"

Another male voice—much louder—called from downstairs. "You home?"

Damn.

She pushed away from Ben, her stomach knotted

under the dusty rose vermicelli silk sheets. "It's my father."

"Oops?" he asked with a half-smile.

Anna felt her cheeks growing red. "I have never been in this situation before. I don't . . . I'm not . . ."

"I'll play it however you want," Ben offered.

"I'll go downstairs and talk to him," she decided, as she went to her closet and wrapped herself in a Ralph Lauren emerald silk robe.

"Tell him he doesn't need his shotgun. I'll leave peacefully."

"Besides, you didn't even get a chance to ravish me yet," Anna pointed out in what she hoped was a light tone. As in: hint, hint. Then she headed out of her room and down the long, carpeted staircase with the polished brass banister.

"Dad?"

"Anna? I'm in the kitchen, sweetie!"

Anna padded into the kitchen. Her father was at the table, nibbling on one of the rosewater brioches from Arminee's Bakery on Rodeo Drive, flipping through the paper. He looked handsome; tall, lanky and boyish, and much younger than the midfortysomething Anna knew him to be. He wore black Ronin cargo pants and a Mongolian cashmere sweater in a rich camel that Anna remembered from when she was an elementary school student in Manhattan. The sweater reminded her of one of the many dictates in the apocryphal *This Is How We Do Things* Big Book: Don't buy cheap.

"Great to see you," he said, motioning to an empty chair. "Coffee's brewing—push the button on the Krups, will you?"

She was hoping for an opening to mention her overnight visitor who was still upstairs. "I'd love some coffee. So would—"

"I'm surprised you're not in school," Jonathan interrupted. "Or did you decide just to blow off the week before graduation? Come to think of it, that's what I did."

A discreet chime signaled that the coffee was ready; Mimi, their cook, didn't come in until eleven, and Consuela had the morning off.

"No class this week." She got out two of her dad's new Laura Smith original hand-painted ceramic mugs—he'd had them done in a Wall Street theme, with huge bulls about to devour cowering bears—and poured them each a cup. Jonathan took his coffee black.

"So what are you going to do with the day?"

"I'm not sure." Anna was suddenly nervous about telling him that she had a guy in her bedroom. "I was thinking that maybe—"

"We'd drive up on the Angeles Crest highway toward Mountain High," came a cheerful male voice from the doorway.

Anna whirled. Ben stood—fully dressed, thank God—with his arms on the doorjambs. Smiling.

Jonathan seemed to bide his time with a long sip of coffee. "Ben."

"Nice to see you again." Ben eyed the Krups. "Mind if I have some?"

Her father nodded, so Anna poured Ben some coffee. Meanwhile, he sat down, apparently as comfortable as if he was in his own kitchen. Then her dad's gaze shifted from Anna, in her robe, to fully dressed Ben, and back again.

He raised one cool eyebrow. "Nice to see you again, Ben."

Okay, that was good. Anna knew that with her father, you could never tell how he'd react. One day he was the hippie, pot-smoking, "call-me-Jonathan" dad; the next he was the uptight money manager in a six-thousand-dollar hand-tailored suit.

"So." Jonathan began in a conversational tone, "did you spend the night here with my daughter?

"I did," Ben acknowledged, setting his coffee on the table and looking her father in the eye.

Silence. Anna felt sick to her stomach. She was about to get busted for bringing her boyfriend home for sex, when no such activity had even occurred.

"I . . . I didn't know you'd be home," Anna stammered. "That is, I should have asked if . . . I mean—"

"When I was your age, my parents would *never* have let me have a girlfriend stay over," Jonathan recalled. "Of course, that was back when dinosaurs roamed the earth."

"This isn't a casual thing," Ben explained. Anna felt him put a hand atop her forearm. The touch made her

feel positively unsettled. It was the gesture of a lover.
But were they still lovers?

"I know that. You two met when? New Year's?
You're doing better than two-thirds of the relationships
in Los Angeles."

As Jonathan rubbed his chin—obviously considering
the facts on the ground: that his younger daughter had
brought a guy home for a sleepover—Anna studied him.
He was a handsome man. His vivid blue eyes sparkled in
his roguish, tanned face. Even the spiky haircut suited
him. She'd never considered it before, but she realized
now that he'd probably had a lot of girlfriends when he
was her age. Was there someone before her mother who
he had been madly in love with? What had his hopes
been, his dreams? Strange, to think about your parents
as real people.

"Ben is welcome here anytime," her father declared.
"Just one thing, Anna. Don't get the idea that I'm going
to be happy if I come down to breakfast and find a different guy at the table every week."

Okay, that was way, way over the humiliation line.

"I would *never* do that." Anna tightened the belt on
her robe.

"She would never do that," Ben echoed putting his
hand on Anna's back.

Her father laughed heartily and got up from the
table. "I believe her. But I'm just being a dad here. Give
me a little credit. I've got some work I can do at the
office." He looked pointedly at his shiny gold Rolex

Datejust with the steel-and-gold oyster band and sapphire crystal. "It's ten-thirty. I'll be back by . . . three?"

The blush spread up Anna's neck and into her cheeks. There was nothing she could do to stop it. No matter how you cut it, her father had just basically said that he would clear out so that she and Ben could retire upstairs and do what he thought they'd done the night before.

She decided she was grateful. They'd actually just been on the verge of—

"Mr. Percy?"

"Jonathan."

"Jonathan," Ben corrected himself. You don't have to leave on my account. I . . . have to get to work, too."

What?

Anna's jaw dropped, and then she immediately put it back into place. He hadn't said anything about having to be at Trieste. What would they want him to do on a Monday morning? Mop the spots on the floor that the custodians had missed the night before? And wasn't the club closed on Mondays? What was going on? Had he had a sudden attack of the nerves just because her father had arrived? No, it was more than that. She *knew* it. Her cold eyes met Ben's.

"I checked my messages right before I came downstairs," he explained, his eyes holding Anna's. "I've gotta get going. I promise I'll make it up to you."

Anna doubted that was possible. She smiled a tight smile, kissed him goodbye far away from his lips on his cheek, as he promised he'd call her later. Then, feeling as if her heart was breaking, she watched him walk away.

The moment Ben was out of sight of Anna's house—past the corner of Foothill Drive and Lomitas—he pulled the Merc to the curb. He had a call to return, immediately. It went straight to her voice mail.

"Yeah, hi, it's Ben. Stop by where I work this afternoon. Trieste. Come at three-thirty. I have a management meeting at four. See you."

He clicked off and started the engine again. It was a glorious day in Los Angeles, bright sunshine and eighty degrees, with that cloudless, gleaming blue sky you never saw anywhere except right up against the Pacific. Off to the east, there had been brush fires burning for the last few days over near San Bernadino—a typical occurrence in Califonia in early summer—but the gentle onshore breeze from the Pacific was pushing all the smoke toward Palm Springs instead of back toward Los Angeles.

It was a day to feel good, but instead he felt like shit. Why did everything have to get so damn complicated?

SOB

Cammie leaned back in Danny Bluestone's office chair, put her fuchsia Manolo Blahnik stilettos up on his desk, and waited for her father's grand entrance. She had no doubt he was about to make it.

Studios were notorious for providing their writers with low-rent furniture, and Danny's windowless office was no exception. The show had provided its co-executive producer with a battered wooden desk and desktop computer, a gray faux-leather seat that was the epitome of used, and a mismatched dark yellow plaid upholstered chair that was supposed to be comfortable but looked like puke. He had a whiteboard on one of the walls and two large rock 'n' roll posters taped to another (Tom Waits and Nine Inch Nails). The other two walls were bare, save for a brown pressboard bookcase loaded with scripts on every shelf.

The wait for Clark felt interminable. What to do, what to do, what to do to pass the time? She opened one of Danny's drawers. It was full of half-written scripts and memos from her dad. She was about to read the one on *Hermosa Beach*'s vacation policy for its writers—that should be really short—when in strode her father.

"You have a helluva nerve."

"Thank you."

"Never—and I mean never—pull a stunt like that again, Cammie."

"It was the only way to get your attention," she shot back hotly.

"I don't respond well to public humiliation."

"No shit." She hesitated a strategic moment, then softened her tone a bare notch. "Look, you didn't leave me much choice. You didn't answer my calls when you were in Europe. You've been hiding out in a bungalow at the hotel, so . . . can we talk now?"

"The sad thing is, you think you know everything about everything, when you don't know a goddamn thing about anything." He kicked the door shut, then sat in the ugly yellow-puke chair. "You want to talk Cammie? Let's talk."

"So why the disappearing act? You *knew* I was trying to reach you."

"You'll read about it in the trades tomorrow. Here's the deal." Clark drummed his fingers on his pants legs. "Paradigm made a huge offer to acquire the agency last week. Strictly hush-hush and strictly off the record until someone leaked it to *Variety*. Margaret and I were meeting with their people in Zurich—we figured that was the best way to stay out of the public eye."

Whoa. Paradigm was a huge agency with a lot of

clout. In recent years, they'd acquired first the Genesis Agency, then Writers and Artists. If Apex joined their mix . . . well, Cammie could practically see the zeros mount up in her dad's bank account.

"Well, that's great, Dad, I guess," she stammered.

"No, it's not. It all fell apart last night."

"Over what?"

"Peter Bart will say in *Variety* that the personal styles of the principals didn't mesh, but the bottom line is that they weren't willing to give Margaret and me offices as big as Norm's. Doesn't matter. On to the next. So as you can see, I wasn't avoiding you. I was looking out for our family."

Cammie twirled a strawberry blond curl around her right forefinger. He'd had her going, right until this "looking out for our family" line of bullshit. Clark Sheppard never talked about *our* family, which made her think that there was definitely something rotten in the state of *Hermosa Beach*. Not all of it—her dad wouldn't have mentioned a story in tomorrow's *Variety* if that story weren't going to appear. Yet Cammie was a good liar, and a good liar can always uncover a not-so-good lie.

Had the circumstances been different, she would have seized on this. Today, though, she had a larger purpose in mind.

"Here's what I want to know. The boat, Dad? What happened out there?"

Clark sighed. "I was wrong not to tell you about Sam's mother. I admit that."

"No shit."

"Enough with the fucking cussing, young lady."

A beat of silence, then they both laughed, and the tension dissipated slightly.

"Okay, you got me." He tented his fingers. "How the hell was I supposed to tell you? You'd lived so long without knowing, I couldn't see where it would have made anything but heartache for you and your best friend."

She swung her feet down from the desk. "Since when do you care?"

"You think I don't care about you?" He eyed her curiously.

"It must be all the quality time we spend together that tipped me off."

"Well, you're wrong," he stated bluntly. "For Chrissake, you're my kid."

"A lot of parents don't love their children, Clark," she pointed out. "You're not the first."

He leaned in to her. "I don't suck at loving you. I suck at showing it."

This tugged at some place deep inside of her, but she reminded herself that he was a master manipulator, and he was damn well not going to manipulate himself out of this one.

"The boat?" she prompted.

"How'd you find out?"

"I . . ." She was on the verge of telling him about the police documents, then stopped. She owed him nothing—no information. "It doesn't matter, does it?"

"No, it certainly doesn't." Clark smiled broadly, but she could see the tension in his brow. "You were just about to tell me, and yet you stopped yourself. I mean it, Cammie. You know, since you're not going to college, I would be happy to put you on a desk at the agency as an assistant. Skip the mailroom. You have a future in the business if you ever decide to quit shopping for clothes and start shopping for talent."

"Nice line, Dad. The boat. *What did you do?*"

"You're so sure I did something?"

She tried to keep her tone measured. "My mother was a wonderful person. She deserved a hell of a lot better than you. And she loved me. She never would have . . ." Cammie stopped and swallowed hard. "She never would have left me on purpose. So don't try to feed me some bullshit about her. Because I know better." She folded her arms, unable to read the emotions that flitted over his face. "Your turn."

"Okay, you're right," he finally said, looking down. He laid his large palms faceup on the table. "It *was* my fault. I was screwing around behind your mother's back."

"I *knew* it."

Clark sighed. "I had a fling with Sam's mother. I had lots of flings, come to think of it. She wasn't happy with Jackson. . . . These things happen."

Cammie gritted her teeth. "Oh, *do* they?"

"I'm not saying it was a mature thing to do, but I've never been a very mature person that way. Jeanne was on the boat that night—"

"I know that." Cammie felt a tightening in her chest and pressed her lips together.

"I thought your mom was sound asleep, but she caught us together. I was drunk. I said some dumb-ass things—"

"What?"

Her father waved a hand dismissively. "That . . . your mom . . . sucked in the sack, if you must know. It wasn't true, but, like I said, I was plastered, so . . ."

Cammie could barely control her vitriol. "And then?"

"And then . . . nothing. She said she was going back to bed. I don't know what happened after that." Clark leaned back slightly in his chair and looked Cammie in the eye.

Cammie stood stiffly—she would *not* cry in front of him, no matter what—and deadeyed him. She let out a forced scoff. "Tell me. How does it feel to have murdered your wife?"

"I was an SOB, I grant you, but I certainly didn't mean for her to kill herself."

"Please." She leaned down and scooped up her bag. "You did everything except push her overboard. I will hate you as long as I live."

Cammie found her best friend just where she thought she'd be, hidden behind black Ray-Bans on a bench that faced the beach, reading the *Hollywood Reporter.*

"So?" Sam looked up.

She didn't even know where to begin, so she just shook her head.

"That bad?" Sam patted the place next to her on the bench and pushed a Hermosa Beach Coffee Express cup toward her friend.

"Worse."

"Drink up and tell me all about it."

Cammie sipped the coffee. Could she even make the words come out of her mouth? As a way of distancing herself, she studied her surroundings. The bench was located on an asphalt path along the beach, like the one in Venice but much bigger and much nicer. Venice Beach attracted bums. Hermosa Beach attracted Yuppies and Guppies, along with the occasional surfer who got lost on the way to Rancho Palos Verdes. As she watched in silence, at least a dozen people in their twenties and thirties jogged, rollerbladed, or bicycled past them, enjoying the magnificent morning by the ocean. Did all these people have such drama in their lives? Did any of them have to tail their fathers to their workplaces just to have a conversation? Had any of them sat with their fathers while said fathers confessed to being monsters?

"I'll tell you. But just . . . not yet."

Sam nodded. "Just tell me this. Was your dad doing my mom?"

Cammie nodded.

"Thought so." Sam patted her cell phone. "I got busy while you were in there."

"Eduardo?"

"I wish. Nope. Adam."

Cammie went on red alert. "You had no right to—"

Sam lifted her sunglasses. "Jeez, chill out. I wanted to talk to his parents. I was looking for the name of a good—no, great—private investigator. To track down my mother."

Jesus Christ. Sam was actually following through.

"They gave me some names, I made some calls. I just hired someone named Melanie Mayes—former FBI. Two hundred bucks an hour. But what the fuck? Buy cheap, you get cheap."

"She says she can find your mother?"

Sam nodded vigorously.

"Good."

Cammie resisted the urge to say "Thank you," because there was only so grateful she could be to one person in the space of two days. It struck her anew, though, as they sat together in the bright morning sun: Sam Sharpe was the best friend she would ever have.

Big Bird Hips

"When in doubt, spend," Sam decreed, as she and Anna took the elevator up from the parking garage at the Beverly Center.

As soon as Ben left, Anna had called Sam. She felt so crazy, so unsure of him, and needed to talk to a friend. Sam said she was with Cammie, but would drop Cammie off, change clothes, and then meet Anna for shopping; it was more a proclamation than a suggestion.

Shopping was not what Anna had in mind. She was thinking deep conversation over espresso and dessert at the Insomnia Cafe on Beverly Boulevard. But Sam said she had an important mission, and unless Anna said yes, she planned to be relentless and obnoxious.

So shopping it was, at the storied Beverly Center across from Ma Maison Sofitel in West Hollywood. The Beverly Center was an atypical mall—instead of being spread out like the ones in suburbia that were surrounded by parking lots, it was a rectangular, multistory struc-ture, with escalators in huge plastic tubes that faced the street, and dozens of boutiques and shops on each of the

levels. The top level featured one of the best movie the-
aters in all of Los Angeles. It was a mecca for shoppers
of every nation, even on a weekday afternoon like this
one. "I'm not talking about dropping two thou on a
Christian Lacroix lime-green miniskirt with an uneven
hem on a whim and then realizing when you get home
that it makes you look like you've got Big Bird hips,"
Sam explained fervently. They were the only passengers
in the elevator. "I'm talking about spending money to
get what you want."

"Which would not be Big Bird hips."

"Precisely. So what was it you wanted to see me about
anyway?" Sam asked, adjusting her slouchy Stella
McCartney sweater (which bared one creamy shoulder),
which she'd paired with brown Daryl K. capris and mile-
high YSL Rive Gauche platforms. Anna was wearing an
ancient Narciso Rodriguez black camisole with her
favorite no-name jeans and black linen Prada slides.

The elevator stopped on the first floor. They stepped
off it and onto the exterior escalator that overlooked
Beverly Boulevard and Ma Maison Sofitel. Anna hesitated. Talking about personal things always made her
uncomfortable, but she had been dying to disclose this
information to Sam all day. "Well, it's about Ben. He
stayed over last night."

"Where the hell is that damn store?" Sam asked,
looking around as they stepped off the escalator onto
the third floor.

"What store?"

"The one I need for Operation Eduardo. I am a woman with a plan and the money to back it up."

Oh, so *that* was what this was about. It must be nice, Anna mused, to feel so certain of a game plan. Where was her Operation Figure Out What the Hell Was Really Up with Ben? Maybe talking about it would help.

"Something is wrong between Ben and me. Last night he—"

"Ass!" Sam yelled as a group of very large women with lots of bleached hair clamored by, their arms full of shopping bags. One of those bags had just clocked Sam in the back. "Did you see that? I swear, tourists should need visas to get into Beverly Hills. You were saying about Ben. What's wrong?"

"I don't know, exactly. He's . . . distant. Last night he stayed over and we didn't . . . you know."

"No kosher kielbasa?"

Anna winced. "Now that's just gross."

"But accurate," Sam guessed, as they walked past Bebe, which was showing orange suede with aqua beading in its main window. "So what?"

"Well, I mean . . . shouldn't he have . . . wanted to?"

Sam shook her head. "Honestly, Anna, how obsessive can you be? Ben didn't want to do it one night. *That's* your concept of a crisis?"

"Well, no, but—"

"I would *kill* to have with Eduardo what you have with Ben right now, do you realize that?"

"Yes, but . . ." How could she possibly explain? Maybe

she really was overreacting. Sam was the one with the more obvious boyfriend crisis. The least she could do was be supportive.

"So you're going to buy something for Eduardo?"

"You could say that."

Anna wasn't sure she followed this logic; last she'd heard, Eduardo was both rich enough to buy anything he wanted and not speaking to Sam.

The mall was crowded, as always, with an interesting soup of the rich and famous, and those who merely hoped to dress like them. Tourists from everywhere ended up at the Beverly Center, languages and accents flowing like a shopping Tower of Babel, because this very famous mall was listed in every tourist guide from California to Zimbabwe. The Beverly Center was eight levels of retail heaven. Yes, it had your basic Banana Republics and Gaps ad nauseam, but it also had Dolce & Gabbana, Dior, and Jennifer Kaufman. Therefore, the wanna-bes on a budget could move like lemmings into the chain stores and brag later that they'd bought such-and-such at the Beverly Center. Meanwhile, girls both in the know and in the chip could wander into Just Cavalli and find one-of-a-kind hand-tooled pink python cowboy boots hand-set with emeralds in the shape of a cactus, with a ten-thousand-dollar price tag.

The Beverly Center was an exercise in Tinseltown egalitarianism. Shop and let shop.

"This morning, I went to the set of *Hermosa Beach*," Sam continued, turning and peering around at stores.

"With Cammie. Where the hell is it? I know it's on this floor. Anyway, she was determined to confront her father about . . . well, that's her story to tell or not." Sam took hold of Anna's arm and pulled her to the right. "Ah, here we are."

"Here *what* is?"

"What I'm looking for. My point—and I do have one—is that Cammie is actively going after what she wants. Which reminded me that I too should continue to go after what I want. Namely, Eduardo. Which is what you need to do with Ben. Be an active heroine. Try it some time and—ah, here we are." She waved a hand toward a Verizon cellular telephone service store.

"You're buying Eduardo a cell phone?"

"No, Anna," Sam replied patiently. "Why would I do that? Follow me."

Anna sighed. Really, she had too much on her mind now to try and follow Sam's flights of illogic. She hadn't been able to eat anything all day. Why did Ben keep insisting that everything was normal when it obviously wasn't? The most obvious answer was the one that made her sick to her stomach, the one she was afraid to say aloud lest she somehow make it true—he had met someone else, and he didn't know how to tell her. One minute the idea of that would fill her with a needy panic. The next it would piss her off so much that she wanted to scream. Was Ben that big of a wuss that he'd skulk around behind her back rather than simply be honest with her? Unfortunately, the two of them didn't have a

very good track record in the honesty department.
Other people felt a need to verbalize their internal
monologues, but Anna did not, and neither did Ben.

Sam had suggested that she be an active heroine.
Hmm. That could be good advice.

After waiting in line at the customer service counter
while a middle-aged platinum blonde in peach-toned
Juicy Couture, carrying a peach-toned toy poodle in its
peach-toned carrying case, got her malfunctioning
BlackBerry replaced, Sam stepped up to the desk, where
a guy in a cranberry polo shirt grinned at her. He looked
to be about nineteen, with spiky blond hair and aquamarine eyes that bellowed, "I wear colored contacts!"

"Can I help you?" he asked.

"Yes. I need a new cell phone plan," Sam replied.

His voice dropped to a conspiratorial level. "Say,
aren't you . . . ?"

"Cell phone plan?" she repeated.

Anna knew Sam was used to getting recognized as
Jackson Sharpe's daughter. Often she liked it, and used
it to her great advantage.

"Oh sure," the guy assured her. "Just wanted to say
that I'm glad you put the weight back on, 'cuz it like suits
you. There are a zillion skinny girls out there. And you
looked really good after you lost weight too. But I just
meant I really like your show. My girlfriend turned me on
to it—"

"What show?"

Anna could see doubt begin to cloud his way-too-blue eyes. "*Less Than Perfect*? You're Sara Rue, right?"

"Wrong," Sam snapped. "I am not Sara Rue. Now can we get back to your actual job? New cell phone plan?"

"Oh sure, sorry. Wow, you really look like—"

"No, I really don't. And I don't look like Kelly Osbourne, either."

"Sheesh, my bad." He plucked a brochure from under his desk and slid it over to Sam. "Lemme just go over the plans with you—"

"I don't need you to go over the plans. Just pick one."

"But there are different options based on—"

"Fine. This one." Sam blindly stabbed a finger at the brochure.

The sales rep looked confused. "Well, okay. Do you already have a phone or will you be needing a—"

"Let's cut to the chase. Any phone plan, any phone. I'll need that for *one hundred phones*, which I'd like programmed now. Now what did you say your name was?"

"The name is Stuart." He hesitated. "Did you say—"

Sam turned to Anna. "Did I not say a hundred phones?"

"You did," Anna confirmed. "I have no idea why, Stuart, but I have a feeling she's going to explain."

Sam hitched a forefinger in Anna's direction. "Stuart, now see, this is a girl who knows me. Fine. One hundred phones on plan whatever. I want every single number on them blocked, except for a single number that I give you. And I want that number programmed into all the speeddials, too."

Stuart looked dubious. "Is this, like, a joke?" He was scratching his head and squinting his eyes.

"No, this is not, like, a joke," Sam replied.

"Well I . . . I'm not . . . I mean, I don't think we can . . . It's going to cost . . ."

"Stewie," Sam said with a grin. "Let me tell you who I am. I'm Sam Sharpe. As in, Jackson Sharpe's daughter. As in, I am not concerned about the cost of this. As in, do you think you could make this happen within the next five minutes?"

Stuart turned beet red. "I . . . I . . . "

"Glad to hear we're on the same page here," Sam said with a smile.

Stuart excused himself to speak with the manager. Sam folded her arms, tapping one patent-leather-plat-form-clad foot impatiently.

Anna tried to fill in the blanks. "You're ordering a hundred cell phones for Eduardo, and the only number he can call on them is yours?"

Sam wagged a playful finger at Anna. "There's a reason you get straight A's."

Anna laughed out loud. "That's actually kind of . . . brilliant."

"Is it?" For just a moment she looked vulnerable.

"Yes, it's great," Anna assured her. "It's sweet and funny and shows how much you want him. I should do something like that for Ben."

Sam threw her hands in the air. "What is your problem? Ben loves you. You don't *need* to do anything."

Anna sighed. Right now, she needed to be about Sam; she got that.

"I'm going to have the phones delivered to Eduardo in a giant box. Any number he pushes on any phone, he gets me. He'll laugh, don't you think?"

"I do. How could he resist?"

Stuart hustled back to them, his manager in tow. She was in her thirties and built like a bowling ball, wearing the same regulation Verizon shirt as Stuart. Sam had told Anna many times that any time you found someone fat in a position of power in Beverly Hills, it meant they were great at their job, because excess avoirdupois in Beverly Hills was essentially illegal.

Ten minutes and one credit card with no spending limit later, Sam had ordered her phones and arranged for them to be delivered to Eduardo.

"So we're here, let's spend," Sam suggested as they exited the store, mission accomplished. "Aveda Esthetique, Donna Karan, Armani?"

"I'll wander around with you if you want, but I don't really feel like shopping."

"You and your vintage Chanel hand-me-downs," Sam groused. She peered closer at Anna. "Wait. Something really *is* wrong; I see it in your eyes."

It wasn't like she hadn't been trying to tell Sam exactly that. Yet Anna couldn't help herself; her knee-jerk reaction was to lie and murmur, "No, I'm fine."

God, she'd been well bred into being a damn robot!

According to her mother, being well bred meant that you never let on that your life was anything less than serene. If you were the center car in a ten-car accident on the 405, you'd say, "I'm fine, thank you," before bleeding on the paramedics' feet.

"Oh puh-lease," Sam challenged. She stopped walking and faced Anna.

"Okay, not fine," Anna forced herself to admit. Then, as they leaned against the metal rail, beyond which they could look down to the floors below because the mall was constructed like a giant angel food cake, she told Sam everything.

"Okay, so it's more than he didn't rock your world last night. What does Ben say is up?"

Anna hesitated. "I haven't exactly asked him."

"That is so you," Sam marveled. "How can you stand not knowing?"

"I can't. That's the problem."

"Here's a novel concept: Ask him. At least you can. Think about me and Eduardo. The guy won't even talk to me. Yet, that is."

"But . . . I did ask him if anything was wrong. He said no. You can't force someone to confide in you . . ."

"That is utter bullshit. He's your guy. You have this serious big-time relationship, starring *you*, Anna."

Starring me, she thought, and felt ridiculous just thinking it.

"I know exactly why you haven't confronted him." They began moving away from the railing and started back toward the escalators. "Come on, let's get out of here."

"Why?"

"Because you're afraid to find out the truth. There is nothing to fear but fear itself."

"Franklin Roosevelt," Anna filled in. "He was talking about the Depression."

"Very apt." Sam agreed, as they started downward. "He fought the Depression like it was a war. So rally your fucking army and ride to the sound of the guns."

"It's just so . . . so not me."

"God, would you just get over yourself? If Ben is cheating on you, then he's an asshole who doesn't deserve you, and I'll help you kick him to Van Nuys. If it's something else, find that out too. Don't give up without a fight."

Anna nodded, feeling emboldened by Sam's fighting words. They were particularly sweet since she knew there had been a time not so long ago when Sam had nursed an unrequited crush on Ben herself.

Sam was right. Anna was in a much better place with Ben than Sam was with Eduardo, and Sam was the one taking action. She reached into her black Chanel quilted purse, fishing through her Kiehl's lip balm, her black leather Coach wallet, and a pack of spearmint gum for her own cell.

"How's this for a saying?" Anna asked, flipping her cell open with her thumb. "'I have not yet begun to fight.' I'm calling him. Right now."

Not a Screw-and-Run Guy

B en's cell phone rang out the first three notes of the Who's "Baba O'Riley," but he ignored the call because Blythe was winding her way through the tables of the outdoor patio section of Trieste to meet him. The inside of the club was a series of enormous themed spaces set up by some of the most famous movie set designers in Hollywood. There was a room set up to look like a giant emergency room, complete with bottles of alcohol suspended in medical bags over the massive bar. Another was decorated like a cave, with a special glass floor that changed colors in time with the music. But the part of the club Ben liked best was definitely the patio; it was set up to look like a wacked-out version of a suburban family's backyard from the middle of the twentieth century, complete with individual barbecues, an aboveground pool where clubgoers could cool off during a hot night of dancing, and life-size cardboard cutouts of President Eisenhower, President Kennedy, and other world leaders. He saw Blythe stop and take a second glance at Winston Churchill.

She was a damn great-looking girl, he had to admit—
on the short side, and very curvy, à la Salma Hayek. In
fact, she looked a little like that actress. Her naturally
raven-black hair fell straight past her slender shoulders,
compliments of her mom, a full-blooded Sioux. As she
had confided to Ben one night, her grandparents still
lived on a reservation in Nebraska.

Blythe was a fascinating girl. She dressed like a pretty
stuck-up bitch. Most everyone at Princeton thought that
was exactly who she was. It was authentic, too, from her
father's Portland, Maine, first-family blue-blood side. Ben
didn't know how Blythe's parents had actually met, but
he did know that her family background was an uneasy
mesh of two very different worlds.

They'd met at the movies, of all places. Blythe had
taken off her shoes during a midnight showing of *Rocky
Horror* that she'd gone to with a girlfriend for nostal-
gia's sake—evidently, back in junior high, she'd been a
fixture at the midnight Saturday show at Portland's sole
art house. Somehow, her black velvet Steve Madden
wedge heels had migrated to the row where Ben was sitting with Jack and two girls they'd met at the Ivy Club
on Prospect Avenue.

They'd ended up going out for coffee, and that
wasn't all they'd ended up sharing. They'd ended up
becoming friends, and then things had progressed.

Shit! Why had he let it happen? How had hanging
out turned into . . . more? Ever since he'd come home
for the summer, Blythe had been calling to discuss their

"relationship." To make matters worse, she'd called over the weekend to say she'd be in Los Angeles in two days visiting her older brother, Derek—a junior development exec at Disney. She couldn't wait to be with Ben again. To Ben's shock, she'd started talking dirty to him; all the things she remembered about him, and all the things she wanted him to do to her when they saw each other.

Ben had been freaked ever since Blythe's phone call. If Anna found out how much Blythe was pursuing him . . . he simply could not let that happen.

He'd picked Trieste because he figured this was as neutral an environment as he could think of. Yet here she was, dressed to kill in a little lacy burnt-orange camisole and the lowest-slung jeans in the history of denim.

"Hi," Ben said.

"Hey, gorgeous." He was sitting in one of the outdoor lawn furniture chairs that were spread around the patio. She leaned down to kiss his lips, somehow supergluing her body to his at the same time. "I missed you."

"Blythe . . ." Ben motioned to a second lawn chair he'd placed near his own.

"Ooh, too much too soon, huh?" She smiled and tossed her inky hair back, sitting down and crossing her right leg over her left. "I can't help it if seeing you gets me hot."

Shit.

Ben was determined to take control of this conversation. "You remember I told you about Anna."

"Sure," Blythe breathed easily, lifting her heavy dark

hair to fan the back of her neck. "Is it warm in here or is it you?"

"Um . . . It's warm. They turn the AC off when the club isn't open. I don't know how to make this any clearer to you, Blythe. You and I had sex one night—that's all—during a time when I thought Anna and I had broken up forever. And that's all that happened."

"That's sweet, Ben." Blythe's thick but perfectly groomed eyebrows rose. "But I know you better than that."

"What are you talking about?"

"You are not a screw-and-run guy," she replied simply. "You care about me too much to be like that. I know you do. "Plus . . ." She ran the toe of one black Chanel stiletto against the leg of his faded jeans. "You can't tell me the sex wasn't great."

"Well, I suppose it was," Ben admitted reluctantly. God, if Anna were anywhere nearby, she would *freak*. "And I *do* care about you. As a *friend*."

She laughed her throaty laugh. "You do what we did with all your friends?"

"No. But we talked about it before—"

"Because I'm not the kind of girl who rolls around with her friends. You *know* that about me." She looked him straight in the eye, her expression suddenly serious.

This was true. During one of their late-night conversations, she'd talked about the two lovers she'd had and how both relationships had been serious. How the hell had he allowed himself to get carried away by a few beers and some steamy kisses?

He ran a nervous hand through his thick hair.

"Blythe, I don't know any other way to say this. I told you this before, at school after I came back from Vegas. I'm back with Anna. You and I are just friends. We have to pretend that drunken one-night thing never happened."

"Wow," she breathed, hurt clouding her eyes. "That stings."

"I just . . ."

He hated the hurt on her face and knowing he'd caused it.

"I—I don't want to screw things up with Anna."

Blythe withdrew her hand. "I see." She stood, tears in the corners of her limpid eyes. "Sometimes the heart and the lips say two different things. I was reading your heart. The reason I'm so sure I'm right is that you're breaking mine." With those words, she turned around and walked away; Ben put his head down on his arms. Why had he succumbed to one drunken night of lust? How had he gotten himself into this terrible predicament? He went back over everything he'd said and done and concluded once again that he hadn't in any way led her on.

Yeah. Great. He felt damn guilty anyway.

Evolution T-Shirt with a Photo of an Ape

On Tuesday night, Dee sat at her vintage mirror-topped desk—straight from the Pasadena Antique Center—in her boudoir-style bedroom (straight from a '40s film noir), nibbling on a hangnail and studying the list she'd just complied in her new pink leather Molini journal.

Keeping a journal was such a retro thing to do; half the people Dee knew didn't even own pens anymore; they just brought their Toshiba Qosmio laptops to school and took notes directly on them. But her primary psychiatrist at Ojai, Dr. Silverstein, had suggested that she keep a journal of her time at the institute; to Dee's surprise and delight, she'd found it helped her to organize her thoughts. She'd filled one and a half notebooks with her musings and observations up in Ojai. Now that she was home, she was quickly working her way through her second one.

Unlike Internet blogs (which were so preadolescent and last week), her journal was private. There was no

"How Hot Am I?" photo section for others to rate, no chain-disses of whomever was the out-of-it *chica du jour*, no I'm-so-cool-look-what-I-can-say gossipmongering by someone too much of a wuss to go by more than her initials.

No way. This was by Dee and for Dee only; it made her feel really good.

She stared dreamily at the list she'd just written.

My bed with my parents home
In a closet at Ron's in Hollywood
At the Getty in a storage room behind the North Italian
   Renaissance exhibit
The ladies' room at the Viper Room
The men's room at Privilege

Let's see. . . . Had she missed any locations? Dee felt hot breath on the back of her neck. She lifted her chin and Jack leaned over, his lips meeting hers upside down.

"We can't go on meeting like this," he murmured.

She rose, turned, and stood on tiptoe to drape her arms around his neck. "Yes, we can." They kissed again. "Who let you in?"

"A short, round woman who told me she was the housekeeper. She's wearing an Evolution T-shirt with a photo of an ape morphing into a man on the front."

"The cover of Evolution's first CD. My mom designed it. A huge box came by FedEx. My dad said to give you one. Isn't it cool?"

"Sure," Jack agreed, tugging Dee toward the bed. "But why is the maid wearing one?"

"Oh, my parents asked all the staff to wear them," Dee said breezily. Jack plopped backward onto her satin pea-green quilted bedspread and ivory silk–sheathed pillows and Dee nuzzled on top of him. "He likes the publicity to trickle down to all segments of the city."

Jack laughed. "You're such a snob. 'All segments of the city'? Is that why I get one? Am I a segment?"

"You're an up-and-coming star producer of reality TV," she reminded him.

"Not unless I can keep my hands off you long enough to work on my pilot." He smiled, caressing her lower back.

"You are going to do amazing things," she kissed him lightly. "I know it."

He arched a brow. "To you?"

"Yes," she giggled, "but that's not what I meant. I meant in TV."

She lay on her back and he propped himself up on an elbow. "Do tell."

"Most of the kids I know don't have to work at anything," Dee continued, "because they're already rich and have great connections. But you . . ."

"Us poor and humble working folk," Jack teased.

"Nothing can stop talent and brains like yours, Jack."

He studied her face in wonder. "How did I get so lucky?"

Dee frowned, unsure. "What?"

"You."

She caressed the stubble on his chin. "It's funny, you know. I'm not like . . . ambitious. Maybe that's why I admire it so much in other people."

"There must be something you want, Dee."

She thought for a moment. "Well, consistent sanity. That's one."

"What else?"

What *did* she want? She so rarely asked herself that question.

"Honestly?" she paused for a few seconds. "I don't know."

"Well, when you figure it out, I'd love to hear it." He meant what he said.

"Why?"

"Because I'm into you for more than your hot little body, my dear," Jack explained, his hands slipping dangerously close to the edge of her gold pleated Reiss miniskirt. "Nice outfit you have on."

Dee smiled. *This* was ground upon which she felt supremely comfortable. She'd worn the skirt, along with a burgundy Valentino tank scattered with golden seed pearls, specifically for this occasion. Under it was a white Cosabella mesh thong.

"You like?"

"A lot, Now . . . up, girl." He lightly pushed her off of him.

Dee rolled over and sat up, surprised. "But my parents are out for drinks with the band's new publicist. I

thought we were going to . . ." She eyed her bed mean-
ingfully.

"We are." Jack rose and beckoned Dee toward the
door. "I saw your list."

She stepped toward him. "And?"

"And . . ." Jack backed slowly toward the door. "Very
nice. Now let's improve it. We're going out."

Dee grabbed her purse and they headed downstairs
and outside to Jack's car, a green Ford Taurus from the
late 1990s. With its New Jersey plates and last-millenni-
um pedigree, it was a vehicle sure to attract disdain from
most Los Angelenos. Dee, though, found it charming
and unpretentious.

As Jack pulled out of the driveway, he pressed a
Coldplay CD into the sound system. Dee giggled.
"Jack?"

He'd motored the car to the edge of her triple-wide
driveway and was about to move onto Elvarado.
"Hmmm?"

She leaned over and kissed him. Then kissed him
again, this time with more intensity. Then their hands
were all over each other. "Want to add 'in the backseat of
my boyfriend's car at the bottom of the driveway' to my
list?" she asked breathlessly.

"Anyone can put 'backseat of the car' on their list,
Dee. I'm thinking bigger. Like, say, what would you
think of the *H* in the Hollywood sign?"

So this was what it was like. To be sane and healthy,
in lust and love with a boy who felt the exact same way

about her. It was as if she'd been behind a huge rain cloud, or stuck in some sort of fog for years and years; but now the fog had lifted, and at long last she could see the sun, feel it shining on her, arcing across her life in a delicious, shimmering rainbow. This was what happiness felt like.

"Brainstorm with me," Sam urged Cammie, as they lowered themselves into the sumac-and-rose-scented water that filled the new redwood hot tub on the deck off the upper bar in the rear of the estate's main house.

Sam's gagworthy stepmother, Poppy, had recently exchanged the old Cal Spa hot tub for this new redwood one because their most recent decorator, Mallory Tsu Goldfarb, had insisted that, according to the principle of feng shui, this spot needed to become Poppy's serene space, redone in her baby Ruby Hummingbird's signature color—red. Then Mallory had charged high six figures to have the tub put in, the deck designed in redwood, and the adjoining walls repainted in an abstract concoction of vermillion, cranberry, and radish.

Supposedly, the redecoration meant that Poppy could bring the baby out here so she could quiet and renew both of their spirits. Sam was certain this was a crock of high-priced shit, not that anyone—least of all her father, the actual owner of the estate—cared what Sam thought. But anyway, along with the hot tub, out had gone the "old" furniture (Sam remembered when it had arrived eighteen months before, courtesy of a different decorator) and in had come the new—mostly redwood chaises covered in red velvet cushions. The cushions weren't weatherproof, but to Poppy Sinclair-Sharpe, things as insignificant as patio cushions were easy come, easy go.

A long, polished bar ran along the near wall, stained deep crimson a day before by a team of woodworkers from San Diego. Seven tall bar chairs were lined up like obedient soldiers, each crowned with a velvet cushion anchored to the legs with four garnet brooches flown in from India. On the other side of the hot tub, a redwood planter exploded with wild poppies and wild-looking American Beauty roses.

An enormous redwood patio table displayed the remains of a dinner feast for two, all in varying shades of red: rare Argentinean steaks, chilled gazpacho, and roasted bell peppers stuffed with toasted walnuts and drizzled in a raspberry vinaigrette. A matching wine-colored linen umbrella stood still in the night air. Every imaginable surface was sprinkled—no, heaped—with rose petals: the bar, the chaises, the latticed side tables. Even the water in the hot tub had to be scented with red-colored flower essences.

Complaining to Jackson would have been an exercise in futility. Jackson had married young Poppy on New Year's Eve, and even after six months, Sam found their marriage just as painful as she had on their wedding night. Well, not quite as painful, since that night Sam had been forced to wear a bridesmaid dress that she was certain Poppy had chosen to make her look like shit.

She splashed one hand through the fragrant, bubbling water. That very morning, Poppy had made an inane comment about how they were "really becoming a family" and how she hoped she and Sam could soon share some mother-daughter bonding moments. It had taken all of Sam's self-control not to spill her coffee on the bitch. For one thing, Poppy was only a few years older than her, and for Sam to be her daughter, Poppy would have had to begin puberty in kindergarten.

For another thing, Sam had a real mother; "real" being in significant air quotes, since said real mother seemed to have forgotten that she existed. Anxiety welled when Sam thought about how she'd hired the private detective. At the time, it had seemed like the right thing to do. A day later, she wasn't so sure. When someone didn't want you, they didn't want you. Her mom. Eduardo. Sam was used to being able to use fame, money, and power to get most anything she wanted, yet she couldn't find a way to get the two people she wanted—needed—most.

At least she and Cammie had the deck and the den to themselves this lovely, hazy night in Bel-Air. Her father was on location in Rome for his remake of *Ben-Hur*. Poppy had taken little Ruby Hummingbird to a girls-only party at the Coldwater Canyon home of a friend on one of the ABC soaps. The pregnant soap actress was throwing this soiree to show the DVD of her sonogram, followed by a late night dinner of egg-themed foods— egg salad, caviar, etc. Sam had seen the little egg-hatchinga-baby-shaped invitation on the white marble table in the front foyer.

Sam reached over the edge of the hot tub, where she and Cammie had brought out Bloody Marys made with Flagman vodka and fresh-squeezed tomato juice. She hoisted hers at Cammie. "Brainstorming inspiration. Want another?"

Cammie shrugged. "Depends what we're brainstorming. What we're going to do to Stefanie at her party to pay her back for her indignities?"

"We can figure that out tomorrow. I was thinking about Eduardo."

"Just keep in mind that you have to finesse this in exactly the right way. You can't just go around doing shit to make him think that he has the power in this situation. You have to make him think he's chasing you, not the other way around."

Sam's eyes flicked over Cammie's flawless body in her teeny-tiny bikini; a baby-blue Dior triangle top edged in silver-tipped lace, and low-cut matching boy shorts that showed more ass than they covered. It was so much hotter than her own aqua Moontide bandeau one-piece. Oh sure, it was easy for Cammie to make such sweeping statements. If she looked in a bikini like Cammie looked in a bikini, Eduardo probably would have pushed Parker out of the way on the beach that night and kissed her himself.

Then the healthy part of her psyche bitch slapped the insecure part. Yeah, right. Eduardo loved her just the way she was. Well, he had, anyway. Losing weight and magically having her fat calves turn thin would not change anything.

"But he does have the power," Sam admitted. "We both know it. I'm the one who fucked up what we had—"

"Oh please. It was prom night. Besides, kissing Parker is not fucking Parker. Someone needs to tell Eduardo that this is not some cheesy *telenovella.*"

Sam gave her a disgusted look. "What would Adam do if he walked in on you kissing Parker?"

"I don't know. Laugh?"

"No, he'd be pissed. Wouldn't you feel horrible if you hurt him like that?"

Cammie leaned her head back against the lip of the tub, careful to lift her curls over the edge so that they stayed dry. She closed her eyes. "I hurt Adam all the time."

"What are you talking about?"

"I don't even know why I do it." Cammie peered at Sam through the gloom of the evening. "Sometimes I wonder . . . what I would be like if my mom hadn't died? I mean, maybe I'd be exactly the same bitch I am, but . . . you know . . . maybe not."

Sam's heart clutched. "At least you know your mom would be with you if she could, Cam. But my mom . . ."

"We're getting maudlin here, Sammikins," Cammie sang out.

"I know, Cammiekins," Sam sang back. She was right. Enough with wallowing in this shit. Gawd, it was all just too depressing. If her mother didn't want to be in her life, didn't care enough to even pick up the phone, send a card, an e-mail, a fucking IM, then fuck her.

"What have you heard from your dick?" Cammie asked.

"I don't have a dick. Not even Eduardo's anymore."

"I believe 'dick' is slang for *detective*, silly girl."

"I've heard nada," Sam admitted. "All I know is that your father was doing my mother. *Ew.* But everyone has sex with everyone in Beverly Hills—that's no reason to get out of Dodge."

"Good point," Cammie agreed, and poured herself another Bloody.

"Maybe the whole thing with my mother makes me more insecure with Eduardo," Sam mused. "You know. Abandonment issues."

"Jeez, you really need to cut back on those sessions with Dr. Fred."

Sam nudged her foot into Cammie's leg. "I love Eduardo. Isn't that worth fighting for?"

"Sure, to prove that you can win. But don't think that if you do win, it's gonna be forever."

"It's a little late for that, for both of us," Sam teased. Cammie didn't crack a smile. "Come on, Cam. I know you don't believe that. If you did, why would you stay with Adam?"

Cammie let her toes float to the surface of the water. "I ask myself that all the time."

"You love him."

"Sometimes," she allowed. "And sometimes I wonder

what the point is. We're going to break up eventually. Everyone always does. My parents. Your parents. Look at our friends' parents, The only ones who are still on their first marriages have so much Prozac in their systems, they should wear prescription bottles."

"Come on," Sam told her friend. She didn't let herself think it, much. But she had to admit to herself that—every so often, usually late at night when she was all by herself—she'd definitely considered the notion of her and Eduardo *forever*. "You're only saying that because of what's going on with your father."

"No. I'm saying it because it's true." Cammie hoisted herself out of the tub and padded over to the redwood stand of fluffy six-hundred-thread count fuchsia-and-bloodred Ralph Lauren damask towels, took one, and used it to dry herself off. "My parents loved each other." She sat on the edge of a velvet-topped chaise and wrapped the towel around her neck. "My earliest memories are of them together. They were laughing, my father dancing my mother around the living room in that crappy little house in Mar Vista we used to live in. Look where *that* shit led. How about we talk about Jackson and *your* mom? That was a match made in heaven. Just a heaven in a parallel univer—"

Sam's cell rang. She'd left it on the lip of the hot tub. *Eduardo?*

"Hello?"

"Sam? It's Melanie Mayes. Your investigator," came a woman's brisk voice. "Do you have a minute?"

Sam watched the fingers of her left hand weave through the water.

Not Eduardo.

"Sure."

Cammie mouthed, *Who is it?* but Sam paid no attention, just kept her eyes on her fluttering fingers, their size distorted by the refraction.

"I found your mother."

Four simple words.

I found your mother.

Sam's gaze drifted past the deck, out to the mustard-colored and squishy lights of the sprawling metropolis of Los Angeles below. Would her mother like the view?

I found your mother.

"Miss Sharpe? Are you there?"

Sam inhaled sharply through her nose. "Yes, sorry. I heard you. You found her." Across the hot tub, Sam saw Cammie's eyes bulge from her head. "That was fast."

"It wasn't all that difficult. She's running the Living section of a local newspaper in western North Carolina under her married name."

Sam was suddenly dizzy. Everything felt not quite real. "Go on."

"I told her you were graduating from high school on Friday. She now has your cell number, as you instructed," Melanie continued.

Sam dug the nails of her left hand into her thigh. "Is she going to call me? Did she say?"

"Actually, she gave me a message for you."

"What . . . message?" Sam could barely choke out the words.

"She said she'll see you on Friday."

Ugly Squared

"Well, this is taking forever," declared an elderly woman with thinning chin-length gray hair and an oversized aqua peasant blouse. She was sitting next to Parker in the medium-sized waiting room full of orange plastic chairs. There were a few Peruvian travel posters on the walls; the far end of the room featured a door and a long glass window, behind which three or four consular officials were methodically processing visas. "What are you here for?"

"Visa," Parker lied. He lied easily; he was very good at it.

"Me too," the woman smiled. "This will be my fourth trip to Peru, relief work with my church. We always go to an Indian village named Indiana. Indiana, Peru. Did you know there's also a Peru, Indiana? I wonder if anyone mixes them up."

Parker laughed, because obviously she expected him to laugh. Fulfilling other people's expectations was something else at which he excelled. A tall, dark-rooted blonde in the chair kitty-corner from him flashed a dazzling Rembrandt-veneer smile. She crossed her faux-tanned legs, which led to her Pucci knock-off miniskirt. Parker knew the real thing and he knew a cheap imitation. He knew a lot of things, most of which no one gave him credit for. One thing he did not know, though, was why he felt quite so determined to do something really, really nice for Sam Sharpe.

He knew he should have a million other things on his mind. First and foremost, what to do after graduation that did not involve the phrase, "Do you want that supersized?" He wasn't old enough to bartend. With his chiseled good looks and easygoing flair, he knew he could be a waiter at someplace upscale, but the idea of serving the "haves" would make him feel all the more like a have-not. He hated that feeling more than he hated romancing a supposedly rich girl and dumping her if he found out she was as poor as he was.

That morning, he'd awakened damn depressed. He was going to graduate from high school in three days. After that, his life was a big fat blank, beyond his burning desire to become a professional actor. His mom was pumped; she considered graduation a big occasion, probably because she'd dropped out of school in the tenth grade. She'd purchased an outfit from QVC and had already modeled it for him—too loud and too tight and too short and ugly squared. There was a matching droopy hat from the same shopping channel—did Parker notice how it picked up the citron in the print of the dress and was the same color as the ankle boots that showed off her legs, which were still her best feature, dammit?

Jeez. Could he pretend that he didn't know his own mother at his graduation? With her around, forget that Robin Williams was the graduation speaker—the Pinelli family would be all the entertainment the audience needed.

As the day had gone on, and Parker had gone through his usual daytime routine when he didn't have to go to school, he found himself thinking more and more of Sam. Not in a romantic way. At least, he didn't think so. Oddly, he had really enjoyed kissing her the night of prom. But what the hell, maybe he'd enjoy kissing any girl that rich. If he got desperate enough, he could probably learn to enjoy kissing a *guy* that rich. But it was more than the money, and more than good acting on Parker's part. He liked her. Yeah, he was very, very grateful that she hadn't blown his cover after figuring out the truth about his depressingly low family income level during their trip to Vegas, but gratitude didn't explain why he was where he was at that very minute.

He'd tried to fight the feeling. He'd gone for a run along San Vicente Boulevard down to the ocean, and then watched DeNiro in a DVD of *Raging Bull*. The movie only made things worse; that much acting talent was intimidating. He even raided his mom's meager liquor cabinet and downed a couple of shots of her el-cheapo bourbon. Then he'd sat in his mother's very used Barcalounger with the bottle by his side, staring blankly at *Animal Planet*, where a lioness stalking a zebra herd spotted a small zebra that had come up lame. In two seconds, that zebra would become the lioness's lunch— just like he would have if anyone but Sam had learned his secret.

Goddamn. He *liked* Sam. He *owed* Sam. Sam had *power*, maybe even the power that could likely give him a break in the business down the road. She was hurting because of their prom kiss, caught in the act by her boyfriend. Maybe there was something he could do for her that would not only be kind, but also be in his enlightened self-interest.

On *Animal Planet*, the Australian guy who looked like Matt Damon's bigger, taller, and more handsome brother was talking directly to the camera, making a big deal about how he was going to cheat death on the Serengeti plain and walk straight into the lioness's den— the same lioness that had just torn the lame zebra several new orifices and checked out the caloric content of its hindquarters.

Bingo. He knew what he had to do. It might not involve eating raw zebra, but it definitely could mean he'd have to consume a good deal of crow.

Fuck it. He'd better do it now, before he lost his nerve.

Parker looked at the paper slip in his hand that had been handed to him by the guard at the entrance to the consulate, which occupied the eighth floor of a nondescript office building. He was number ninety-one. The electronic sign above the long glass window in front of him said that number eighty-five was being served.

"*Numero ochenta y seis, numero ochenta y seis,* number eighty-six to the visa window, number eighty-six to the visa window."

His seat companion bounded to her feet with the energy of someone much younger, brandishing her navy blue American passport. "Well, see you in Peru, young man. What airline are you flying?"

"TWA," Parker replied. He'd never flown internationally and only a few times within the United States. TWA was the first airline he could think of.

The elderly woman frowned. "Young man, TWA went out of business at least five years ago. I hope you didn't actually pay for a ticket." With that, she departed.

Her departure was a good omen. Numbers started to be called in rapid succession. Eighty-seven. Eighty-eight. Eighty-nine. Ninety.

Ninety-one. Parker got his old Campmor green knapsack from the floor under his seat and went up to the glass window, where a beautiful Peruvian girl with thick dark hair and Angelina Jolie lips smiled at him.

"How may I help you, señor?" Her voice was soft and melodious; Parker had to remind himself of his mission and restrain himself from flirting. Besides, if she had any money, she definitely wouldn't be behind that damn desk.

"May I speak with Eduardo Muñoz, please? He's working here for the summer."

The beautiful young woman looked puzzled. "You want to speak with Eduardo? You don't want a visa?"

"Nope. No visa."

"You could have come up to the desk to tell me this sooner."

Great. Now that he'd wasted a fucking hour and a half with his ass in one of those ugly-ass plastic chairs.

"Could you tell him that Parker Pinelli would like to see him? For just a few minutes. Tell him it's important. It's . . . Tell him it's about Sam."

"Okay. Please sit. I'll call him. If he's available, that is . . ."

Her voice trailed off, and Parker was tempted to up the flirt quotient again. How could he be sure that Eduardo was even here? If he wasn't, why shouldn't he ask this lovely señorita for a drink? He doubted that anyone had yet taken her to the Viper Room, or the Derby, or even a salsa place, like Club Bahia on the dicier part of Sunset.

He sat, folded his arms, and waited some more.

Ninety-three. Ninety-four. Ninety—

The wooden door next to the long glass window opened. Eduardo peered out. He was wearing a dark suit, white shirt, and yellow tie, a stark contrast with Parker's battered Levi's, white T-shirt, and red baseball jacket from a minor-league team in Las Vegas.

"Parker Pinelli?" he asked, his voice impersonal.

Parker stood.

"Please." Eduardo motioned with one hand for Parker to join him behind the door.

Again, Parker grabbed his backpack. Ninety seconds later, he was sitting with Eduardo in a small conference room ringed by file cabinets, plus a small TV with a DVD player and a couple of computers.

Eduardo's face was impassive; neither pleased nor displeased to see Parker here on his own turf. Then he smiled thinly. "What do you want? Did Samantha send you?"

Parker shook his head. "I came here on my on my own."

"That is good to know. Do you know what she did this morning?" Without waiting for Parker's response, he reached under the conference table and extracted a white documents box that normally held files. "Look."

It was the strangest thing. The box was filled with brand new cellular telephones phones—there had to be at least fifty or a hundred, maybe even more.

"Try one," Eduardo instructed. "They're all charged. Call your own cell."

Parker took one at random from the open box—a Samsung SGH-E635, punched in his own digits, and pressed send. Nothing. Just a Verizon voice saying that the call could not be completed.

"Didn't work, right? Try any other number. On any phone you want."

Parker switched phones, this time to a red Verizon 5200. His cell. His brother's cell. His mother's cell. Nothing. Strange.

"None of these phones work?"

"Oh, they work." Eduardo smiled that thin smile again. "Try the speed dial. Any speed dial."

Parker pressed the digit *4*. It dialed Sam's number. Eduardo yanked the phone from Parker's hand, ending the call before it connected.

"I must say this for Samantha. She is . . . What is the word in English? Indefatigable."

Parker was impressed. Sam really wanted Eduardo back. Well, he could try to do his part too.

"She is," Parker agreed. "And I just wanted to tell you, Eduardo, that what happened after prom was totally my fault. We were drinking, and I was the one who made the first move. She was a little toasted and a lot depressed."

"Depressed about what?"

Parker pointed to the DVD player and TV. "Do you mind? I want to show you something."

Eduardo looked skeptical, but nodded. "Go ahead, but keep the volume down."

Parker got his backpack and rooted around in it for a certain DVD. Then he brought it over to the Bose player, popped it in, and turned on the TV. Almost instantly, a picture appeared—it was film taken by Parker's brother Monte at the Beverly Hills High School prom, on the set of *Ben-Hur* out in Palmdale. The film was from the pivotal moment of prom, when the prom queen and king were announced. Parker saw that Eduardo was transfixed by the images: the impossible moment when Sam was named queen of the prom. Monte had come in close on Sam and focused on her face—shock, disbelief, and finally, amazed pleasure as she mounted the stage at the far end of the Coliseum movie set to frenzied cheers from the thousand-plus crowd of students and faculty. He zoomed in even closer at the climactic moment when the glittering tiara was placed on Sam's head, and Fee Berman stepped to the microphone for an impromptu speech:

"I think we all know that Sam Sharpe single-handedly saved our prom," Fee recounted into the mike.

As Fee's words echoed around the Coliseum, Monte had panned the crowd: every head in the place was nodding fervently. Parker snuck a glance at Eduardo. He was rapt.

"I mean, how great is this?" Fee continued. "Here we are on the set of Jackson Sharpe's next unbelievable movie. Sam, we all just want to thank you for taking lemons and making lemonade!"

Parker turned off the DVD and TV. "Sam was a hero that night, Eduardo." He took the disk out of the player. "A real hero. I don't know how much you know, but our prom was completely ruined. It was supposed to be at the Bel-Air Grand Hotel, but that hotel burned down the week of prom. Sam was the one who figured out what to do. Sam was the one who made all the arrangements. Sam was the one who thought of everything. Sam was even planning to make a movie about it. You're asking why she was so bummed out, so upset that she'd let me kiss her . . . and maybe even kiss me back? The answer is simple: Because you weren't there to see it."

Whew. Parker hadn't intended to go on that long. He didn't want to seem like he was overplaying his hand. Yet the passion of his words got the best of him. Sam *had* saved the day, and she'd been planning to make a movie of the prom do-over. When she'd won prom queen, the movie had been ruined, because she knew no one would take seriously a documentary where the filmmaker ended up as the belle of the ball being filmed.

"She didn't tell you, right?"

Eduardo nodded.

"Yeah, didn't think she would. That's why I came here. That's why I wanted you to see that. It hurt her that she couldn't make her film, but it hurt more that you weren't there to see her moment of glory." Parker stood. "Look, the girl really, really loves you. She's special. Hell, she doesn't even know how special she is, but she's . . ." He stopped, then started again. His eyes met Eduardo's. "You don't just throw something like that away, man."

Eduardo's eyes clouded. "What she did . . . you did . . . It was still a betrayal."

Parker shrugged. "Like I said, we were drunk. But it didn't mean shit." Then he switched to Spanish. *"Si yo podría vivir esa noche otra vez, no habría hecho lo que lo hice. Y de la manera que me has recibido aquí hoy, debo decir que mi amiga Sam es afortunado tenerle. Gracias, Eduardo. Yo significo eso."*

The look of shock on Eduardo's face pleased Parker greatly. His high school grades had always sucked . . . except in Spanish, where his twelfth-grade teacher was a fox. He'd just told Eduardo that if he could do it over again, he'd do it differently, and that from the way Eduardo had allowed him—Parker—to make his case here, he thought Sam was lucky to have him as a boyfriend.

"Where did you learn to speak Spanish like that?"

"We have schools in America too. But there's one thing they can't teach, no matter how good a student you are."

"Okay. What's that thing?"

"To get your goddamn head out of your ass, Eduardo. Before it's too late."

Celebrity Gawk Session

When Anna went to meet Ben for breakfast the next day at Nate'n Al's delicatessen on North Beverly Drive in Beverly Hills, she was determined to be what Sam had described as an "active heroine." There was something off between her and Ben, but she wasn't just going to wait around miserably and see what would happen. She would take matters into her own hands and address it. "I can't pretend everything is fine when it so obviously isn't. It's insulting to both of us."

Yes, that was what she would say. If it meant that she and Ben were done, so be it. It would hurt. It would hurt a lot. But there were other guys in Los Angeles, and it wasn't like their relationship had been a plate of . . .

Oh God. She was so full of it. Ben was her first everything. Her *only* everything. How could he have stopped loving her?

What did one wear to confront one's boyfriend? Her mother would have insisted on high-priced battle armor—Chanel would be perfect. So Anna did just the opposite. She pulled a plain white T-shirt from her

175

drawer and an ancient pair of cargo khakis. She did opt for Chanel, but only on her feet—comfy ballet flats. With her hair back in a ponytail tied by a black silk ribbon, a little Stila brown mascara, a slick of Smith's Rosebud Salve on her lips—that was it. Take her or leave her.

Nate'n Al was the most famous deli in Beverly Hills, with a simple storefront that boasted its name in bright orange script. The interior was spacious, with booths and tables all variations on orange and white. Off to the left was an actual delicatessen counter, with glass cases full of herring, lox, pickled tomatoes, and other delicacies.

The place was popular, an industry hangout for decades. In fact, as Anna stepped through the door, it seemed like Nate'n Al was packed to well over its human capacity. She knew that Ben was supposed to be here already to find a booth, but how was she going to find him in this mass of Hollywood hipsters, ladies-who-lunch out for breakfast instead, waitresses in their fifties and sixties in orange dresses that must have been high fashion forty years ago, and tourists enjoying a celebrity gawk session? Just to her left, in fact, a tight knot of foreign visitors surrounded one table, talking excitedly to one another and pointing. All Anna could understand were the words *American Idol*, which meant that someone from a show even she had heard of was dining at that very moment.

She felt a strong male hand on her right shoulder.

"Table for two, madame? Come right this way." She turned. Ben wore a green V-necked Fila rugby shirt with khaki pants. He looked great. More than that, he looked different, and not just because he'd gotten his hair trimmed between the last time she'd seen him and now, or because he sported a scruffy growth of beard that Anna found very sexy. It was his eyes—as she looked into them, all she saw was love.

"I might have to hit on the maître d'," Anna mused, as Ben led them through the restaurant. "Or is he taken?"

"Very taken. But since when have you ever 'hit on' anyone?"

"Oh, you'd be surprised."

"You don't say? No, wait. Come to my table and tell me every titillating detail," Ben suggested. He tried to force his brows and mouth into an impression of Jim Carrey, but failed miserably. Still, Anna giggled as he helped her into a vacant chair at a table for two with a RESERVED sign on it. Just like that, all was right with the world again.

A well-past-middle-age waitress with dangerously tall brown hair and legs like tree stumps lumbered over to their table. She wore an orange Nate'N Al uniform that had likely looked good twenty pounds ago, but miraculously didn't restrict her movement as she poured coffee for them both. "The matzo brei will be out in a minute, Benny," she reported. "Ditto the sable platter."

Ben grinned and pointed to his watch. "I'm timing you, Myrtle."

"Timing, shmining," Myrtle scoffed in her warm yet

gravelly voice, obviously unfazed. "Remember, I control your breakfast between the kitchen and here. I could tell you stories about what Phoebe did to a certain notorious Oscar-winning actor's tongue-pastrami-roast-beef sandwich when he was rude to her, but I'd hate to ruin your appetite. How're your parents?"

"Great. And don't try to blame Phoebe, either. I heard this unnamed actor has your picture up on his dartboard."

"I ain't saying I did anything, but whatever happened, he deserved it." Myrtle lumbered back toward the kitchen.

"She's been a waitress here since I was a kid." Ben leaned over the booth, grinning. "She used to be an actress in Roger Corman's horror films."

No doubt. Ben was back. Apparently, better than ever.

"You're different today," she declared.

"Yeah?"

"Yeah." Myrtle had also poured fresh-squeezed orange juice. Anna took a sip; slightly tart and slightly sweet, it was delicious. At the next table, a couple of producers were arguing over possible casting for their next feature, an action flick about a lonely female cruise ship captain who decides to quit her job and enter the competitive world of speedboat racing. One wanted Angelina Jolie, one wanted Renée Zellweger. Their voices got louder and louder.

"It's the talent, Richie. It's the talent. Renée has the talent!"

"Screw that, Freddie. What would you rather see? *Cold Mountain* or *Tomb Raider*? I tell ya, Jolie's butter!"

In best *This Is How We Do Things* Big Book fashion, Anna was doing her utmost to ignore the distraction. Ben, however, leaned over toward them. "Hey, guys? I write for the *Hollywood Reporter*. What's the picture? Maybe I can do a story for tomorrow?"

The two squat-looking men—both in standard-issue jeans, T-shirts, and baseball caps to cover their candidacy for the Hair Club for Men, backpedaled furiously.

"We're still in preproduction—"

"We're not ready to be in the trades—"

"We'll be greenlit any day now, I swear it."

"Fine," Ben replied, nodding. "Then please keep the volume down. You see this girl?" He hitched a thumb toward Anna. "Gorgeous, huh? I think I'm in love, and I need a little quiet here so that I can tell her."

The thinner of the Hair Club men nodded. "Okay, wise guy. Just don't get married. Ruins everything."

"I'll certainly keep that in mind," Ben assured him.

Myrtle brought them the sable platter—bright pink slices of fresh lox, golden pike, sliced tomatoes, and the sable itself, which Anna discovered was close to smoked cod but altogether wonderful. There were two sliced everything bagels shedding sesame and poppy seeds, plus small brown chunks of roast garlic and flecks of salt.

She leaned close to him as he prepared a section of bagel, cream cheese, and sable for her. "Do you know what's funny?"

"What?" He forked up a piece of sable and tasted it. "Perfection."

"Something was bothering you over the last few days, and you wouldn't say what. But now I realize; it didn't have anything to do with me. I'm right, aren't I?"

"Yeah," he agreed, and put the bagel section on her plate. "I'm sorry, Anna. I acted like an asshole. A rude and distant asshole."

"Can you tell me what it was about?"

"Just some personal stuff." He spread cream cheese on his own half a bagel.

"With your family? Your dad?"

"I swear it's not important. I just really don't want to go into it."

She was a little taken aback. "Okay. It's just . . . maybe I could help."

Ben shook his head. "It's . . . not really appropriate for you to help. Anyway, it's handled and it's over." He lifted her fingertips to his lips and kissed them. "Okay?"

Anna considered pressing him for details, but thought better of it. In the social circles of the WASPy Upper East Side of Manhattan, there was a difference between what was and what was not her business. Couples didn't need to share *everything*. Besides—if she was going to be perfectly honest—she hadn't been without at least a slight interest in Caine during the brief time they'd spent together. It wasn't like she'd confessed that to Ben.

Perhaps some things in relationships were better left unsaid.

"Got plans for today?" Ben asked. He sipped his coffee.

"I don't know. Do I?"

He grinned. "Well . . . I thought it might interest you to know that my parents are not only not home, they're not coming home, because—"

Anna's cell rang. "Don't you dare change the subject," she warned him, then fished her phone out of her classic butter-colored Marc Jacobs hobo bag. "Hello?"

"Anna? It's Dad."

"Hi, Dad."

"Where are you right now?" Jonathan asked.

"Nate'n Al. Having breakfast with Ben."

"I hope you ordered the sable."

"I did . . . I mean, Ben did. And matzo brei."

Jonathan's happy laughter rang in her ears. "Well, that's a good thing. Now, I want you to do four things, and no is not an option. One, pack up the sable to go. Two, pay the check, though I suspect your dining companion will cover it. He'd better. Three, come home right away. And four, bring Ben with you."

"But—"

"No buts, Anna. *Now.*"

"A summons to Foothill Drive," Ben joked, as he and Anna stood on the doorstep of Jonathan's mansion. "Just when we were about to make up for lost time."

Anna tried to force a smile, but the truth was, she felt uneasy. From the exterior, everything at home looked normal—her father's third car, a bright yellow Lotus

Exige, stood sentry in the driveway that circled the front
of her father's two-story classic white mansion with two
bay windows that looked out over the front of the prop-
erty. Anna's own room was in the rear, on the second
floor. Behind and around the house was something more
rare in Beverly Hills than a child who had to walk to
school—a sizable plot of land. An old maroon pickup
from their landscaping company was parked behind it; a
crew of workers was hard at work cutting the lawn and
trimming the shrubbery before they went to work on
the landscaped grounds behind the building that featured an artificial stream, a footbridge, and a wooden
gazebo. But who knew what was going on inside?

"Shall we?" Anna asked tentatively.

"We shall, but I'm not carrying you in this time."

Anna smiled sweetly and found her keys. "I think we
can go in under our own steam." She opened the door.

"Happy graduation!"

Anna stopped dead in her tracks. Barely five feet from
her, in the middle of the foyer, were not just her father,
but her mother, Jane; her sister, Susan—who had just
made the big surprise announcement—and a mystery guy
with a brown bushy beard and wiry, unkempt hair. He
wore blue drawstring pants and a sort of white tunic.

Susan rushed forward to embrace her sister, words
tumbling out of her as she did. "Surprise! Mom came
from Italy and Gordon and I came from the East Coast
to surprise you for your graduation! So say something.
Oh wait, I should introduce you. Anna, this is Gordon

Freed. Gordon, meet my little sister, Anna." Then she
threw her arms around Ben. "It's so good to see you!"

"Uh, nice to see you again too, Susan," Ben acknowledged with a sudden grin. "You seem . . . like you're doing
well."

When Ben had first met Anna's sister, she'd been
consistently bouncing between very and totally fucked
up. Now she was apparently sober.

"Yep, I'm different," Susan acknowledged. "Welcome
to the real me!"

A moment later, Jane Percy moved in toward Anna for
a double French-style air kiss that came no closer than
three inches to Anna's cheeks. "Let me look at you,
Anna." She took her daughter by the shoulders and
frowned, taking in the ancient white T-shirt/ancient
khakis combination. "Have you been . . . beachcombing?"

Have you been beachcombing? Quintessential Jane
Percy.

"No, mother. Surfing."

"Well then." Her mother's voice turned surprisingly
upbeat. "Perhaps sometime you'll show me to how to—
how do they say it here?—hang . . . ten?"

Everyone laughed. The notion of Jane Percy on a
long board—not to mention uttering a painful cliché
like "hang ten"—was so comical as to be absurd. Then
Anna rubbed both temples, as visions of the next few
days *en famille* flashed through her head. She got along
okay with her mother, but Jane Percy was always so
judgmental, it was sometimes hard for Anna to maintain

her sangfroid. As for her sister, Anna loved Susan fiercely. But Susan had a lot of problems—she always seemed to mess things up. Over the years, Anna had been the one to clean up those messes.

"Why don't we all come in and get acquainted?" Jonathan suggested. "I've had Mimi put a little spread out in the living room."

"Great idea," Gordon exulted. His voice was high, almost girlish.

With a grand gesture, Jonathan pointed the way to the living room, and the pack moved off.

"So, Ben," Jane began, bringing up the rear. "Anna has told me a bit about you. But I'd so much rather hear it in your own words. Tell me about yourself."

"Well, I just finished my freshman year at Princeton."

Anna's eyes slid to her mother and saw that she was impressed. How nice. Wait until she found out that Ben's father was in Gamblers Anonymous. Strike one. His mother had been hospitalized in January for a nervous breakdown. Strike three? He wouldn't even need one.

When it came to Jane Percy, two strikes, and you were out.

Anna sat on the claw-footed beige couch in her father's living room and watched as her family and their significant others helped themselves to the magnificent buffet brunch. The room itself was opulent enough, with its marble floors and Steinway grand piano. Light classical music tinkled out of the custom-installed sound system. What her father had referred to as a "little spread" was laid out on the Greek marble side table—the feast leaned heavily toward the cuisine of Ethiopia, because Jonathan's latest cook was from that eastern African nation. There were soft, flat breads called injera, yesmir wat (made with spices and stewed lentils), yehabesha gomen (cooked collard greens with other spices), and kitfo—a very spicy concoction made of lightly cooked ground beef, which Anna had learned was most often served raw back in Addis Ababa, the capital city of Ethiopia, where Mimi was born. But Mimi had also added eggs Benedict and cheese omelets to the menu, along with an enormous crystal pitcher of Mimosas and a silver carafe of French-press coffee.

She saw Gordon tear off a morsel of injera and pop it into her sister's mouth. Susan was beaming. Too weird. The Susan she knew and loved would never have eaten food from her boyfriend's hand in front of her parents. Susan had been the rebel without a cause, the downtown rock 'n' roller who never met a controlled substance she didn't crave and who, according to Anna's best friend, Cyn, changed boyfriends more often than Anne Heche changed sexual orientation.

Now look at her. After her last stint in rehab, she'd moved to the Kripalu Institute—a heavily spiritual hangout in the Berkshire Mountains of western Massachusetts—where she worked in the kitchen, ate macrobiotically, and attended as many yoga and medita-tion classes as possible. Gone were the seductive black eye makeup and the platinum-bleached spiky hair, the generous curves, and the overpriced black punk clothes with more rips than intact seams. In their place was a short, almost boyish haircut in her natural honey color, plus clothes that looked more Yoga Booty than CBGB—white linen drawstring pants like Gordon's, Birkenstock sandals, and a blue cotton pullover top that was somewhere between tank top and short sleeved.

If the internal transformation was even a bare facsimile of the exterior, Anna felt confident she was looking at a completely new Susan.

She shifted her gaze to her mother, who was talking with Ben as she ate a small plateful of scrambled eggs— no injera or yesmir wot for her, since Ethiopian food was customarily eaten with one's fingers. Her sleek blond hair was parted in the center and fell to her collarbone; her makeup was so subdued as to appear to be nonexistent. Her outfit was classic Upper East Side of Manhattan let's-go-gallery-gazing Jane Percy: a cream Oscar de la Renta blouse that tied at the neck, a Caroline Herrera skirt that ended midcalf, opaque hosiery, classic camel Manolo Blahniks, and 4.48-karat flawless diamond stud earrings that that Anna knew had been insured for a hundred and fifty thousand dollars. Everything about Jane was understated, tasteful, and suffocatingly perfect.

It made Anna want to push Ben down on the couch, climb aboard, and give him a lap dance.

"You're not eating," Jonathan pointed out to his daughter when he returned to the living room from the kitchen, martini glass in hand. He was in a dressed-down phase, in Levi's 505s and one of his white button-down cotton shirts. "What do you think of the big surprise?"

"When did you arrange this, Dad?"

Jonathan smiled slyly and raised his glass to Anna. "You don't give your father enough credit. Here's to you. It's a big deal, graduating from high school."

Anna shook her head. "No, it isn't."

Her dad took a swallow of his Grey Goose and vermouth. "You're right. It isn't. But when you get your doctorate at Yale in nineteenth-century European literature and a teaching fellowship at the University of Chicago, that'll be a big deal—don't look at me like that, I know you better than you think. Look, I just thought this would be a great excuse to have the whole family together."

"I'm so appreciative, Dad." Anna hugged him while sneaking another look at her mother and Ben. It made her remember the last time Jane was in Los Angeles— she and Anna's father had embarked on a brief and torrid affair. Which was *so* disgusting. They didn't even like each other.

"Are you and Mom . . . you know?"

Jonathan's laugh boomed, but he didn't answer.

Just then, Ben caught her eye and winked. He looked happy and perfectly comfortable talking to her mother . . . even more comfortable than Anna was most of the time. She knew she should be thrilled to have a family that cared enough show up for her graduation.

"Excuse me, Dad." She got up and edged over to her mother—Susan and Gordon had just joined Jane and Ben's conversation.

"Mom? Excuse me."

"Yes?" Jane raised her eyebrows.

"I just wanted to say thank you for coming. It was really sweet of you."

"You are absolutely welcome," Jane replied, with a demure twinkle in her eye.

No subterfuge, no sideways dig, no subtle expression of disappointment. Wonder of wonders, Anna thought. She really means it.

Paired Up Like Penguins

S am pulled her Hummer into the only open parking space left at Will Rogers State Park, one of the nicest beaches between Santa Monica and Malibu. She shifted the car into neutral as she took out her cell and left a long-overdue message for Anna.

"Hey, good morning. Why aren't you answering your phone on a Wednesday morning? Busy with Ben? As for me, I'm sitting here like a beached whale in the parking lot at Will Rogers. I was thinking seriously about plunging into the Pacific to rejoin my brethren in the great blue. You know, Free Willy and all that."

Sam rubbed her bottom lip as she cradled her Motorola between her MAC Studio–powdered cheek and silk-clad shoulder. "Anyway, the update is, still no word from Eduardo. Do you think he didn't get that he was supposed to call me? Or do you think that nine dozen cell phones was overkill? Okay, so now I'm thinking about a billboard outside the Peruvian consulate. No. That's a shitty idea. I could use some inspiration."

She sighed morosely and glanced at her La D De

Dior diamond watch, set with sixty diamonds and sapphire crystals.

"Okay. This sucks. I was really hoping he would come to graduation. But there is a mystery guest coming I want to tell you about. No, *not* a guy. But I'll wait to tell you in person. Kiss kiss. Call me in a couple of hours. I'm not taking my cell to the beach."

Well, that was the world's longest voice-mail message.

She stashed her cell in the glove box, opened the Hummer door, and stepped down to the gravel of the parking lot. Though the beach was usually ten degrees cooler than Beverly Hills, today was warm and there was practically no breeze. Sam was wore a strategically ripped Rock & Republic denim miniskirt, along with a pin-tucked Y&Kei cream silk cami and long gold David Yurman necklaces hanging to her navel—perfect clothes for a perfect June day.

When she'd awakened with still no word from Eduardo—what was wrong with him? He couldn't take a goddamn hint like a life-size cardboard cutout? From a hundred cell phones?—she knew she had to do something to get her mind off things. She'd considered some of the prime hashish stashed in her father's nightstand but had decided on ocean air instead.

The beach was just a few steps from the parking lot; she carried a white rattan beach mat under her right arm and kicked off her black flip-flops once she reached the sand. Everywhere she looked were people having fun—flying kites, playing Kadima with wooden paddles and a rubber ball, building sand castles. Out on the water, dozens of surfers waited for the perfect wave. Sam, who often thought in cinematic terms, realized it was the perfect establishing shot for an ocean-side movie scene, maybe that climactic moment of the film where the two star-crossed lovers finally reconciled after their long estrange—

Shit. Stop it, she told herself. Just stop.

Shit. It wasn't working.

It didn't help that the sand seemed entirely populated by couples in various states of flirtation. She stopped for an errant Frisbee tossed by a pretty girl in a pink string bikini who was goofing around with her boyfriend, who looked like Chad Michael Murray, only younger and better looking. They had matching mandala tattoos—when Chad tackled his girlfriend lightly to the ground to tickle her, her shrieks of joy reverberated in Sam's eardrums.

Double shit.

Farther along was a cute blond girl vaguely in the Cammie Sheppard mold, pre-implants, who was posing for her baby-faced boyfriend. He was using his camera phone to snap a photo of her and an elaborate sand sculpture she'd created.

Everywhere she looked: couple, couple, couple.

Jesus. Everyone's paired up like penguins. Except for me, still wandering across Antarctica by my jackass self.

She stopped near a rock jetty and spread out her beach mat. She wouldn't even look at people. She would just gaze at the water. Yeah. Maybe that would help.

It didn't. Guys kept coming into her line of view—

swimming in the ocean, fishing on the jetty. Each of them reminded her of Eduardo. One had his chiseled chin; another his piercing dark eyes. Even a guy walking along the tidal line maybe thirty feet away . . . same golden skin. Sexy crinkles around his eyes. Same elegant way of carrying his body, like something out of another era, one where dashing princes carried beautiful maidens off on white horses, where the girl got the guy and they went to live happily ever after. Unlike real fucking life, where—

The guy was just ten feet away.

Holy shit.

He didn't just look like Eduardo. He *was* Eduardo.

"Hello, Samantha."

Eduardo was barefoot, just like Sam, wearing a maroon Randolph Duke shirt and casual white pants with a knife crease from Harrods. He gazed at her as if she was the most beautiful girl on the planet. Or was that part only her imagination; wishful thinking?

"What are you doing here?"

"An excellent question." He turned to gaze at a seagull squawking overhead. "Perhaps you are wondering how we are on the same square meter of sand at the same time." He said it as a statement, not a question. "It must be more than coincidence, don't you think?"

She nodded, not quite believing this was actually happening.

He regarded her thoughtfully. "One theory is that a cosmic planetary alignment brought us both here, to this spot, at this moment. The same cosmic alignment that allowed us to meet in the first place."

"Or maybe you have the Peruvian secret police tailing me," Sam teased. She had to keep her edge. She couldn't just stand there like a lovesick puppy, even though that was how she felt.

Eduardo laughed. "There is no one else quite like you. You realize that."

"Yes," Sam replied with mock seriousness. "I am utterly unique and completely without parallel in my ability to walk the fine line between the highly creative pursuit of something deeply desired and criminal stalking. It's the reason that my father thinks I should run a studio instead of becoming an outstanding film director. And I still don't know how you found me."

"Not so complicated. Your highly creative pursuit succeeded. By the way, dinner the other night was excellent, though my dinner companion was a bit of a cardboard cutout. I called you this morning. You didn't answer. I called Anna. She said you were here."

Sam dug her toes into the sand. "I guess the next question is, what were you planning to say?" She kept her head down, afraid to hope. Because, God, it would hurt so much if she got her hopes up only to have them dashed again.

"I was determined to forget you, Samantha. But you're a hard habit to break. Would you like to take a walk?"

Would she ever.

The beach was the same show as before: couples flying kites with multiple tails, drinking beer furtively out of bottles in paper bags, sunbathing and flirting. They were just a blur to Sam, background actors in a movie where she was one of the two leading stars.

"You know, the calls and the dinner and the phones were just the start," she told him, reaching out and taking his arm. "Tomorrow, I've got a thousand geishas prepared to storm the consulate wearing masks of my face. On Friday, ten thousand carrier pigeons will home in on your condo, all with my profile tattooed on their fat little bellies. Saturday, NASA—"

Eduardo laughed. "I believe you actually would have done all that."

"Defeat isn't in my DNA." She stopped and looked into his eyes. "But evidently, stupidity is."

He put a finger to her lips, implying that he knew exactly how she felt; that she didn't need to say it. "Your friend Parker came to the consulate yesterday. Not for a visa. To see me."

"Parker?" Sam's heart quickened. "What did he say?"

"He showed me film from your prom. He explained some things to me, about how you were feeling that night." He stopped and ran his knuckles tenderly over her cheek. "Samantha, I wish I could have been there to see you win your crown."

Sam blinked back tears, of joy this time.

His arms went around her. "No more kissing anyone else. Drunk, sober, lonely, angry—it doesn't matter. We don't do that. Do we have a deal?"

She nodded, afraid that if she opened her mouth at that moment, the tears would begin and she wouldn't be able to stop them. She swallowed hard and smiled. "I could have my dad's attorney write up a deal memo if you want. It's legally binding, you know."

"I like this kind of binding better." He pulled her close and kissed her softly, then sealed that kiss with the sizzling kind.

"Yep, that pretty much does it for me," she laughed.

"Me too."

As he kissed her again, an important thought somehow formulated itself in Sam's insanely happy and endorphin-flooded mind:

I owe Parker Pinelli one big-ass graduation present.

Granny Pants

Cammie looked around aghast as Sam pulled her Hummer into the massive parking lot at the MegaMart in Panorama City, on the northern outskirts of the San Fernando Valley. The vehicles in the lot were scary—an ungodly mix of Fords, Chevys, and the occasional Pontiac. Not a Beemer or Lexus in sight.

"Wow, this is kind of like a sociological experiment," Dee mused, staring out the window at the customers with overflowing carts heading toward their cars.

"You're sure this is the best place to go?" Anna, who sat in the front seat next to Sam, looked to her friend for confirmation.

"Here's everything I know," Sam began. "Stefanie called this morning and laid it down, after she waxed poetic about her vacation last month in Antigua. Beyotch. Anyway, the theme for the party tomorrow night is "cheap." Not cheap chic, either. Just plain cheap. No one can spend more than forty bucks on her outfit. Winning outfit gets to pick a girl from the opposing school to be her slave for a day. She said to bring price tags and receipts as proof. If cheap is the goal, MegaMart is the place."

"Fair enough," Anna acknowledged. Meanwhile, Cammie slipped on her Versace N86 H sunglasses as they got out of the Hummer, unwilling to face this experience without something between her eyes and reality.

Penetrating MegaMart was like entering Fort Knox. The girls walked past a phalanx of uniformed security officers, a bank of cameras just above the door recording their faces for posterity. Then they passed three more guards who were checking the receipts of everyone against their purchases before they were allowed out of the store. A stoic cluster of customers with screaming kids waited to be checked out.

"That's terrible," Anna muttered as an old lady with a cane fumbled for her paperwork. "They act like the customers are criminals."

"Hey, if I just got released from San Quentin, this is where I'd shop," Cammie countered.

"It's a class thing," Dee decided. "Less fortunate people don't get treated very well."

Cammie shot her a look. "How would you know, Dee? You've been painfully overfortunate your entire life."

"I've watched TV." Dee sniffed self-righteously. "Which way is the women's department?"

Sam pointed and grabbed a shopping cart. "There it is. Come on."

Cammie put a restraining hand on her arm. "Sam,

those clothes will be the size of pup tents. Even you don't need a pup tent. Don't these people do Juniors?"

"'These people' is kind of an insulting thing to say," Anna pointed out.

"Thank you, Miss Politically Correct," Cammie countered, not in the mood to deal with Anna Percy's righteousness. Not that she ever was.

"Just think, Cammie," Dee chirped, fingering a small chartreuse handbag with beads and rhinestones glued to it as they walked past. "If you do decide to design handbags, stores like this will be knocking you off. No wonder they say that imitation is an affront to flattery."

"That's 'imitation is the *sincerest form* of flattery,'" Sam corrected.

They passed the MegaMart lingerie department, which featured thin polyester granny gowns with Halloween pumpkins on them on sale for eight dollars, ultrasheer baby doll nightgowns in jewel tones with matching G-strings with some sort of fake marabou crap around the neckline, and a delightful selection of white cotton industrial-strength bras large enough to house a small island nation. There were granny pants and fuzzy lime-green socks and more ugly intimate wear than Cammie would have believed possible.

How could anyone actually feel desirable in this stuff?

"Okay, this must be it," Sam announced. They'd reached an area where the mannequins had been made to look like teenagers clad in low-cut jeans and wide pleather belts. They were surrounded by racks of clothing that imitated various hip looks of "the moment," if said moment had passed in the previous millennium.

"How about this?" Dee displaced a black lace miniskirt approximately the size and shape of a postage stamp. The material was rough, but not in a hip meant-to-be-unfinished way. "It's kind of cute, don't you think?" She fingered the price tag. "Eighteen dollars. This could work."

"What about a top and shoes and underwear?" Sam asked. "You'd go way over the limit."

Cammie shuddered. "Please don't tell me we have to buy the underwear here, too."

"You do if you want to make Stefanie your slave for a day."

Cammie gave a long-suffering sigh. Fine. She'd get through this somehow, and it had better be quick. She was supposed to meet Adam for dinner; she hadn't seen him since her confrontation with her father, though she'd told him a little about it on the phone. Even that had felt too raw to share. It was as if she was too drained from what was going on with her father to muster the energy to discuss it with him. What she'd said to Sam in the hot tub also stayed with her. What was that again? What was the point? She and Adam would break up eventually.

For the next ten minutes, all four of them pawed through endless six-dollar tops: kelly green and beige striped terry cloth, purple with Mickey Mouse dancing with Minnie Mouse, and endless printed T-shirts—YOUR

BOYFRIEND WANTS ME, 100% HOTTIE!, and SUPERSTAR in gold glitter on a red baby tee.

Dee nabbed the SUPERSTAR shirt. "What about this?"

"Maybe," Sam mused, holding a shirt printed with a giant HELLO MY NAME IS label with SEXY written on it in script.

"What if we all get them?" Dee suggested. "It'll only cost us twenty-four dollars out of our total."

"If we dress alike, none of us will win," Cammie declared.

Anna frowned at a low-cut brown-an-aqua print shirt made of some shiny slippery material. "You know, winning isn't such a big thing,"

"You're right," Cammie corrected. "It's the *only* thing. Stefanie is going to be my slave. She deserves it. You guys just choose what's least horrible, okay? I'll be right back."

This was not going to do. Cammie knew she'd never find what she wanted in this assortment of dreck. But at least she had something in mind as she strode through the store to the boys' department. Bingo—plain white cotton T-shirts. A large should fit her nice and tight. Price? Six-fifty. Take that, Stefanie. Now for bottoms. She found some Winnie the Pooh boxer shorts—if she cut the legs apart and had one of her housekeepers resew the pieces into a miniskirt, it would be quirky enough to be cute. Stefanie had made no dictates about alterations.

Ready to go with everything but shoes, Cammie returned to the juniors' department to see how her friends—and Anna—had fared. Not too badly, actually. Sam had come up with black boot-cut stretch pants and a fuzzy red off-the-shoulders sweater that would show off her pretty shoulders. Dee had chosen a pair of Daisy Dukes (evidently they hadn't sold well after that execrable film with Jessica Simpson) and a sleeveless white polyester shirt. Washed once, the shirt would undoubtedly fall apart, but for one party it would be fine.

Then there was Anna, who had found an oyster-toned polyester satin bias-cut slip with spaghetti straps; perfectly plain, perfectly simple, in which she looked perfectly fabulous.

So Cammie wasn't the only one who'd come up with the creative-shopping concept. Damn.

Last stop—shoes. Cammie had the most money left, and found a pair of sky-high clear plastic heels for eighteen dollars. She knew that her legs would look a mile long in those heels with her soon-to-be-created miniskirt. Dee, whose feet were tiny, dug out some girls' red plastic cowboy boots. Twelve bucks. Sam went for black wedge espadrilles, which would help elongate her legs. Which left only Anna. Cammie felt smug. No way was the girl going to find shoes for under seven dollars, and that was all she had left to spend.

"I think I got it!" Anna stepped around the edge of the last shoe aisle, displaying a pair of red velvet flip-flops. "They were in a bin in the bedroom slippers section. On sale, four ninety-nine."

"Do they fit?" Dee asked.

Cammie already knew they would fit perfectly, because Anna was fucking Cinderella.

"Kind of small," Anna pronounced.

Cool. Cammie peered at Anna's feet—her sheer oyster OPI–polished toenails hung over the edges of the flip-flops. The sight cheered Cammie considerably. "Oh well, too bad."

Sam fiddled with the Carl Blackburn gold earring in her right ear and contemplated the situation. "Look, Anna. Just try to walk in them. If you can, then all you have to do is to make an entrance. After that, go bare-foot."

Anna stood up and took a step. And another. "Well, I can sort of walk. It's not very comfortable—"

"Comfort is not the issue," Sam reminded her. "One of us winning *is*. So?"

"So . . ." Anna took a couple more steps, then laughed. "What the hell, I can handle it."

Okay. Fine. Anna Percy was willing to take one for the team. Cammie had to give her that much.

Shopping completed and outfits assembled, they dumped everything in their cart and pushed it toward an endless checkout line. The girl who rang up their items—her name tag indicated that she should be called Jolene—wore a pink shirt so lowcut it that her massive bosom strained to plop out onto the conveyer belt. This was no shocker—Cammie had noticed that almost all the girls and women in the MegaMart were curvy-fat. Didn't they want to be thin? Didn't they feel the pressure?

Sam asked for separate receipts for each item they bought, pissing off everyone in line behind them. Meanwhile, Cammie watched in fascination as a heavily tattooed, grossly overweight guy with an exceptionally hairy chest and an unlit cigarette dangling from his lips charged up to Jolene.

"When you getting off work?"

"Regular time, honey,"

"I'm goin' to Bud's tonight. Play pool."

Obviously, there was some sort of romantic relationship between Jolene and the hairy behemoth, who also apparently had not showered in a number of weeks. His body odor was rankling.

"Aww." Jolene turned to him. "You're never home! How you gonna show me that you love me?"

"Hey, I told you I'll be at Bud's. That's love!" He belched loudly; Cammie stepped back another few feet from this loathsome representative of the species.

Then she stopped and congratulated herself on her genius.

Oh yeah. I've got it, she marveled. Revenge, payback, retaliation, counterattack, reciprocation, reprisal, anti-pardon, vengeance, petty spiteful behavior that made a person feel great. In other words, how to make Stefanie sorry that she ever, *ever* messed with Cammie's best friend.

Mermaids and Mermen

I t took a lot to impress Anna. Not because she was a snob, but simply because of the many and varied experiences that had been a part of her life since . . . well, since forever. She'd attended parties at the White House, Buckingham Palace, and the Palais de l'Elysee, not to mention nine of the ten top hotels in the world. (Yes, she had stayed at the Hotel Caruso in Ravello, Italy, but not after the recent renovation.)

Still, after Anna and Ben had ridden together through the warm, dry night on the double-decker London-style shuttle bus ferrying passengers up through the hills of the Pacific Palisades (the seats were covered in faux-mink slipcovers embroidered in pink thread with Pashima and Stefanie's names, the date, and the coat-of-arms of Pacific Palisades High School), and then finally onto the long private drive up to Pashima's estate high above the Pacific, Anna had only one word to describe what she was seeing:

"Wow."

"I gotta agree." Ben laughed. "This rivals Sam's digs. Only better, because it's right over the ocean."

"Well then, I'm sure Sam will buy an ocean immediately," Anna joked snuggling into his shoulder.

"Welcome to the estate of Pashima Nusbaum," the driver announced over his intercom system as the bus rolled to a stop. He was round and red-cheeked, with a nose almost as big as Adrian Brody's. "Please feel free to take the fun-fur seat covers with you as a souvenir. Watch your step climbing down, please."

He opened the front and rear double doors; happy partygoers spilled down into the night. The boys looked normal, Anna noted, since the cheap clothing contest was girls only. Parker Pinelli's date—he'd introduced her as Raisin, something like that—had on a Day-Glo orange polyester backless minidress so short that her lack of underwear would be displayed anytime she bent over.

Ben helped Anna off the bus onto a circular driveway large enough to support a fleet of fighter jets. The patio surface was illuminated by rose-colored floodlights high atop stanchions. Remarkable. She realized they weren't standing on asphalt at all.

"It's mosaic," Ben exclaimed. "Can you imagine how much work it was, laying this down tile by tile?"

Anna pointed. "Look closely. It's full of mathematical formulas."

"Well, I guess we shouldn't be surprised." Ben swept back the lock of hair that had flopped onto his forehead. He was dressed comfortably in jeans and a blue work shirt. "Pashima's father gets a penny every time someone clicks a computer mouse. Or something like that. Ready to head in?"

Anna nodded. To get to the front door, they trod a mica path that followed the curvature of the building. The structure itself was magnificent. Perched at the edge of one of the promontories that gave Pacific Palisades its name, Pashima's house was as long as two football fields, with the side closest to the ocean almost entirely made of glass.

As they approached the front door, they had to give their names to a guard in a black uniform, dark sunglasses, and a Secret Service–style earpiece. He typed their names into his Sidekick and waited for some kind of confirmation. Then he waved them toward a black glass door that slid up as they approached.

"Welcome! You're Ben Birnbaum and Anna Percy, right? We've been expecting you! Welcome to my house!"

The girl greeting them was built like a midget sumo wrestler, with dark hair that had been flat-ironed into submission, and smooth olive skin. She wore a bowling shirt from the Mar Vista Bowl-O-Drome and white cotton painter's pants from OSH Hardware. "I'm Pashima, your hostess. I'm *so* glad you're here, Anna. You too, Ben!"

Anna was a bit taken aback. Clearly, the security guy had warned Pashima that she and Ben were about to enter. "Thank you. It's a pleasure to be here."

"Don't thank me, thank my daddy. He's a genius!" Pashima exclaimed. "He practically invented the Internet."

All righty, then. Anna gazed around the amazing foyer, which featured a floor-to-ceiling saltwater aquarium complete with coral reef. Huge parrot fish dominated the seascape, along with various other tropical fish. The rest of the entryway was stark and white, with sea-themed sculptures atop white marble stands dotting the gleaming white tile floor.

Pashima looked Anna up and down. Then her eyes narrowed, her gracious hostess face a thing of the past. "Didn't anyone tell you about the price tag rule for outfits? You don't want your school to forfeit, do you?" Then she touched the fabric of Anna's dress. "Oh, I see. It really is cheap shit. Well, okay, then." She smiled, the radiant hostess once again. "Have fun. Dee Young and her boyfriend are out there. What is she taking? I swear, she was totally coherent when she arrived. And Sam Sharpe's with that hot Spanish guy. Just between you and me, is she *paying* him to pretend to be her boyfriend?"

"The hot Spanish guy's name is Eduardo," Anna filled in, her tone frosty. She was quickly learning to despise Pashima as much as Sam and Cammie did. Sam had called her the night before, giddy with the news that she and Eduardo were back together. Anna had been thrilled to hear it—almost as thrilled as she'd been to share the word that the weirdness she'd felt with Ben was over. "He's lucky to be her boyfriend."

"Oh, relax, Anna. I was only *joking*! You'll see that Pacific Palisades kids don't bite. Food's on the second floor, fashion-contest photographer at the first guesthouse, and the band is supposed to start in forty-five minutes. Here's a schedule and a map, cuz this place is, like, huge." Pashima pressed a piece of heavy parchment paper into Anna's hand. "Okay, you two, go have fun!" She was already moving toward a group of girls who had just entered, all of whom wore cheap cotton shorts with faux Fendi scarves twisted into bra tops. "Natalie! Kendall! Madison!"

Anna and Ben took that as their cue to wander off. The room adjoining the foyer was an art gallery, featuring dozens of late-twentieth-century works from such downtown New York City artists as Keith Haring, Jean-Michel Basquiat, Futura 2000, and Kenny Scharf. Anna could almost hear her mother's approving cluck-clucks as she checked out one of Rodney Alan Greenblatt's cartoon-inspired paintings.

The next room, though—an indoor picnic area with teakwood patio furniture, an actual bubbling spring, and a skylight roof that opened to the second floor—had plenty of action. There were lots of people drinking beer and dancing to Fall Out Boy being piped through a hidden sound system, while waitresses in 1950s carhop uniforms with exceedingly short white skirts circulated with plates of picnic-style foods: tuna sandwiches, hot dogs on buns, plates of potato salad and cole slaw, and actual s'mores. The s'mores made Anna smile—she hadn't actually eaten one since the summer after seventh grade. Then she heard her name. "Anna. Anna!"

She turned—Sam was coming toward her, grinning

happily, wearing her black stretch pants and fuzzy off-the-shoulder sweater. "I'm so happy, even in this piece-of-shit outfit!" She threw herself into Anna's arms. Eduardo stood just behind her, gazing at Sam as if she were more precious than all the art in this outsized home. Anna knew that look from Ben—she had missed it so much earlier in the week, when things were so peculiar between them.

Thank God that's over.

"It's good to see you again, Anna," Eduardo told her, and kissed her lightly on the cheek. He wore jeans and a baby-blue T-shirt under a blue Polo; perfectly under-dressed for the occasion. "And thanks again for telling me where Sam was."

Sam put her hand on her boyfriend's shoulder. "Now I get to introduce you to one of the truly great guys in the world. Eduardo, I want you to meet Ben Birnbaum."

Finally.

Eduardo stretched out a hand; Ben shook it firmly. "I've heard a lot about you," Ben declared. "You've got a great girlfriend."

Eduardo put his hands on Sam's waist. "I know that."

Anna recalled Sam telling her how she and Ben had made out at the party after a bat mitzvah once—that Ben was the first boy she had ever French kissed. Funny, the story hadn't made her jealous then, and it didn't make her jealous now. It just seemed sweet.

"What do you think of the place, Anna?" Sam asked. "Have you guys been out back?"

Anna shook her head. "Not yet."

"Well, come on. Prepare to be blown away. Who knows? You might even meet the definitely-not-divine Miss Stefanie."

Facing north toward Malibu, Anna could see the twinkling lights of communities all the way up the coast to Santa Barbara. There were three aquamarine swimming pools, each one jutting out over the one below it by some miracle of engineering. A five-foot-high waterfall flowed from the third-floor pool into the second-floor pool; another waterfall spilled from that pool into the main pool. Meanwhile, a tiny computer console embedded in the wall was programmed to change the underwater lighting scheme, as well as fire a series of lasers into the waterfalls. Lilies and rose petals floated on the pool surfaces, while beautiful long-haired models dressed as mermaids and mermen sat around the perimeters, fins swishing in the water.

The rear area teemed with partygoers, and the waitstaff continued the nautical theme, going from group to group with seafood appetizers—jumbo prawns on braised endive leaves, Beluga caviar with *fromage blanc*, cracked lobster bites wrapped in maple-infused bacon. What these pricey foods had to do with the theme of cheap, Anna had no idea.

Just beyond the pool, a band was setting up on a portable stage. Anna checked the schedule to determine that this was Goes to Eleven—graduating senior Felicia Finn ("*Felicia is a proud member of the Pacific Palisades graduating class whose father wrote Goes to Eleven's first smash college-radio hit, 'Inside Doubt'—thanks, Mr. Finn!")* was responsible for the band's appearance.

"How excessive," Anna commented, still scanning the schedule. "Let's see, we can have our tarot cards read and get henna or real tattoos in the second guesthouse. Swedish massage and reflexology are in the third guesthouse."

"That's nothing," Ben scoffed. "The United States Olympic women's gymnastics team is in the home gym giving floor exercise demonstrations."

Just as Anna was going to suggest they get some food, a brief but dazzling fireworks display erupted overhead, to oohs and aahs from the crowd. When it was over, a tall girl with blunt-cut platinum-blond hair hurried toward them.

"Anna! Anna!"

"Who's that?" Anna mouthed to Ben.

"Not a clue," Ben admitted.

The girl, though, knew exactly who they were.

"Anna Percy, right? I'm Stefanie Weinstock. Thanks so much for coming, I've heard so much about you."

Stefanie took Anna's hands in hers. She had high cheekbones and a longish face, with slightly too much chin, looking not unlike a much younger version of Cher, if Cher had had her plastic surgery as a teenager. Her lips were absolutely perfect—whether they were natural, plumped up with silicone, or fortified with fat sucked from her butt was impossible to determine—and her eyes were Bambi-esque and honey-colored, with eyelash extensions. She wore a burnt-orange faux-silk sheet wrapped in a complicated fashion that resulted in a pretty authentic-looking sari; and there was a small orange jewel in the middle of her forehead. "You're even cuter than everyone said you were. I *mean* it."

How to respond to this flattering comment?

Stefanie gave Anna no chance to respond. "You know that Sam, Cammie, Dee, and I used to be dear friends. Then we moved and lost touch. I've missed them so much. This is like a big, happy family reunion."

Either this girl was the greatest liar Anna had ever met, or her ability to rewrite history with a straight face was impressive.

When in doubt, do what the Big Book says.

"Nice to meet you, too," Anna replied. Before she could introduce Ben, Stefanie was hugging him. "Of course I know who you are. Girls at my school drooled over you. How's Princeton?"

"Great." He extricated himself from her embrace. "Uh, nice party."

"Well, Pash and I tried to make it really special for you guys. So listen, Anna. You need to get down to get your photo taken for the contest, because the voting will happen in an hour. Think of it as running for antiprom queen. I heard Sam won at yours. That must have been something. Got your receipts?"

"Definitely."

"Great. Well, tonight it all about making memories,"

Stefanie gushed. "So Anna, scoot scoot scoot down to guesthouse one for me, will you? You're a sweetheart!"

Anna watched Stefanie rush to another group of kids and embrace them like long-lost family. "My mother has friends so plastic they could rival Barbie. But Stefanie makes them seem genuine."

Ben winked at her. "I say we just laugh the whole thing off and cut out of here early." He brushed some hair from her cheek. "I was thinking of us, alone, a roaring fire . . ."

"Hopefully in a fireplace."

"Hopefully in my fireplace. My parents are still out of town."

"Lucky us," Anna murmured.

Ben kissed her softly. "No. Lucky *me*."

Anna sighed with happiness. Thank God everything was right between them. As long as she had Ben, she could make it through graduation with both of her parents, her sister, and her sister's extremely crunchy boyfriend swarming around her.

No matter how insane it got with her family—and it was bound to get insane, because it always did—Ben would be the calm at the center of the storm.

"Girlfriend" Material

"HELLO TO PASHIMA AND STEFANIE'S FRIENDS. ARE YOU READY TO ROCK?" Jett James, the lead singer of Goes to Eleven, posed the challenge to the crowd—the response from the party-goers was deafening as they streamed to the dance floor that that been laid down in front of the stage.

When the band launched into its monster hit, "Inside Doubt," Ben couldn't help but smile: The girls who were usually the epitome of chic were now the epitome of cheap. The ones with a sense of humor had left the price tags attached to their clothes, the 99 Cent Store and Kmart markings flapping in the breeze as they danced.

Funny how much could change in a year, he mused. Last year he'd had a blast at the version of this party that had been held at the Malibu beach home of an outrageous 1970s glam rocker whose daughter was in Ben's class. This year, he couldn't wait for Anna to come back from the bathroom so they could retire to more comfortable quarters.

Two very soft, small hands clamped down over his eyes. "Guess who?"

Fuck no, Ben thought. That's impossible.

It wasn't. Blythe launched herself into his arms. "Surprise! Glad to see me, lover?"

"No." He immediately pulled her hands off of him. "What are you doing here?"

"Same thing you're doing. I got invited." She twirled to show off her outfit; her jet-black hair swished against her high cheekbones. "Like my dress? It's Yamamoto. I figured since I'm in college I can wear what whatever I wanted."

The Yamamoto was a low-cut coral baby doll. She'd paired it with thigh-high melon-and-raspberry suede boots. The combination was devastating.

Ben didn't give a shit. "Is this some kind of a joke?"

"Do I look like I'm laughing? Come on, lighten up, Ben. It's a party."

"I can't believe you would show up here and—"

"Ben and Blythe! I knew you two would find each other!" Stefanie came over to them practically on the dead run, shouting to make herself heard over the pounding music.

"Excuse us a minute," Ben told Blythe, then took Stefanie's arm and led her toward the pool and away from the band and Blythe.

"What's she doing here?" he asked urgently, once they were out of earshot.

Stefanie looked hurt. "I invited a bunch of college

kids because I thought you and some other people would be more comfortable. My friend Blake Goldenberg who goes to Princeton told me that you guys knew each other."

"That's all?"

"That's all."

Ben frowned. It seemed like a reasonable explanation, though he had no more interest in spending time with Blythe at this party than he did in *Groundhog Day*ing his life to repeat his high school graduation experience.

As Stefanie drifted away, Blythe slid over to Ben again. "Well?"

"Well, what?"

"You see this isn't a setup."

What could he say? Or do? He felt foolish and more than a little self-absorbed.

"It's just that Anna is here."

"I hope you two are very happy."

One of the wait staff—a guy this time, dressed in 1950s greaser clothes—offered them broiled monkfish hors d'oeuvres. Ben waved him off and peered at Blythe.

"You're sure?"

"What do you want, Ben, a papal blessing?" She tossed her hair back. "You hurt me and you know it. But I'll live. It wasn't a fatal wound."

Well, that was a relief.

"We never should have hooked up," Ben declared fervently. "You can't imagine how much I regret it."

"Gee, thanks."

"I didn't mean it like that!"

"Jesus, Ben. Why don't you just take a bucket of kosher salt and rub it in? Do you have any idea how that makes me feel?"

Goes to Eleven launched into a ballad about lost love. Blythe stepped closer, gazing into his eyes. He saw the hurt and knew he'd caused it.

God, I can be such an asshole.

"So what is your deal, anyway? You put girls into mental compartments—this one is 'friend' material and this one is 'girlfriend' material? How did I not rate in the girlfriend box? Not good enough, not hot enough— what was it?"

"It wasn't like that, Blythe. You're gorgeous. The sex was *great*. But—"

Fucking bloody hell.

Ben froze midsentence. He'd seen a flash of wheat-colored hair and beige faux-silk out of the corner of his eye, and knew—without moving a muscle, he *knew*, because that was just how life worked—that Anna Percy had overheard his last sentence. If ever there was a moment when he craved an earthquake that would swallow him whole, it was now.

He turned slightly. Anna's face was ghostly white.

"Anna," he whispered.

She shrank away, tears of betrayal hanging in her eyes. Then she fled.

Just Sex Buddies

"How could anyone seriously wear this more than once?" Sam asked Eduardo. She scratched her stomach under the itchy red MegaMart sweater—the cheap material had actually given her a nasty case of the hives.

"I promise to take it off as soon as possible," Eduardo murmured into her shiny dark hair. They stood in line at guesthouse one, where a photographer was taking pictures of the competitors in the cheap-threads competition, while his assistant was carefully checking each girl's receipts to insure that no one had cheated.

Jasmine Eckels—one of the weenies whom Sam had helped to save the Beverly Hills High School prom—had just been photographed in a sheer hot pink baby doll nightie/G-string combination, with a sleazy black bra underneath. With her was tall, thin Ophelia Berman, the other main prom organizer, who wore what looked like a cheap green army camouflage rain poncho tied just over the bust.

The prom weenies had already hugged Sam like a long-lost best friend—only because Sam was in a fog of love did she suffer the embraces. Okay. She had learned during prom prep that Jazz and Fee weren't all that bad. But it was one thing to work with the prom weenies, and quite another to *befriend* them.

"Good luck, Sam!" Jasmine called as she finished. "You won prom queen; maybe you'll win this, too!"

"And I'll be here to see it if she does," Eduardo quipped, rubbing Sam's back.

"Next," the photographer's assistant called, and Sam gave her an envelope full of receipts as she stepped in front of the photographic backdrop—a wall-size mural of Pacific Palisades High. Truth was, she was irritated at herself. No way was her piece-of-shit red-sweater-and-black-pants outfit going to beat some of the outfits she'd seen, especially some of the skimpier ones from the girls at PPHS. One PPHS girl was walking around in a black string bikini that she'd purchased in Thailand for the baht equivalent of five bucks.

"Name?" the assistant asked.

"Sam—"

"Sharpe," the middle-aged photographer filled in, smiling for the first time since Sam had seen him. Three digital cameras hung around his neck and bounced against his substantial paunch. "Tell your dad that Stan Mackey sends his regards—I did some publicity stills for *Ben-Hur.*" Then he fired off two quick pictures with two different cameras, explaining to Sam that the second shot was for insurance in case there was a problem with his camera's media card. From here, all the photos would be printed and posted in the Skylight Room, an open space on the third floor of the main house, where all the high school partygoers would vote for the best cheap outfit. Dark purple ink on a finger would prevent double voting.

It was hokey, yes, and it did remind Sam of the vote for prom queen. But being prom queen didn't mean she could make Stefanie her slave for a day; being queen of the cheap threads meant she could. It was unnatural, and it was silly, but she found herself wishing desperately that she would win tonight.

"Dance?" Eduardo asked as they reached a wide space on the red brick path that led to the various guest cottages.

"Definitely."

There was no dance floor, but Sam didn't care. She swayed in Eduardo's arms. "I missed you so much," he confessed.

"That feeling was mutual," she whispered, running her fingers through the back of his cropped dark hair.

"Sam, hi!"

Sam turned. Dee and Jack were coming down the path hand in hand. "Having fun?"

"Sure." Sam noted that Dee's hair was smashed to her head in the back, as if she'd been rubbing it into a carpet. Her lipstick was gone too. She smiled knowingly. "And where have you two been?"

"Oh, they're doing some repairs in one of the

cabanas," Dee explained, waving a hand vaguely back toward the pool. "We found an empty one."

Sam had to smile. It was so good to see Dee happy and healthy.

"I'm going to get my picture taken. We'll see you guys back at the house." Dee and Jack started down the path to guesthouse one.

"They are in love," Eduardo noted.

"Well, at least in lust. How do you know the difference?"

"One only makes the other better."

Sam shivered deliciously. "Maybe we should track down that cabana."

Eduardo shook his head. "I want you in a proper bed. With time and privacy and all the luxury you deserve, Samantha."

"Works for me. Let's go join the party, then."

But they didn't make much progress up to the main house before Anna came barreling toward them, eyes on the brick path, oblivious to anyone and anything.

"Anna?"

Anna looked up. Her face was the color of Corrasable bond.

"Are you okay?"

"No, I'm not okay." She was holding her elbows, her arms pressed against her stomach like she'd just been punched.

"What the hell happened?"

"I . . . Ben . . ."

Sam held up a finger. "Wait." She turned to Eduardo. "Can you give us a few minutes?'

He agreed, telling her he'd meet her in the Skylight Room in fifteen minutes. They were standing just a hundred feet or so from a small redwood structure with inviting lighting, so Sam led Anna toward it. It was open—some sort of dimly lit meditation room, with a huge gold Buddha at the far end of an enormous straw mat, no furniture to speak of, and a dozen soft red throw pillows on the floor.

Sam pointed to one of the pillows. "Sit. Then speak."

Anna did sit, cross-legged on one of the pillows, and put one balled fist inside the other. Sam had never seen her like this. "Just tell me what's going on."

"Okay. . . . Bl . . . Blythe is here."

Who was Blythe? Then she got it.

"The Blythe who Ben was dating at Princeton when you guys broke up?"

Anna nodded vigorously.

"Okay. Weird that she's here. But BFD. That can't be what you're so upset about."

"I overheard them taking. He said she was gorgeous. And the sex was great."

Sam winced. "Ouch. That had to hurt a little."

"A *little*?" Anna echoed, hot tears welling up in her eyes again. "He told me they were barely involved with each other; that there was nothing to 'end' about their relationship, that they didn't have a relationship."

"Well, maybe they didn't," Sam mused. "Maybe they

were just sex buddies."

Anna recoiled. "I *hate* that."

"Well, fine, hate it all you want. But that doesn't mean everyone else does."

"How could he tell me they weren't 'involved' if he was sleeping with her?" Anna demanded.

"Because that happens sometimes with people and—"

"You're defending him?" Anna was incredulous. "You're actually *defending* him?" She flung one of the pillows across the room. "He *lied* to me. He had the right to do anything we wanted with anyone he wanted after we broke up, but he should have told me the truth."

"Just . . ." Sam scooched closer to her friend. "Listen to me a minute, will you, please? You might be totally right—"

"I *am* right."

"But you also might not be. You guys need to sit down and talk."

Anna shook her head vehemently. "There's no point. On some level, I've always worried about something like this with him, ever since that very first night when he dumped me on his father's yacht."

"That was different."

"He wasn't honest with me then, he isn't being honest with me now, and I'm sick of it." She stood up. "I'm going to call a cab and go home."

Sam stood, too. "Just listen to me, will you? Know what you're doing? You're pulling a goddamn Eduardo."

"Oh, thank you, Sam, very supportive—"

"And it's goddamn stupid. After he caught me kissing Parker, he just walked away. He wouldn't talk to me for days. It sucked."

Anna shook her head. "Nope. It's not the same."

"What the fuck are you afraid of?" Sam exploded. God. Anna was being so dense. "If you care about Ben, give him a chance to explain. If you don't like his explanation, *then* tell him to fuck off."

Anna put one slender hand over her heart. "It just hurts so much."

"I know, sweetie," Sam agreed. "Talk to him."

"I can't. Not yet. I refuse to do it when I'm feeling all shaky and betrayed. Because I will *not* cry in front of him. You think there's a phone in here? I left my pocketbook up in the cloakroom at the main house."

"Probably."

Sam turned up a dimmer switch and saw a white phone on the wall near the front door. Moments later, Anna had called a cab to meet her in front of the mansion.

"I'll call you tomorrow," Anna promised.

"If I don't call you first." Sam hugged her friend. "Take my advice. Don't throw it all away over hurt feelings before you find out what's really going on. Promise?"

"I can't promise," Anna admitted. "But I will think about what you said. That's the best I can do."

Miss Priss

"Yo, people!" Jett cradled his microphone, his face covered in a thin sheen of sweat. "Just five minutes left to vote for the queen of cheap threads." He glanced down at the index card that Pashima had handed him moments before. "So . . . get your asses to the Skylight Room. Tonight's ballots will be tabulated by the accounting firm of Weiner, Paulson, and McWilliams—special thanks to Mercedes Weiner's dad. This next tune was written by our lead guitarist, Igor. It's called 'Alone.'"

The ballad began, bluesy, haunting, and irresistibly danceable. Some couples followed Jett's advice and headed back toward the main house, but most converged on the dance floor. Cammie and Adam were already there, she in his arms.

"Nice outfit," he murmured, and squeezed Cammie's butt through the Winnie-the-Pooh miniskirt. "Where's the honey?"

That afternoon, one of the new maids—Bridgetta or Biscotti or something like that—had done an amazing job of turning Cammie's cheap boxer shorts into a hot little micromini that went perfectly with her sleeveless white T-shirt. She'd been surveying her competition ever since she and Adam had arrived; she thought she had it in the bag.

God, winning tonight would be so satisfying.

"The honey? You know very well where it is, and you can't have it until later. Unless I win. Then I'll have Stefanie make Pashima's bed for us."

Adam kissed her neck. "How about you make Stefanie take the SAT for you?"

"God no. I told you, I'm not going to college, and I haven't changed my mind in the past forty-eight hours. I have about as much interest in college as you do in a sex change."

"Good to know you're not ambivalent." They swayed to the hypnotic music.

"It's not like I need to get an education to make money, Adam."

"How about education for the sake of education?"

She shrugged. "I hate school. Always have. Bores the shit out of me." She snuggled closer to him as Igor ripped off an amazing guitar solo. "You'll see. I'll design something fabulous, like handbags. I'll get my dad's clients to carry them. Next thing I know, I'm an overnight sensation on *Entertainment Tonight*. Why should I study ancient civilizations?"

"If that's what you want."

"It is," Cammie said emphatically, acting on the

theory that if the outside made a statement, inner feelings would follow. The truth was, every so often, she had
a weird thought: Go to college and get a teaching
degree—carry on her mom's career. It would be a kind
of homage. Her mother had been the kindest, most
altruistic person in the world. She'd been everything
good and kind and sweet and loving in this world. If
only she were here to see her daughter graduate. . . .

She shook her head, as if that could make that painful
thought disappear. Better to concentrate on the here and
now. Yes, it would be great to win the contest and make
Stefanie her slave. But even if she didn't win, she and
Sam had something cooked up that would exact long-
overdue justice.

"You nervous about tomorrow?" he asked.

"Graduation?"

"No. Meeting Sam's mother. She's still coming to
Los Angeles, right?"

Trust Adam to bring up the one thing that she did *not*
want to think about.

"No," Cammie lied. "I mean, she's coming, but I'm
not nervous."

"I told you before, I can be there if you want."

She shook her head. "I can handle it. We'll talk afterward. But that's a really, really nice off—"

Suddenly, Ben broke through the crowd on the dance
floor—his forehead was creased with tension. "Have
you guys seen Anna?"

"No," Adam replied. "Why?"

"We just . . . I need to find her. If you see her, tell her
I'm looking for her and we have to talk and . . . Just tell
her, okay?"

"Sure."

Cammie was more than a little curious about why
Ben had to find Miss Priss. Could they be having trou-
bles? The thought brought her considerable good cheer.

In fact, the only thing that could make this night better than winning the contest and humiliating Stefanie
would be if Anna and Ben broke up.

Yeah, it was schadenfreude. But it was worth it.

In a home of magnificent rooms, the Skylight Room
was the most magnificent of all. The roof and two walls
were glass, the whole thing bisected by platinum support rods in geometric patterns that dazzled the eye.
The view ranged from Malibu in the north down to
Long Beach in the south; there were banks of telescopes
for guests to use at their leisure. The floor was glass too,
permitting the guests to see what was happening in the
game room on the second level. All the furniture had
been removed for the party, and the empty room easily
held two hundred people.

There was a small stage at the east end. Cammie, Sam,
Adam, and Eduardo stood near it—Cammie didn't want
to have to work her way through the throng if she won.
As they watched, Pashima climbed onto the stage to
cheers from the crowd; their hostess held a wireless
microphone.

"Hey, everyone! Stefanie and I want to thank you guys sooo much for coming tonight!"

The crowd cheered; then Pashima went on and on about how the balloting had been so close, they'd had to count and recount the votes.

"Who's going to win?"

Cammie turned—Stefanie had stepped up behind them.

"Oh, you, definitely," Cammie declared, catching Sam's eye at the same time. They knew what was coming later, after the winner was crowned. Stefanie didn't.

"Sam?" Stefanie asked. "You know who the slave's going to be no matter who wins from my school? Go look in a mirror—if you can find one big enough."

"Could you suck any harder?" Sam swallowed slowly, trying to restrain herself.

"Yeah, I could have invited that girl Blythe tonight just to mess things up between your buddy Anna Percy and her boyfriend. Oops!" Stefanie smacked herself in the forehead. "How could I forget? I did!"

Cammie stifled a grin. Well, that explained the Ben/Anna drama. Not that she still wouldn't make Stefanie her slave.

On the stage, a bald accountant type handed Pashima a large white envelope, then stepped to the back of the stage. "Okay, time to announce our winner!" Pashima gleefully tore at the envelope. "The winner is . . ." She pried the envelope open. Stared. Squinted. Stared at it more closely. Frowned mightily.

It's me, Cammie thought gleefully. Across the room, one of the boys from PHHS she'd flirted with gave her a big thumbs-up.

"Fee Berman?" Pashima shrugged. "Who the hell is Fee Ber—?"

"It's me, I won!" Fee squealed. She pushed through the crowd, leaped onto the stage, and threw her arms around Pashima. "I really, really won!"

"B-but . . . you're wearing a poncho!" Pashima sputtered.

"Not anymore!" Fee flung the poncho over her head; it fluttered like a parachute out into the crowd. Underneath was a matching camouflage bikini . . . that had been painted onto her naked skin.

In other words, she was naked.

"I totally underestimated that girl," Cammie marveled, as the guys in the audience whooped and cheered; Fee held her hands overhead like a boxer.

"She's got nerve, I'll give her that," Sam agreed.

"Not to mention a killer body," Adam added. "Who knew?"

Fee stepped down from the stage; Cammie watched with not a little pleasure as Stefanie confronted her. "I really do not think this is fair. You didn't buy cheap threads. You bought body paint."

"I bought both. Hurts to lose, doesn't it?" Fee crooned sympathetically. "But this is going to hurt even more." She turned to the crowd and cupped her hands. "As my personal slave for the day, I pick . . . you! Stefanie Weinstock!"

"No fucking way," Stefanie spat, over the cheers from the Beverly Hills kids. "I only invited you as a *joke!*"

Fee retrieved her poncho, dropped it over her head again, and peered down at her feet. They were shod in cheap bamboo thongs. "Wow. Right now, I need a foot massage before dessert. What are you doing standing up? Sit on the edge of the goddamn stage and rub my goddamn feet!"

"*Fine.*"

Cammie grinned. She hadn't won, but Stefanie was going to be the slave to a prom weenie. Better than that—

"Stefanie Weinstock, where the hell are you?"

The room fell silent, as a behemoth of a man—easily six-foot five inches, two hundred and seventy-five pounds—pushed into the Skylight Room. His curly hair was disheveled and his beard was five days overdue for a shave. He wore a ragged T-shirt that advertised PEACE THROUGH SUPERIOR FIREPOWER and cutoff jeans. His flip-flops left a trail of mud on the glass floor—the same mud that was caked on his feet. In each hand, he carried a huge, open blue-and-white Foster's beer can.

"Stefanie? Where are you?!" The behemoth didn't speak. He bellowed.

Instantly, Stefanie was on her feet to confront the intruder. "Who the fuck are you? How'd you get in?"

"Oh sure," the guy sneered, stomping toward her. "Act like you don't know me, after you were all over me and spent every night with me last month in Antigua! And promised you'd come back after school was over and spend the entire summer with me?"

A murmur ran through the crowd. Everyone at PPHS knew that Stefanie had been on vacation in the Caribbean. She'd met this guy there?

"I never met you in my life!" Stefanie's face was bright red.

"Oh, really? How about this? 'Give me more, Damon! Give me more! Do it to Stefi, do it to Stefi! I love you Damon!'" The huge guy made his voice as high-pitched as he could, imitating Stefanie in the throes of passion, which made the crowd—even many of Stefanie's classmates—burst into laughter. "'Ooh! Ooh!'"

"Omigod, who is this dude?" Sam asked Cammie with a profound wink.

"Beats me," she gasped back with a giant smile on her face.

Stefanie looked around for support, but there wasn't any. Even Pashima seemed to have slunk away to parts unknown.

"I mean it," she told everyone, her voice coming out in a tinny whine. "I've never seen this guy before in my life!"

"He sure seems like he knows you," Fee commented. "And who said you could stop working on my feet? I sure didn't."

The huge guy shook his head in disbelief, then lifted

one of the Foster's to his lips and took a drink that seemed to go on forever, then flung the can against one of the walls. "This is bullshit. Total and complete bullshit. And could someone back me up on that goddamn beer?"

"That's it," Stefanie fumed. She dug in her pocketbook for her cell. "I'm calling security."

"What for?" the behemoth roared. "To take you to the fucking zoo?"

Once again, the crowded room broke up in laughter.

The guy drained the second Foster's can, dropped it at Stefanie's feet, and belched loud enough to be heard in Swaziland. "Know what? You don't have to call security. 'Cause I'm outta here." He took a step back toward the door, then stopped and whirled back toward Stefanie. "Aw, shit."

With those words, he projectile vomited the contents of the two Foster's cans—and probably several others— in Stefanie's direction. As Stefanie screamed in disgust and outrage, Cammie smiled knowingly at Sam.

Yep. Revenge really was better served cold.

Please-Forgive-Me Flowers

Anna stared out her bedroom window. As she watched a leaf sail down from a eucalyptus tree, she ruminated on how peculiar it was to live in a place where the seasons never seemed to change, yet a leaf could die and fall from a tree in early June. It made no more sense than Ben and Blythe's Princetonian sex life. Anna had a hard time with things that didn't make sense.

When she'd returned home the night before, there were already a half-dozen messages from Ben. "Please call me." "Please let me explain." And the proverbial "It's not what you think."

She hadn't called him, but rather had just thrown her horrible cheap clothes in the trash and stood in a scalding shower for what felt like hours. There'd been no tears just then. She felt that if she allowed herself to cry, she'd just melt into a blubbering puddle.

But when she'd gotten into her bed and curled up in a ball trying to sleep, the tears had come, trickling onto her silk pillowcase until she fell into a deep, dreamless sleep. A knock from her sister had woken her up. Susan was wearing her pristine, white cotton yoga clothes and was carrying a bouquet of fragrant tulips and freesia. Anna's first thought: Please-forgive-me flowers from Ben.

Her second thought: Fuck him.

"I don't want them," Anna told her sister. She punched her pillow into a new position. "I'm going back to sleep."

"Who's Caine?"

"Who—Why?"

"They're from him. Card was already open. You are in a terrible mood. Ever tried chamomile tea in the morning? I can brew some."

Anna realized there was no reason to take her misery out on her sister, who had traveled all this way to see her and had clearly gone through enough misery of her own. "I'm sorry. I'm just . . . I had a fight with Ben last night."

"Well, someone named Caine wants to make you feel better."

Anna lifted the small white card nestled between the branches of baby's breath.

"All of us are in the gutter, but some of us are looking to the stars." Oscar Wilde wrote that. It was the quote under my senior photo and I'm still trying to live it down. Hope graduation tonight is endurable.

Time to move on to real life.

—Caine

Anna took a deep breath. *Time to move on to real life.*

"Is he cute?" Susan asked, stretching her arms over her head.

"Yes. He's your type. Your type last year, I mean." Anna tapped the card against the back of her hand. "I can't believe he sent flowers for graduation. What a thoughtful thing to do."

"How'd you meet him?"

"Dad's intern, believe it or not. We're just friends."

"Of course," Susan agreed with a laugh. "You're too straight to do one guy behind another guy's back. Want them in a vase?"

"Sure, thanks." Anna handed her the flowers back and then hesitated a moment. "You don't do that anymore, Sooz. Do you?"

"What are you talking about? I'm doing pretty much the entire kitchen staff at Kripalu," she cracked. "Is that what you think?"

"I don't think anything. I'm asking."

Susan stood, her mouth pressed shut in a tight line. "Look, I'm together now, get it? I prefer to forget that the old me ever existed. In fact, if you tell Gordon, I'll kill you." She turned around and promptly walked out with the flowers.

"Gee, swell way to start the day," Anna told the ceiling.

The flowers were nice, but Caine wasn't the guy on her mind at the moment. She was thinking about what Sam had said to her the night before, and about what she'd said earlier in the week about being an active heroine.

Well, all right. She would take Sam's advice and listen to Ben. Unlike last night, she felt like she could do it with a modicum of dignity.

She reached for her cell on the antique oak nighstand before she could change her mind.

"I should have told you," Ben muttered.

He stared at the tiny espresso cup in his hands; they were sitting together but quite apart on a huge green velvet couch at the Cameo Bar in the Viceroy Hotel in Santa Monica. The Viceroy was extremely popular—just steps from the beach—but at ten on a Friday morning the bar was nearly empty. Ben could have chosen one of the white tables with the high-backed white upholstered chairs out on the exterior poolside deck. Instead, he'd opted for this couch, which faced two white stools and a round Lucite table. There was an area rug underneath in swirls of white, black, green, and gray. Anna could see what a fun and romantic place the Cameo Bar would have been at another time—the green-and-gray palette with Lucite and chrome accents was beautiful in an off-kilter way. But not now.

I should have told you.

Anna sighed. How many boyfriends had used those exact same words with how many girlfriends? Funny how they never got used until the person got caught.

"I'm being as honest as I can, Anna." Ben was leaning forward with his arms resting on the table. He raised his eyes to her. "Blythe and I were just friends. We got wasted one night and had wasted-friends sex. That's all it was. We both agreed."

"I guess she didn't get the memo," Anna said coolly.

Ben shook his head. He wore baggy jeans and a sky-blue polo shirt. His hair was disheveled; he looked as if he hadn't slept. "I've been asking myself over and over: Did I do or say anything to make her think we had something going on?"

"You had *sex* with her, Ben." She leaned back on the couch and crossed her legs away from him. "Most girls take that as a sign of involvement." She'd dressed down in khakis and a plain white T-shirt. But just to make sure Ben would eat his heart out while he drank his coffee, she'd put on a touch of Stila brown mascara and a quick slick of clear Chanel lip gloss. Then she'd sprayed Chanel's Allure perfume into the air and stepped through the mist so that only the subtle aroma would linger. Diamond studs in her ears, a quick brush through her hair, and she'd been good to go.

"Actually, you're completely wrong." He sipped his espresso, then set it down on the round Lucite table. "I know you do, but other people don't. When it happened, you and I weren't together. I had no way of knowing we'd get back together, either."

Oh. That was just so disingenuous.

"You just don't get it, Ben. I don't think you should have had sex with her unless you loved her. You can call me old-fashioned or the moral police or whatever flip thing you want to call me. I don't really care."

"I wasn't going to—"

"But that's between the two of you," Anna went on, keeping her voice low. "When you came to Las Vegas to see me, I asked you again and again what was going on between you and Blythe—"

"I told you the truth—"

"No, you didn't—"

"Yes, I did," Ben insisted in a loud whisper. "I told you she and I had barely gotten started and there wasn't a real relationship to end. One night of drunk sex didn't make that any less true." He ran a hand through his disheveled hair. "I don't know why she showed up here with this delusion that there was more going on with us. I swear to you, I did *not* lead her on."

Anna glanced over at the empty bar, realizing all this could well be true. She wasn't sure, though, what difference that would really make.

"Even if I accept that," she began slowly, "it doesn't change this: You hid this whole affair from me. Literally and figuratively, I mean."

"Jesus, Anna. What do you want from me? I know you. I knew you'd make it into way more than it was. Which is exactly what you've done. Look, I'm not perfect. And I'm sorry."

"Sorry that I found out," Anna translated, trying to keep her voice from trembling.

He rubbed his collarbone. "The truth? Yeah. I'm real sorry you found out. We weren't together then, which means that what I did and who I did it with had nothing to do with you. You don't see me asking for a blow-by-blow of your time then. Do you?"

The bluntness of his statement stung, because she sensed he really was telling her the entire truth. No. He wasn't asking for a blow-by-blow. But if he did, there wasn't anything she'd done with anyone that came close to what he hadn't shared about Blythe. Sometimes she thought that the two of them had been marked by some strange, two-pronged Shakespearean curse. Just when things were good, they fell apart. No matter how often they pledged honesty, what got delivered was deceit. Which was more painful? she wondered; to constantly hope and hope and hope things changed? Or to just accept reality?

"If you had only trusted me with the truth, we wouldn't be sitting on opposite sides of this couch right now," she said softly.

"I'm sorry, Anna." He put his hands on his knees. "I should have told you, but it wasn't really such a big thing. I would hate like hell for this to break us up."

She managed a small smile. "Me too."

His eyes brightened. "So we're good?"

"I don't know what we are. I need to think."

"Okay, okay, that's reasonable," Ben agreed, head bobbing. "How about if I pick you up after graduation tonight? We'll go someplace quiet and romantic. Up to Malibu, maybe. Jeffrey's restaurant, or—"

Anna shook her head, her heart tightening in her chest. "I don't think so."

"What then?"

"I don't know. I need some time." She stood; Ben did too.

"How *much* time?" His eyes bored into hers.

"I don't know. I'll call you."

"You're not really going to let this mess us up, Anna. *Come on!*"

She raised her chin and kissed him softly. "I'll call you. And Ben?"

"Yeah?"

"Don't follow me."

Anna was going to drive straight home from Santa Monica. She really was. But when she reached the inter-section of West Olympic Boulevard and Avenue of the Stars, she impetuously turned her loaner red Acura TL onto the Avenue of the Stars, and then into the parking structure below one of the immense high-rises that made up this incongruous L.A. neighborhood known as Century City.

There was the ubiquitous valet to take her car, and the ubiquitous garage elevator that swooshed her up, up, up to the thirtieth floor—the floor that housed the offices of Percy Tweed Partners, her father's investment firm. Their striking offices had been designed by the Dutch architect Rem Koolhaas; they featured exposed beams and pipes, irregular walls, and a gleaming parquet wood floor.

The receptionist had straight chestnut brown hair

and a button nose with a smattering of freckles. She wore a sleeveless gray cashmere sweater and gray pants over her lean frame. "May I help you?"

Funny, in all the time that Anna had been in Los Angeles, she'd never been here.

"I'm Anna Percy."

"Mr. Percy's daughter?" the young woman exclaimed, taking off her phone headset for a brief moment. "He talks about you all the time."

Anna was taken aback. Her father talked about her all the time?

The woman looked something up on her computer. "I'm Claire. It's such a pleasure to meet you. Your dad . . . is in a meeting with clients from Oman. He probably shouldn't be interrupted, unless it's an emergency, of course."

"That's okay. I didn't come to see him, actually. Is Caine Manning around?"

"Your dad's intern? Absolutely," Claire told her. "I'll buzz him."

She typed something on the keyboard—a bare minute later, Caine pushed through the mirrored doors into the reception area, carrying a stack of manila envelopes. He wore black trousers, a crisp white dress shirt, and a red- and-black striped tie. His tattoos were covered, and his ears were earring-free.

"Hey, stranger!" He dumped the envelopes on the reception desk into the wire basket for outgoing mail.

"Hey, yourself. You're looking quite corporate."

"I told you, protective coloration," Caine replied easily.

"You have a minute?"

"Sure. Come on back."

He opened one of the doors and led the way through a warren of trapezoidal gray cubicles, until they came to a conference room with a spectacular view east toward downtown and the San Bernardino Valley. He pulled out one of the high-backed black suede chairs for Anna on the side where she could take in the landscape.

"I wanted to thank you in person for the flowers," she told him as he sat down across from her. "That was unbelievably thoughtful of you."

"I have my moments. Glad you liked them." He leaned back in his chair and stretched his arms out. "So, ready for your big night?"

"Not really," Anna admitted. "Kind of . . . fraught, actually. My mother and my sister showed up to surprise me."

"Good surprise or bad surprise?"

"Um, peculiar surprise."

"Oh hell, everyone's family is insane, don't worry about it. Do the cap-and-gown thing, kick back with your friends, and realize that everyone will be gone on their merry ways in a couple of days."

Friends. All week, Anna had just assumed that after graduation she would go someplace with Ben and they'd spend the summer together. Now that was out. What were the alternatives? Sam would be with Eduardo. Even though Anna liked the new and chemically balanced Dee, they weren't really friends yet. Besides, she was completely involved with Jack. And of course, forget Cammie. What was Anna going to do all summer? And then what about after that? She'd be heading off to Yale to start all over again, make all new friends and start a whole new life. Would Ben be a part of it?

Caine laced his hands behind his neck, clearly at home in his skin and damned okay in both of his worlds.

Why not? She could almost hear Sam's words in her head: *"Goddammit, Anna. Be an active heroine. What would an active heroine do in your situation?"*

Anna took a deep breath.

"I like that idea. Kicking back with friends." She nodded, putting her hair behind her ears.

"Well, I hope you have a great time. And maybe we'll run into each other over the summer." He stood up and smiled as if to go back to work.

"Hold on."

Caine looked at her quizzically.

"I was wondering if . . ." Damn. This active heroine thing wasn't so easy. "I was wondering if . . . well . . . would a friend like to hang out with a friend tonight? After graduation?"

"Could be." He peered at her more closely. "But the friend who's good at reading people is wondering if there's a motivation for this invitation."

"There is," she admitted.

"It being . . . ?"

"I had a fight with my boyfriend."

"Ah, yes. Scowling Dude from the movie line. Got that preppy thing goin' on."

"We didn't break up," she added hastily. "And I'm not inviting you on a . . . *date* or anything, so I would completely understand if you don't want to be with me under the circumstances—"

He held up a hand. "Got the picture. Rashomon is playing Redrum tonight. You into it?"

Anna looked bewildered.

"Redrum—a new club in Hollywood. Rashomon—Asian fusion rock. They kick ass. We'll have fun."

How had the tables turned? Now she felt like she was the one considering an invitation. Okay. She could deal with that, as long as Caine truly understood her situation. Lies of omission could be just as painful as lies of commission.

"I love Ben."

"Glad to hear that. How about after we hit the club—I know this amazing guy in Venice—you can get I LOVE BEN tattooed someplace it will really hurt."

Anna laughed. "You're crazy."

"We on?"

"On," Anna agreed. "Do you want to pick me up? Say around eight?"

"Call me after you get handed your diploma." He reached across the table for Anna's hands and helped her up. Once she was standing, he didn't let go and his smile disappeared. "I even promise not to hit on you."

Anna arched a brow. "Good to know."

"I'll wait until you hit on me."

She giggled. Instead of wallowing, paralyzed with inner angst, she was making decisions. She was acting like a goddamn active heroine, in fact. Sam would be proud of her.

Acid-Green Faux-Fur Shrug

Cammie was aghast as she took in the low-slung building ahead of them. "The ZurichHaus hotel in Sherman Oaks? Gawd, who stays at a place like *that*?"

"My mother, evidently," Sam replied nervously. There'd been no valet; they'd had to park behind the hotel and walk to the entrance. In some ways, Sam didn't mind. She'd been so nervous about this meeting that she'd scratched all the polish from her last manicure at La Prairie off her nails, then nibbled them practically to stubs. She couldn't believe this moment was actually real.

Last night, after the party, she'd gone back with Eduardo to his condo and they'd reconnected in every possible way. Afterward, he'd held her while she poured her heart out about this reunion with her mother. How freaked out she was. How angry.

The hardest part, she reluctantly admitted, was how little she remembered of her life *with* her mother. She had vivid memories of sixth grade, seventh grade— everything that had come after her parents divorced. But before that, it was a blur, with only the occasional birthday party, vacation, or movie opening clear in her mind. She lamented to Eduardo how she didn't remember a single intimate moment with her mother—sitting on her lap, coloring with her, shopping . . . all the things that girls did with their moms.

How sad and pathetic was that?

Ironically, Eduardo had offered the same advice she'd given to Anna. "You can't change the past. Just listen to what she has to say. If you are so busy resenting what you think she did or didn't do, you will not be able to hear anything she says now."

Okay. Good advice. But it sure as hell was easier to give than to take.

And how did one dress to see a mother who walked out of your life nine years ago and never looked back? Sam had put on and rejected a dozen outfits. She'd finally settled on dark-wash Seven jeans and a pleated black silk Imitation of Christ shirt, with round-toed taupe-and-black snakeskin Prada pumps. She wanted to look put-together and independent, like someone who didn't care that her mother had been missing for the last nine years. As for Cammie, she'd gone in completely the opposite direction. She wore a citron leather miniskirt that barely covered her ass, and a paisley Chamoni nylon-and-antiqu-lace bustier that laced up the back, under an acid-green faux-fur shrug. Her four-inch-high shocking pink velvet platform shoes matched her Pout lip gloss. Her eyelash extensions were heavily done with mascara, which couldn't be good for their longevity.

"Don't be surprised if men in the lobby ask your price," Sam told her, as they pulled open the glass doors of the ZurichHaus, which had no doormen.

"I'll ignore that dig. You're nervous."

"More like petrified. We're supposed to meet her in the café. I have to tell you, I feel like barfing."

"Sam." Cammie stopped and took Sam's wrist.

Sam turned to her. "What?"

"It'll be okay. Really."

Sam managed a small nod. "Thanks. And I wanted to thank you for something, too."

"What?"

"Your idea for last night. How to get back at Stefanie."

"Hey, you hired the actor," Cammie grinned. "One who could barf on cue."

"It was your concept, though."

Cammie shook her curls off her face and winked at a cute blond FedEx guy leaving the building. "Like I always say, that's just the kind of bitch I am."

It wasn't hard to find the café. The room was utilitarian—white stools around white tables, one walnut-stained wall of shelving with souvenir tchotchkes and knickknacks from various Los Angeles attractions, a small bar at one end. Just as Sam was thinking, What if I don't even recognize her?—she found herself looking at the table in the rear corner. No doubt about who was sitting there.

"Sam," her mother intoned with a smile. "And Cammie Sheppard. I'd recognize you anywhere. Sit, please."

Almost mechanically, Sam took the stool across from her mother; Cammie sat between them. She was a little shocked. Her mother probably had been pretty thirty pounds ago, but now looked so *old*. But she couldn't be more than . . . what? Late forties? Sam realized that no one in Beverly Hills ever looked like they were in their late forties, because they began having work done in their late twenties. She wasn't used to seeing a female face with actual *lines* on it.

The former Mrs. Sharpe had thick, lustrous dark hair streaked with gray, cut into a simple bob. She had a pleasant face with a nose kind of like Bridget Fonda's if Bridget were a lot older. Her lips were narrow, her face round. She wore a simple blue blazer over a white T-shirt, and the kind of jeans that probably had elastic at the waist. As for makeup, all Sam noticed was some coral lipstick that had already crept into the corners of her mouth. A quick flick of the eyes took her to her mother's lower body. Yep. That was exactly where Sam had gotten her fucking fat ankles. The woman had left behind nothing but her bad gene pool.

"You grew up," her mother observed. Her eyes held Sam's—Sam had the uncanny sensation of looking into her own.

There was a carafe of coffee and three cups on the table, plus a sad-looking basket of defrosted-looking sweet rolls and croissants. Sam's mother poured coffee for Sam and Cammie, then gently pushed the cups in their direction.

"I guess that's what happens when you don't see your daughter for nine years," Sam offered awkwardly but firmly. She stirred a packet of Splenda into her beverage. "I'm going to call you Dina. I'm not comfortable with 'Mom.' Okay?"

Her mother nodded and turned to Cammie. "Camilla. It's been a long time."

Cammie crossed her legs and let one shocking pink platform shoe dangle from her toes. "It has. I've had a lot of time to think about things. So tell me, Dina. Were you fucking my father?"

Dina raised her eyebrows. "You're direct and to the point, I'll give you that."

"Oh, so sorry. Would you prefer polite and meaningless chitchat?"

Sam would have laughed if she weren't too busy trying not to cry. Cammie was not taking her own advice. "Let's start with this, Dina," Sam said to her mother, deciding that the only way to remain tear-free was to take control. "Why'd you decide to come? Why are you here?"

Her mother put her hands in her lap. "I shouldn't be surprised at your hostility, I suppose. I'm here because you wanted to see me, correct?"

"I wanted to talk to you, yes. I didn't expect a maternal visit as a graduation present."

"Sam. There's so much you don't know." Dina sighed, tapped a red-painted fingernail on the tabletop, and then laid her hand flat as if to stop herself. Her eyes were welling up with tears. "Let me tell you about myself. Would that be okay?"

Sam raised her palms as if to say, *I won't stop you.*

"I live in a small town, about a half hour from

Asheville, North Carolina," she began tentatively. "It's called East Flat Rock. I run the Living section at our local newspaper."

Sam nodded. "And?"

"My husband's name is Victor Weller. He sells life insurance."

Sam hardened and glanced at the simple gold band on her mother's ring finger. "How many stepbrothers and sisters do I have?"

"None."

"You might take Ruby Hummingbird, then," Cammie offered, readjusting her legs. "Jackson and Poppy's new spawn. Sam's house would be much more pleasant without her."

"I don't think that would be a very good idea." Dina shook her head. "Different people are good and bad at different things. I think I'm a very good wife, and I'm a very good editor. I tutor immigrants from Mexico in English, and volunteer at the hospice in Hendersonville. But the truth is, I was a terrible mother."

Sam was shocked by the blunt honesty of her mother's remark. "Good to know we agree about something."

"Sam." Her mother laced her fingers. "I came to Hollywood right out of Penn State. I got hired at the *Times*, but I wanted to be a screenwriter. Instead of finding a career I loved, I found your father."

Sam eyed Cammie. "Should we set this sob story to music, Cammie?"

"I haven't seen you in nine years; I'm only trying to explain." Dina pressed on. "I got caught up in the glitz

and the glamor. It's so seductive. Some people can handle it; thrive on it, I suppose. I'm not one of them.
Drugs and booze and sex . . . I thought it was what
everyone did. It nearly killed me."

"You want *me* to feel sorry for *you*?" Sam's voice was
small. "I didn't ask to be born."

"You're right, of course," Dina agreed. "You deserve
better."

The table was silent.

"That's *it*?" Sam queried. "That's all you have to say?
What about Cammie's—"

"I've got it, Sam," Cammie interrupted. "The night
my mother drowned on the Strikers' yacht. You were
there. We know that."

Dina nodded.

"You were screwing my father," Cammie said, her
tone as pleasant as if she was discussing what to order
for lunch.

Dina hesitated, then slowly nodded again.

"Here's my question, Dina." Cammie leaned forward.
"Who killed my mother? You, Clark, or both of you?"

Dina recoiled. "My God, is that what you think? We
had nothing to do with it! We were young and stupid
and shallow. I don't have any excuses. Sleeping with
Clark was an idiotic thing to do." She turned to
Cammie. "But you must know that had nothing to do
with why your mother died. She never even knew about
it. Your mother was clinically depressed. Surely your
father told you that."

Clinically depressed? What was Dina talking about?

Sam snuck a glance at Cammie—her friend's eyes were open wide and she looked horrified. Sam had never seen her make quite that expression before.

"No, she wasn't."

"Cammie, you only knew your mother as a little girl. Which means that you only saw one side of her, the side that a child sees. I met your mother soon after Jackson and I were married. Before she had you and I had Sam, we did everything together. Skied at Lake Tahoe, hiked in the Alps. I loved her. I adored her."

Sam found herself leaning forward—it was as if her mother was giving her a window into another world.

"She loved you, Cammie. She used to carry you everywhere. I used to be riveted just watching her with you, especially considering my own . . . shortcomings . . . as a mother. It was amazing."

"She doesn't sound clinically depressed," Cammie pointed out her voice tight.

"Things changed," Dina went on slowly. "When you were in second grade, about."

"What changed?"

"Your mom. There were days at a time when she wouldn't go out of the house. Weeks, even."

Sam had known Jeanne Sheppard. She wracked her memory for any sign that her mother was telling the truth. Nothing.

"No." Cammie was adamant. "Mom was not like that. She was a schoolteacher. She had to go to school. She couldn't just stay at home."

"It wasn't that she couldn't leave home. It was that

she was clinically depressed. She saw many therapists. Ask your father, Cammie. He'll tell you."

"He told me something else."

"To protect you." Dina's voice was gentle. "I'm sure he did it to protect you. If I'd thought you didn't know, I might have lied, too."

Cammie shook her head. "No. I would remember *something. . . .*"

"She got worse and worse. By the time you were starting third grade—that was the year of the accident, I think—she was in bad, bad shape."

Was she lying? Sam honestly didn't know. Cammie had said something to her about her father and mother having had a terrible argument that night—how Clark had been the instigator. Had Clark concocted that story to protect Cammie from the truth? Clark Sheppard had never fallen on his sword before, but there always was a first time.

"I know this has to be a little hard to take, Cammie." Her mother's voice was soothing. "Disappointing and disillusioning, maybe, all at the same time. Don't take my word for it. Talk to your father again. Tell him you talked to me. I think he'll tell you the truth."

Cammie raised her eyebrows. "And I should believe you because . . . ?"

"I'm telling the truth, Cammie. Your mother was a wonderful woman—"

"Then why were you doing her husband?" Sam couldn't stop herself.

"Everyone at that time was doing inappropriate things that they should have thought long and hard

about before getting into. I'm not proud of it, but . . .
there it is. Your mother loved you so much, Cammie.
She was as good a mother as I was bad. Some people
don't deserve to take credit for how wonderful their
children turn out to be."

Dina shifted her gaze to Sam. "Unfortunately, one of
them gave birth to you. I came to see you because I
hoped—now that you're about to graduate from high
school—that we might get to know each other as adults.
I hoped that was why you wanted me to be here now. I
was a weak mother; it's why my husband and I never had
children. But I can be a really good friend."

Sam leaned over the table toward her. "I'm very glad
you came here. I really am. But I can't forget that the
only reason you're here is because I had to hire a detective to track you down. I have friends." She looked
pointedly at Cammie. "Good friends. Friends I'd do
anything for. What I don't have is a mother. I know you
said you're a terrible mom. Well, little kids have moms.
Grown-up women have mothers. When you're ready to
be my mother, I'd love to talk to you some more."

She stood up and looked at Cammie. Shit. Her friend
was finally reacting—her face that of someone who'd
just been handed a diagnosis of pancreatic cancer, or
something else life-altering. Shocked and stunned.

"Come on, my friend," Sam said to her softly. "I
think we should go."

Two Surgically Enhanced Basketball Breasts

"Ladies and gentlemen." Principal Kwan's voice boomed out over the Broadway-level sound system in Beverly Hills High School's two-thousand-seat Streisand theater. "It is an honor to present to you the fiftieth-anniversary graduating class of Beverly Hills High School!"

With that announcement, every student—they were assembled on high-rise Plexiglas bleachers on the stage in black graduation caps and gowns designed for the occasion by Osuro Miko, an up-and-coming designer who had previously been with Gucci before branching out on her own with her Santa Monica boutique—rose in their seats as thunderous applause rocked the auditorium.

Anna peered out into the darkness of the theater, trying to find her family. Impossible. It was a sea of darkness, made more difficult to penetrate by a series of spotlights that played over the graduates as though they were at the opening of a studio blockbuster.

256

"I'd like to thank all the little people who made this possible," Sam whispered to Anna, as Kwan asked the graduates to take their seats once again.

Anna smiled. The best thing about this graduation was that the students didn't have to enter or sit in alphabetical order. It meant she could sit on one side of Sam, with Cammie and Adam on the other side. As for Dee, she wasn't officially graduating because of her hospitalization—she'd have to take summer school classes. Anna felt a little bad that she couldn't participate.

"You haven't won the Oscar yet, Sam," Anna finally whispered back.

"Is Ben out there?"

Anna shook her head, though the whistling and applauding continued.

"Do you know that bitch Stefanie Weinstock set him up?" Sam continued.

"What are you talking about?"

"She made sure Blythe was at the party just to fuck with you."

Oh my God. Was that true? How did Stefanie even know about them? How did she even know Blythe? What if she lost Ben over this, because she couldn't accept his explanation of what had happened with Blythe. Was she being too hard on Ben?

"Yo, Anna," Sam called, waving a hand in front of Anna's eyes. "Enough with the angst. Obsess later. Be here now, 'kay?"

Sam was right. Be here now.

"Okay."

The Streisand Theater, named for one of its largest benefactors, was certainly the most lavish inside any high school in the country. With both a main floor and a mezzanine, it featured rich, floor-to-ceiling wood paneling with acoustic reflective boxed insets, real gold paint trim, a beveled acoustic ceiling, and a raked stage. There was fly space above the stage for scenery changes, rehearsal rooms large enough for a small army, a full scenic shop, and an orchestra pit that could hold an eighty-five piece ensemble. Small wonder that the school was regularly contacted by impresarios wanting to rent it.

"Can you believe they brought Kwan back for this?" Sam quipped. "I just hope she doesn't spend her entire speech obsessively clearing her throat the way she always did when she was principal."

Anna giggled; it was still nice that they'd brought back Kwan, who had been tabbed by the governor as the latest state commissioner of education. The alternative would have been the new principal, a woman whose name Anna could never remember, known best for her two surgically enhanced basketball breasts.

As the applause and cheering finally died out, Kwan announced that it was time to bestow the diplomas. Could the audience hold its applause until the end, and could each graduate please step forward?

"Ashley Elizabeth Abbey. Armondo Giancarlo Abbruzzi. Ntozange Sayrah Adams." The president of the Board of Education—a tall, striking woman with a booming voice—announced each graduate in turn.

"Get her name," Sam whispered to Anna. "I want to cast her in something."

Though Anna had never attended a high school graduation before, she was sure that this one set the standard. Not that she should have expected anything less, considering the showbiz connections of the student body and the glamorous alumni pool of the last fifty years.

The graduation speaker had been a representative from the office of the Dalai Lama—the famous Tibetan spiritual leader had been scheduled to give the address, but had to jet off to New York City at the last minute for a meeting of the United Nations Security Council. His young replacement—spellbinding in orange monk's robes, and with a command of the English language worthy of a literature professor—had given a brilliant address about consumerism and the responsibility of America's youth to stem the tide of conspicuous consumption.

If anyone present appreciated the irony of this topic for *this* audience, it wasn't apparent from the reaction: he finished to a standing ovation. Following the speaker was a video featuring greetings from many of the school's most famous former attendees and graduates.

After the video came the musical performances. Best received was Lenny Kravitz, who happily announced that he was a BHHS alumnus, then launched into his hit "Heaven Help." Contrary to the rumor that swept through the bleachers, Monica Lewinsky—who'd also attended the school—didn't come out to sing backup.

"Charles David Dimmerman. Beijing Lynne Dinnerstein." The litany continued.

Anna saw Cammie look at her watch and peer into the wings of the theater. "Ah, there she is."

"Who?" Sam asked.

Cammie grinned and motioned to the wings. Peeking out from behind one of the black side curtains was Dee, in a tiny little cap and gown. Anna smiled. She'd really come to like Dee. There was justice in Dee's sitting with her friends for the ceremony, even if she wouldn't be getting an official diploma.

"Who arranged that?" Anna asked Sam.

"Cammie."

"Nice."

"You know that thing about blood being thicker than water?" Sam asked. "Total bullshit. Family is who you choose."

Anna knew exactly what Sam was talking about, since Sam had told her all about her strange encounter with her mother. It made Anna think of her own family, out there somewhere in the darkness. She didn't understand her sister and felt as if she was a constant disappointment to her mother. Her father . . . well, she'd hoped to get to know him better by moving out here, but he was still pretty much a mystery, too.

"Anna Percy."

Sam nudged her. "Get your ass up there!"

It was the strangest thing; Anna felt like she was watching herself as she edged her way across the floor-boards of the stage toward the podium, where Kwan was standing with the Board of Ed president, handing parchment diplomas to the graduates as they filed by.

Life is a series of passages. And now I am on to the next.

Was it worth it? To leave her New York friends and life behind? So much had changed. There'd been a boy in Manhattan she'd had a terrible crush on. She'd thought about this guy all the time, once upon a time. She realized now it had been weeks—months!—since he'd crossed her mind at all.

There was Ben. She thought—hoped—that they weren't over. Shouldn't real love—the right love—be easy? It was never easy between her and Ben. They'd be sailing along just fine and then . . . *wham!* They'd be hit by some rogue wave out of the past. Well, she'd wanted to shake up her life. She'd certainly accomplished that.

"Congratulations," the board president told Anna, shaking her hand.

"Thank you." She took the diploma and headed back toward her seat, knowing it was the end of an era.

Okay. The scroll in her hand meant the era was officially over. What would the next one hold?

Active Heroine

J ack stood in the deserted second-floor hallway of Beverly Hills High School and unfolded the small note that Dee has slipped into his hand just after the graduates came off the stage. Dee had been heading into the tightly packed throng of family, friends, and well-wishers to find her parents, who had come to support her even though she wasn't actually graduating. It didn't make a whole lot of sense to Jack, but whatever.

"Go to the second floor," she'd whispered. "Then read this."

It was no problem getting to the school's second floor—there was no security. Who would figure that anyone would visit classrooms or their lockers on this night? Jack went through the double wooden doors, up a stairwell illumined only by blue emergency lights, and emerged onto a long, carpeted hallway. Classrooms and offices lined both sides; strung across the hall was professionally printed banner: GOOD LUCK, GRADUATES!

Like they needed luck. Bunch of richies totally set up for life.

He unfolded Dee's note

My great big Jack—
Walk down the hallway to the teachers' lounge. It's the fourth door on the right. It should be open. I checked. Before I leave this high school for the last time, there's something that I want do, so I'll never, ever want to forget the night I didn't graduate with my friends.
Be patient. I'll be up as soon as I can ditch my parents.
Your Dee

Well, well, well. He'd thought the *H* in the Hollywood sign had been the ultimate, but the teachers' lounge at Beverly Hills High School on graduation night? That was one for the record books.

He counted the doors as he walked; the fourth one on the right was unlocked. Teachers' lounge, just as Dee had promised.

Yeah, baby. Dee had done her planning.

There was a small bottle of champagne in an ice bucket on the main table. The two floor lamps had been draped in blue and red material to temper their harsh lighting. One of the couches had been covered in a silky white sheet—whether Dee had found it, or whether she'd brought it from home, Jack didn't know—and some strategically placed pillows.

"Hi."

She stood in the doorway—he hadn't even heard the door open.

"Impressive," he commented, indicating the trans-formation in the lounge.

"Thanks. I couldn't stop thinking about you all dur-ing the ceremony."

He moved toward her, swept her up in his arms, and carried her to the couch. How great was his life? He had the whole rest of the summer with this amazing girl.

That was the last coherent though he had for the next half hour, until she whispered, "You're the best."

"I think I'd have to say the same thing about you." He'd certainly had never met anyone like Dee before. She was so unapologetically open.

"Well . . . can I make a suggestion? Promise you won't you get mad?"

He held her closer. "Of course I won't."

"I was thinking . . . you're going to get mad."

"No way." He nuzzled the top of her head, burying his face in her tousled blond hair. "But hurry up. I don't want your mom and dad looking for us."

Jack felt her move away from him, far enough so she could look into his eyes. "Okay. I'll just say it. I think we should go back to New Jersey so that we can do it in your bed where you grew up."

What?

"Come again?"

"I'd really like to meet your family. You know, your par-ents," Dee continued earnestly, "and especially your sister."

"I don't really think sex in my very kid-sized bed is the best idea—"

"I think your parents should meet me," Dee went on. "That's what you do when you're really in love, right? We're going to be together forever and ever, Jack. I can just feel it, can't you? We're going to be *so happy.*"

Jack sat up. Talk about your curveballs. Where had "forever and ever" come from? He liked her. Maybe even more than liked her. But he was light years away from thinking about forever with her or anyone else. She had the sweetest, most hopeful look on her face, and it was the night of what would have been her graduation if she hadn't ended up in a freaking psych ward. Definitely not the time to explain to her that *forever* was not a part of his vocabulary. At least not until after he made his first million.

"Sure, Dee." He kept his face neutral. "I totally know what you mean."

"That's fantastic!" she cried, and threw her arms around him.

Shit. Tomorrow they'd have a serious talk. He really did care about her, but those words . . . he could practically feel the noose tightening around his neck.

Tomorrow. Tomorrow he would set her straight. Hopefully without breaking her heart in the process.

Cammie was with Adam and his parents in the teeming theater lobby when Anna strolled by with her entourage—one father, one mother, her formerly slutty sister-gone-crunchy, and slutty-sister-gone-crunchy's even crunchier boyfriend. They were beaming, chatting, and congratulating her—Cammie noted that crunchier boyfriend had one of the most annoying voices she'd ever heard. Something between a eunuch hamster and a vinyl record album played at seventy-eight revolutions per minute.

No Ben, she noted. Very interesting.

On the other hand, she had—count 'em!—no one. Not her father, who'd announced at dinner that a feeding frenzy had developed around Apex in the wake of the collapse of the merger with Paradigm, that two guys named Ari from Endeavor wanted to take him out for dinner and drinks, and that the economic best interests of the *family*—there was that word again—made dinner and drinks absolutely mandatory. He'd promised he'd make it up to her somehow.

"Besides," he'd added, "graduating from high school isn't such a big deal."

So Daddy was eating Periscope Pasta at the Parkway Grill in Pasadena. As for another distinguished representative from her immediate family, forget it. Her stepmother, Patrice, and stepsister, Mia, had gone to the movies. They probably didn't even remember what day it was.

At least Adam's parents were making an effort. They'd suggested that Cammie and Adam join them for a late dinner at Meson G in Hollywood. Cammie had almost suggested Parkway Grill—it would have been so much fun to sit two tables away from her father and distract him while he was trying to make the deal of his lifetime.

She looked up at Adam, whose father actually had an arm around his shoulder and was whispering something—some choice words of life advice?—in his ear. Her heart twisted. She knew she'd neglected him lately, too, so caught up had she been in the mystery of her mother. She'd talked to him after seeing Dina in the morning; talked about how awful it felt to imagine her wonderful, amazing mother the way she'd been described—in so much pain that she'd had to take her own life. Adam had been supportive as always. However she wanted to proceed—to talk to her dad again, to talk to some of her mom's old friends—he was with her.

She'd wanted to reward him in some way, for standing by her in spite of all the craziness. She'd figured out the perfect way to do it too.

"Mr. Flood? Can you excuse Adam and me? For just a few minutes?" Cammie asked. "There's something I want to show him."

The Floods traded a look.

"Sure, I guess," Alan Flood told her. "Our reservation isn't for an hour and a half."

Adam raised a quizzical eyebrow, but when Cammie crooked her arm and beckoned, he took it; they wended their way through the lobby and out into the night.

"Where are we going?"

"Someplace," she said mysteriously. "What are you wearing under that gown?"

"Jeans," he answered, still puzzled. She led him around the side of the building toward the school playing fields—the baseball diamond and football stadium. "And a T-shirt. Why?"

"Do you have any idea how great you are?" she asked.

"Oh yeah, I tell myself that all the time."

"It's just that I know what a bitch I can be."

"It's okay," he assured her as they neared the outdoor basketball court. "I know this has been a tough time for you."

She took his arm tightly. "No. Really. You've been like my . . . my guardian angel. I think sometimes—if you ever tell anyone I said this I will deny it and pass a lie detector test, too—that my mother sent you to me."

He swallowed hard. "That's about the nicest thing that anyone ever said to me."

She turned him toward the basketball court again—the court was floodlit in the night. On the foul line closest to them rested a single orange basketball.

"Go for it," she suggested.

"You dragged me away so that I could *shoot hoops*?" He wrapped his arms around her. "I can think of better things to do."

"If the lady says for you to get out there and shoot, I suggest strongly that you get out there and shoot."

The deep, very familiar voice had come out of the night.

The owner of the voice stepped forward until the

outdoor lights shown on him. Adam's jaw dropped. Cammie smiled.

Perfect. Just perfect.

The guy was easily six-foot six, with a shaved head. His red basketball jersey had number twenty-three in white numerals. "You ready to do some damage?" he asked.

Adam turned to Cammie. "Do you know who that is?" he hissed.

"Multiple All-Star, multiple NBA championships, shoo-in for the Hall of Fame, maybe the most famous face on the planet?" She'd done her homework.

Adam yanked his graduation gown over his head and flung it into the bleachers. "How did you pull *this* off?"

"My dad owed me a favor." Cammie ducked her head toward the famous basketball star. "He's in Los Angeles for a charity thing tomorrow. Voilà."

"Yo! Adam! You gonna chat with the fine fox or you gonna show me what you got?" Number twenty-three threw Adam the ball. He caught it.

"You are . . . I can't even find the words."

He gave Cammie a quick kiss, dribbled toward the basket, then fired a jump shot at the hoop.

Swish. Adam punched the air.

In the halo of lights that shone golden against the Beverly Hills night, a skinny high school kid and a huge superstar shot around together for the next half hour. It was one of the most beautiful things Cammie had ever seen in her life.

Family is who you choose; that's what Sam had said.

At this moment, Cammie knew that she was right.

The stage was empty, the graduation ceremony ended. Still, one lone graduate sat in the chair she'd occupied through the night.

Sam couldn't face what awaited her outside the auditorium doors—her father and Poppy—she'd seen them depart. Even worse, her mother, who had shown up. Eduardo was out there too. Thank God for that.

If only the two of them could slip invisibly past the family psychodrama. How great would that be? She'd had a chance to talk to him briefly about all the family insanity, but he'd been too busy at the consulate to hear all the details. What was he witnessing at that very moment in the foyer? The reunion of Jackson with Dina, as Poppy stood by with fire in her eyes?

That would be too good to miss, Sam decided. Plus, she hoped Parker was still in the lobby so she could tell him about his graduation present—she was going to make sure that her father found a decent role for him in the last couple months of the shooting of *Ben-Hur*.

Just as she rose to join the Jerry Springer theatrics that were certainly under way outside the theater, Eduardo stepped through the double doors. He wore a black V-necked cashmere sweater and black pants. He looked, as usual, perfect. "The coast is— What's that quaint expression? The coast is clear. I suggested to your father and Poppy that they go home; you'll see them there. They were happy to oblige. Your mother would like to have breakfast with you before she goes back to North Carolina. That will be on Wednesday."

Sam was flabbergasted. "But . . . but how? I mean, I didn't even introduce you!"

"Not difficult. I introduced myself. Congratulations, graduate."

She flung herself into his arms. "You are the best. Beyond the best. Light years beyond the best."

"Yes," Eduardo agreed. "It all seemed quite over-whelming. So I'd like to suggest an alternative. Dinner with my parents."

Sam frowned. "They're here in Los Angeles? Why didn't you say something?"

His answer was to extract an envelope from his pants pocket. "For your graduation."

Sam tore it open—it held a pair of old-fashioned plane tickets. "Lima . . . *Peru*?"

"We leave in four hours," Eduardo said calmly. "I apologize, my father's jet is in use. We have to fly com-mercial, but we'll be in first class."

"This kind of stuff only happens in movies with Jennifer Aniston."

Eduardo laughed. "Stop home and pack—you can see your dad. We'll be back on Tuesday, in time to see your mother. If you want, that is."

"Is this really happening?"

"If you want it to."

"But . . . but what about a visa?"

Eduardo laughed heartily. "You forget where I work.

Your visa is all arranged. There's only one thing for you to do. Say yes."

Sam smiled a smile so big she thought her face would break. "Yes, Eduardo. A hundred times, yes!"

The front of Beverly Hills High School featured a circular driveway, just like so many other buildings in a city addicted to the heroin of the internal combustion engine (with the exception of Prius owners, who'd replaced it with hybrid methodone). Most mornings the driveway was vacant, since the vast majority of students owned their own vehicles and queued up at the parking lot.

Not so on graduation night, when the circular drive did its best impression of Hollywood Boulevard and Cahuenga an hour before the Academy Awards. As Anna and most of her family stepped into fresh air, the roadway was already packed with Beemers, BMWs, and Hummers—the urban-assault vehicles of the rich and famous.

They stood in a little knot, waiting for Jonathan to arrive. Anna had already called Caine to come and pick her up.

"I'm so proud of you," Susan beamed. "Really."

"Thanks, Suze. I mean it."

Susan linked her arm through Gordon's. "And this is amazing: Gordon got a fantastic idea at the exact moment that you were getting your diploma."

Anna raised her eyebrows. She noted that her mother was making the exact same dubious gesture.

"Tell her, Gordon," Susan implored excitedly.

"I'd love to." Her sister's boyfriend looked at Anna as if he was about to offer the Nobel Prize in literature. "You sister and I were wondering if you'd like to come back east for the summer. To work at Kripalu, before you start at Yale in the fall. There's a summer opening in housekeeping that I'm sure I could arrange for you to get. I have a lot of clout around the place."

"Wouldn't that be great?" Susan prompted. "We could spend the summer together!"

Anna smiled sweetly, though it was hard to imagine anything more insufferable.

"That is a very kind offer, Gordon. And it would be great to see Susan every day. But no. I'll be here in Los Angeles until I come back east."

Gordon looked disappointed. "Thought I'd ask, is all. If it was me, I'd definitely leave all this superficial pap behind."

"Me, too," Susan echoed.

"What will you be doing for the summer, Anna dear?" her mother queried.

What, indeed? Anna wasn't sure. She'd hoped to just have fun with Ben, to be young and carefree—well, as carefree as she ever got—for one last summer before she became a serious college student. But now what? She knew that if she were a different kind of girl, she could easily forgive him. A different kind of girl wouldn't even have gotten mad at him. But she wasn't that different kind of girl, and doubted that she ever would be.

And that, she decided, was okay.

"Sam mentioned the possibility of our working as production assistants on *Ben-Hur*. Her father is shooting through August."

"That sounds very educational," Jane declared, clearly a lot more comfortable with that course of action than with Anna in yoga threads scrubbing other people's toilets with all-natural toilet brushes. "I'm leaving for Florence on Monday. You must keep me posted on how it's going."

"Our chariot awaits." Gordon pointed to the driveway, where Jonathan inched up in the Mercedes and flashed his lights a few times. Then he frowned. "Anna, do you think your father has any idea of the evil history of Daimler-Benz, or how much it hurts the Earth to drive one?"

Jane gave Anna a thin little smile. Anna knew exactly what it meant: I can put up with this young man for the duration of this visit. *I would rather have your sister be with this young man than be drugged out in some squat on the Lower East Side. However, if they decide to get married, I might have to reassess.*

"I'll see you in the morning, dear." Jane kissed Anna's cheek. "Enjoy your evening. I'm sorry it won't be with Ben, but your father says that Mr. Manning really is quite an interesting young man."

How typical of her mother to be so diplomatic in public. Anna waved as Jane, Susan, and Gordon got into the Mercedes and rolled away into the night.

The line of vehicles coming for their passengers was

endless; Anna realized it could be quite a while before Caine arrived. There were stone benches close to the auditorium doors; she decided to wait on one of them.

"Congratulations on your graduation."

Anna looked over at the next bench. Ben was sitting there, in faded jeans and a white T-shirt under a light red cotton jacket. She felt herself turn to something less than solid, the ground sliding beneath her feet. What good was it to say she was in control with him when just seeing him made her want to fling herself into his arms?

"I came. Feel any different?"

So. He'd been there. Funny how she hadn't sensed his presence.

"Relieved, I guess," Anna responded carefully. "To have it behind me."

"You weren't a big fan of high school, huh?"

"It was an art I never really mastered," she admitted. "Pep rallies and gossip and who broke up with who . . ."

"Snob," he teased.

She nodded seriously and flexed her calf muscles. "I suppose I am in some ways. Not about class—at least, I hope not. But about . . . I don't know . . . seriousness of purpose? Intellect."

"You have to admit I brought fun into your life."

She smiled. "Yes. You did."

"Woohoo! I'm outta here!" a graduating senior with an ill-advised mohawk screamed out the passenger window as his Jeep circled the driveway.

276 ZOEY DEAN

"If I could go back and do things differently, I would," Ben said softly.

"Which part?" Anna asked. "Sleeping with Blythe or not telling me about it?"

He puffed out some air. "Both, I suppose. I swear, I was honest with her. When I told you that she and I agreed to just have friendly sex—nothing more—I wasn't lying to you. She said that was all she wanted too."

Anna thought about this a moment. "Maybe she was being honest, too; at the time. Maybe afterwards, she had all these feelings. For some people, it's hard to have sex without love. Impossible, even."

"You're talking about yourself," Ben proclaimed gently.

"Yes. What did you think I would have done if you just told me about it?"

He looked off into the distance. "Thought less of me. Definitely."

Well, that was honest, at least.

"Can I take you somewhere? Not my house or the boat; I mean some place to celebrate your graduation. How about Grace on Beverly Boulevard? The bartender makes this killer drink called an Orange Blossom Special. You have to try one."

One part of her wanted to call Caine, say that she and Ben had reconciled, apologize profusely. And another part of her . . . didn't. Not because she didn't want to be with Ben, and not because she didn't love him. So what, then, was keeping her from flinging herself into Ben's muscular arms?

"I'm always . . . reacting to you, Ben. You saved me on the airplane. You whisked me off to Jackson Sharpe's wedding."

"You're still thinking about that?"

"I am," she hesitated for a second. "It's almost as if . . . you're the center of the universe for me. It's been like that ever since I met you. And now I think maybe . . . I should be, instead of you. The heroine of my own life."

"From where I sit, you always have been."

She was surprised. "Really? Well, that's good. But I need it to be true from where I sit, too."

"Hey, there."

Anna looked up. Caine was leaning out the driver's window of his blue F-150 Ford pickup. His eyes flitted from Anna to Ben and back to Anna, questioning.

"The guy from the movie line?" Ben was aghast. "Tell me you're not going out with him."

"I'm not," Anna assured him. "Not in the way you think. He's my friend."

Ben reached for her hand. "C'mon. Blow him off."

"I could," she agreed. She got up and kissed Ben's cheek. "But I'm not going to. Thank you for coming. We'll talk soon, okay?" With that, she walked around to the passenger side of Caine's truck and got in, doing everything she could not to turn back and look. She wasn't sure what she was doing exactly, but inside somehow, it just felt . . . right.

"Juggling guys?" Caine wondered aloud.

"He just showed up. We talked."

The truck inched forward. "So, you good?"

Was she? Tonight was an ending; not so much with Ben, but of her high school self. Tomorrow would be . . . something else. She hoped Ben would be a part of that. But this time she'd be the active heroine, the one behind the wheel.

Was she good?

"Yes," she told Caine as they finally made it to the end of the driveway. She realized just how true it was. The summer, new adventures, Yale, her entire life—all of that lay ahead of her.

She was very, *very* good.

If you like the A-List, you may also enjoy:

Bass Ackwards and Belly Up by Elizabeth Craft and Sarah Fain

Secrets of My Hollywood Life by Jen Calonita